P9-AGG-365

SE

WITHDRAWN

The Proposal

LORI WICK

MONTEREY COUNTY FREE LIBRARIES

MARINA CALIFORNIA

HARVEST HOUSE PUBLISHERS
Eugene, Oregon 97402

All Scripture quotations are taken from the King James Version of the Bible.

Cover by Terry Dugan Design, Bloomington, Minnesota

THE PROPOSAL
Copyright © 2002 by Lori Wick
Published by Harvest House Publishers
Eugene, Oregon 97402

ISBN-13: 978-1-60751-617-0

All rights reserved. No part of this publication may be reproduced, stored in a retrieval system, or transmitted in any form or by any means—electronic, mechanical, digital, photocopy, recording, or any other—except for brief quotations in printed reviews, without the prior permission of the publisher.

Printed in the United States of America.

For Todd and Becki Barsness.
You've worked hard, and we have been blessed.
You've shared yourselves and your life with the
church family, and we've grown richer.
This dedication comes with my love.
God bless you both.

Acknowledgments

The first book in a new series! I'm so excited. I fell in love with this time period in England's history while watching some of my favorite Jane Austen films. I returned to England with my husband and a friend, able to look at that old place with new eyes. Since that time the stories in my mind have come alive for me. I hope you enjoy this first volume, and also enjoy reading about the people I need to thank.

—*Julie McKinney*. I couldn't have done this without you. Thank you for a trip we will never forget. I love your enthusiasm for my work and that delighted sparkle that fills your eyes. Thank you for the family name.

—*Shelly Alilunas*. Thank you for all your help on the home front, especially when we were so many miles apart. You were a real lifesaver. The information has been so valuable. Also, thank you for launching me into finding the Internet for myself.

—*Ian, Steve, and Steve*. It was wonderful meeting you and talking to you about England. I'm not sure if my England looks exactly like the real one, but I still hope the people there who have a chance to read my books will enjoy this series. Thank you for all you do to promote my work.

—*Tim, Matt, and Abby Wick*. Thanks for one of the best summers we've ever had. After you all worked so hard, we had more time to play. Never forget how much I love you, or how huge our God is.

—*My Bob*. Thank you for going to England with me. You made it so fun and special. I'm going to go back to England again sometime. It's simply lovely knowing you'll go with me. Actually, it's simply lovely having you with me every day.

Prologue

Tipton

Collingbourne, England

April 1810

Seated in the north sitting room, her letters in her lap, Lydia Palmer read the missive in her hand one more time before looking across the room at her husband. He was studying the daily news, but only a moment passed before he glanced her way.

"What is it, love?" he asked kindly. Frank Palmer was always kind.

"My cousin has died."

Mr Palmer frowned. "I'm sorry to hear that, but I must admit I didn't think you had any cousins left."

"Godwin Jennings. He lives near Bristol, or should I say 'lived.' It was not a close relationship, but he was family."

"I know who you're talking about," he said as light dawned. "Who contacted you, by the way?"

"His solicitor," Lydia said, her eyes going back to the official letter.

"And did Mr Jennings have children?"

"Yes. Three of them." Lydia chewed her lip a moment. "I wonder where they'll end up."

"I was wondering that myself. You have so little family of any kind left."

For a moment, Mr and Mrs Palmer were quiet. A few seconds later, however, their eyes met, both faces showing some shock.

"No, Frank. It couldn't be."

"I don't know who else, Liddy. Your brother is the only male heir left in your family."

"But three children, Frank? You know how William Jennings enjoys his independence."

Mr Palmer shrugged. "I'm just stating the need, Lydia. Unless you're hiding someone that I don't know about, by law Jennings would be responsible for Godwin's children."

Lydia shook her head. "It's too fantastic to be real. Jennings barely tolerates women. I can't think he would have any more interest in children."

"Well, he wouldn't have to love them—just support them."

The room grew quiet again, only the ticking of the mantel clock making itself known.

"Will you write him?" Mr Palmer asked.

"Jennings? I don't think so. He hasn't acknowledged a single one of my letters in seven years."

"But you don't write to him so that he'll answer, Lydia. You write so he'll know you still love him."

Lydia took the gentle rebuke in good grace. Even before reading the letter in her hand one last time, she determined to write her brother by the end of the week.

Chapter One

Aydon
London, England
May 1810

"And where did you say this was?" Mr Collins asked as he frowned fiercely at the new help, a young man who was now sweating from every pore of his body.

"It was on the floor in the back hall, Mr Collins."

"The postmark on this letter is five days past. How could it have been missed in the hall all these days?"

"I don't know, sir. Betsy just gave it to me."

"Who is Betsy?"

"We were hired at the same time, sir. I believe she works upstairs."

Mr Collins' eyes narrowed with even more danger.

"Mr Jennings will hear of this. You may be discharged."

"Yes, sir."

The crushed but humble face of the young man before him softened Mr Collins' heart a bit. He continued more kindly, "As you know, Mr Jennings is out for the evening. He probably won't receive this until morning. If I can put a word in for you, I will, but know this, young Geoffrey, it will not happen again."

"Yes, sir. Thank you, sir."

"You are dismissed."

As Geoffrey walked away, Mr Collins, long in the employ of Mr William Jennings, stood thinking about his next move. He had several options and after just a moment's deliberation, took the second one and turned to locate Bates, Mr Jennings' man. It didn't take long. He ran him to earth in the servants' dining area, where he sat with a cup of tea and the day's post.

"This just surfaced," Mr Collins informed him, setting the letter on the table.

"It's five days old," Bates responded with a frown.

"Precisely. Do I tell him tonight?"

Bates looked up at his old friend and smiled wryly.

"You forget, Collins, that when he returns from Lady Wendt's dinner, we won't be doing anything tonight but keeping the house quiet."

Mr Collins had a smile to match his friend's before leaving to secure the letter on his desk, knowing he would have to face his employer come morning.

≈ ≈ ≈

"Jennings?" Knightly called out as he entered the veranda. "What are you doing out here?"

Mr William Jennings, the man he sought, glanced over his shoulder, not at all sorry to be out of Lady Wendt's stifling ballroom and in the fresh air.

"It was a bit warm in there," Jennings said briefly as Knightly joined him at the railing.

"Yes, and getting warmer. Did you see Louisa Dent tonight? Her husband leaves for France, and she throws off every inhibition."

Jennings shook his head in disgust and said, "I've known for many years what Dent has yet to find out: Most women cannot be trusted."

"I'll say," Knightly agreed fervently, draining the glass he'd brought out with him.

"Knightly?" a female voice called from behind the men just as they were beginning to enjoy the silence. "Are you out here?"

"Yes, Augusta, I'm here." Knightly turned from the railing. "Are you coming back in, Jennings?"

"I think not," that man replied. He was tired and wished to go home.

"We'll see you later," Knightly said and moved toward his wife.

Jennings did not reply. He was in need of solitude and knew that home was the only place he could be guaranteed of that.

≈ ≈ ≈

The carriage delivered Jennings to the front of his London home precisely on time, but that man barely took notice. Though footmen in attendance and his man, Bates, didn't often see him elated, at times they sensed a lighter mood. Not tonight. Tonight he seemed far away, his mind in deep thought.

In the eyes of Jennings, Lady Wendt's dinner party had been dreadful, full of women who had nothing more on their minds than catching a rich husband or gossiping about a woman who had. His dinner companion had been a vain, blonde creature so occupied with herself she had never stopped speaking. It had given him a headache.

Now in his dressing room, having stated that he wished to be alone, Jennings slowly loosened the cravat at his throat, telling himself that tonight's dinner party would be the last. In truth, he didn't know why he'd gone in the first place.

His mood growing more pensive by the second, he waited only until his throat was free to retire to his study to sit by the fire. No other lights burned, and for long moments he stared into the flames.

Jennings had not been reared to distrust women, but his own good mother was dead, and his sister, a woman he'd admired for many years, had changed since she'd found God, cementing Jennings' belief that women were not all that trustworthy.

Jennings hated to even think about the change. It made him angry. That anyone with half a brain would embrace the teachings of an ancient book and say they were life-changing, was incomprehensible to him.

Prior to her religious experience, his sister had been a brilliant woman. Articulate and keen—why, that's what had drawn Frank Palmer to the altar thirteen years ago. They'd been a promising couple. But Jennings couldn't stand to be around either of them any longer. For him, the relationship was over.

Warm from the fire, Jennings felt fatigue creep over him. The blaze lulled him as his irritation drained away. At moments like this, when his sister and her family came to mind, and only if he was very tired, he asked himself if he'd made the best choices. Maybe he should have looked into a family for himself. Maybe having sons to carry his name would have been worth taking a chance on a wife, but he would be thirty-four on his next birthday, and though not old by many standards, Jennings felt he was now too set in his ways to accommodate a family.

Sleep began to crowd in, and Jennings fought it. Just when he thought he could nod off in the chair, Jennings, a man of discipline, made himself rise and find his bed. The cool touch of the linens against his skin was enough to rouse him for a time, but the day's activities and the busyness of his mind were catching up. Asleep before the clock struck one, he never heard a sound.

～ ～ ～

"How did he take the lost letter?" Bates asked.

"I can't tell you. He didn't want the post with breakfast."

The two men looked at each other before going on about their duties.

The staff was accustomed to a life of order and discipline, so this was a surprise to them. Jennings was not an unreasonable man, but he liked his routine. And since he rarely stepped from the routine himself, it left his servants in something of a quandary. They carried on as best they could.

Bates went soundlessly into the room to see to his master's needs, but clearly Mr Jennings' mind was elsewhere. He seemed to be eating the breakfast in front of him without notice or even taste. All over the house, people were moving about quietly and for his comfort, and faint sounds of this activity drifted even to the small dining room where he sat, but there was no outward recognition of anything.

This went on for an hour before Jennings reached for the day's newspaper. He had only just immersed himself in an article on finance when Bates came to the dining room, this time to interrupt.

"I'm sorry to disturb you, sir, but a situation has arisen."

Jennings, wanting his solitude at the moment, still put the paper aside.

"Yes, Bates, what is it?"

"Some children have been delivered to our door, sir. The coachman insists that they are to come here to Mr William Jennings." Bates paused a moment but then went right on. "And if I may be so bold, sir, I have also brought you the post. On top is a letter that was given to Mr Collins yesterday. It was misplaced for a few days."

As keen as the sister he admired, Jennings was lifting the letter and opening it to read just moments later. The news that a cousin he barely knew existed had died was surprising enough. Learning that the man was leaving his three children to him was staggering. Jennings sat utterly still for a full three minutes before standing to face Bates.

"Where are these children right now?"

"In the foyer, sir. The coachman would not be swayed."

Jennings consulted the letter again.

"Three children?"

"Yes, sir. Two boys and a small girl."

"And their father's just died," he said almost absently.

Bates remained quiet.

"Ready a room they can all sleep in tonight."

Jennings made his way toward the foyer. It didn't take long to identify his guests. Standing in a sober mass were three children. The boys stood side by side, but the girl tried to stand behind her older brother. Upon seeing Jennings approach, the older boy gently pulled his sister out to stand next to him.

Jennings went directly to the oldest child.

"I'm William Jennings, your father's cousin," he said, putting his hand out to shake the boy's. "I'm sorry for your loss."

"Thank you, sir. My name is Thomas Jennings. This is my brother, James, and my sister, Penelope. We call her Penny."

"Hello, James," Jennings greeted him, shaking his hand as well. But when he turned back to the little girl, she was already trying to hide behind her brother.

"May I ask you a question, sir?" Thomas, pale from the events of the last weeks, took the courage to ask.

"Yes, you may, Thomas."

"Were you expecting us, sir? Is this where we are to stay?"

As though a present had been dropped from heaven, William Jennings saw what had been given to him. The answer to the boy's question came from Jennings' mouth just heartbeats before it entered his mind.

"Yes, Thomas. This is where you're to stay."

The young man, near his thirteenth birthday, bowed slightly in acknowledgment. His ten-year-old brother and six-year-old sister made no comment or movement at all.

"How are they?" Jennings asked, hovering near the base of the main stairway and waiting for Mr Collins to descend.

"Settling in, sir."

"Did they need anything?"

"No, sir. Young Master Thomas assured me that he would see to things and make us aware of their needs."

"Are they coming down?"

"I don't believe so right now, sir. I heard Master James say that the little girl needed to sleep."

"What's her name again?"

"Penny, sir."

"That's right."

"Is there anything else, sir?"

"No, Collins. Thank you."

Mr Collins had all he could do not to shake his head. He'd never seen his employer so anxious or animated. He couldn't wait to learn Bates' opinion on the matter.

Left alone at the bottom of the stairs, Jennings debated his next move. The children needed time to settle in to their new surroundings—they'd been through quite an ordeal—but at the same time he wanted to get to know those boys. Many times in his life he had yearned for this very thing: sons to share his life with, and now he had two of them! It was almost too fantastic to be real. Last night he'd been mourning his choices, and now he had two sons without the trouble of a wife.

His mind ran with the things he wanted to tell them and show them. Not sure when they would be ready to come down, Jennings retired to his study to prepare for such a time.

≈ ≈ ≈

"It's all right," Thomas said to his sister as he stroked her hair and tried to believe his own words. "Just go to sleep."

"I'm cold," she sobbed.

Thomas shifted the covers up closer to her face.

"The fire is high; you'll be warm soon. Just close your eyes, Penny."

The little girl did as she was told, but not before whispering, "I need Papa."

Thomas didn't reply. He wanted their father too. From his place at the edge of the bed, Thomas looked over to where James sat by the fire. Normally rather bookish, James hadn't read a word since their father's death. Even now he looked into the flames, seemingly unaware of much else.

A glance down at Penny told Thomas she was asleep. She'd traveled in wide-eyed terror all the way to London, and he knew she was exhausted. Moving quietly to the fire with James, Thomas took a moment and looked at the room they were in. It was a large room with two wide beds. They would be very comfortable in here, but something in his young heart told him not to get too relaxed.

"Is she asleep?" James asked quietly.

"Yes."

"I'm hungry," James admitted.

"I am too."

James looked at his brother. "Do you want me to ask for something?"

"I thought I'd wait until Penny woke."

James looked surprised. "She could sleep for hours."

Thomas nodded, knowing how true that was. He could see they had little choice.

"I'll go, but we might need to take turns so one of us can sit with Penny."

"All right. You go first."

"Well, we'll see," Thomas said as he made for the door.

Jennings had tried very hard to find more to do in the study, but a sudden need to move about found him in the large entryway. For this reason he spotted Thomas' descent almost as soon as the lad was on the stairs.

"Is everything well, Thomas?" Jennings asked as soon as Thomas finished the last step.

"Our room is very nice. Thank you, sir."

"Is there something you need?"

"My brother and I find we're a little hungry."

"Of course you are," Jennings said immediately. "Why don't you go and get James, and the two of you can join me for tea."

"Actually, sir, I feel that one of us needs to sit with Penny, so if we could eat separately, that might be best."

"Very well," Jennings said, his face giving nothing away. In all his plans for the boys, he'd forgotten their sister again. "I'll just have something sent up, shall I?"

Thomas paused but still managed to say what was on his mind.

"At the risk of sounding ungrateful, sir, I don't wish to have Penny disturbed."

For the first time Jennings actually looked at this boy. His eyes were red while the flesh around them looked bruised from lack of sleep. He was pale, even to his lips, and he looked as though the world had been set on his shoulders. Jennings knew a compassion he'd not felt in years.

"Of course you don't want her disturbed, Thomas. Come with me and eat something, and then James can take your place."

Knowing nothing but relief that he'd been understood, Thomas went gratefully, planning to eat swiftly so that James would not have to sit hungry much longer.

He wouldn't have hurried so much had he realized the day was going to be spent in their room watching Penny sleep.

~ ~ ~

Thomas Jennings woke slowly the next morning. He could feel James' warmth beside him and realized that he'd slept hard all night. Shifting his neck a bit after feeling its stiffness, he pushed up against the headboard before looking at his sister's bed.

Penelope Jennings, dark hair a mass around her face, sat looking across at him.

"Are you awake, Thomas?"

"I'm awake."

"Do they have food in this house, Thomas?" she asked.

"Come here," he said, motioning to her with his hand.

Not a very large six-year-old, Penny slipped off her bed and climbed up onto the one her brothers shared. Thomas had curled his legs in, and Penny sat on the counterpane in front of him.

"You slept all night," Thomas said when she looked at him, reaching to push some of the hair from her face.

"Do we go home today?"

"No, Penny, we're staying here."

"Will they let us have food?"

"Yes. Are you hungry?"

Penny nodded and Thomas looked at her face. If the portraits didn't lie, she was a picture of their mother as a child, the mother who had died having her.

"Is Papa happy with Jesus, or does he miss us, Thomas?" Penny suddenly asked.

Rested as he was, the oldest Jennings child still felt tears sting at the back of his throat.

"He is happy with the Lord Jesus, Penny, and he trusts the Lord Jesus to watch over us, but I think if Papa had had a choice, he would have wanted to stay and take care of us."

James rolled over then to face his siblings.

"I was thinking about that too. I think if Papa knew he was going to die, he would have told us about William Jennings, so it wouldn't have been such a surprise."

"Did he know William Jennings?" Penny asked.

"He knew of him," Thomas said. "I'm sure of that, but I don't know if they had much contact."

A noise in the hall just then gave the children hope. It was hard to tell if it was too early for breakfast, but they wouldn't know until they dressed and ventured forth. And that plan went well until they got to Penny's hair. Mrs Murch had seen to things before they left Morehouse, the children's home, so this was the first time Thomas had been left with the task. He found in a hurry that the tresses had a mind of their own—just curly enough to be difficult and just thick enough to make it a challenge. Thomas ended up brushing Penny's hair out and leaving it to fall down the little girl's back. It was never left that way at home, but they were all growing more hungry by the moment, and it would do for now.

Hungry as Penny was, leaving the room was hard. The house was large and strange, and she didn't want to see William Jennings again. He didn't look at all like her papa, who had been a man who smiled most of the time, and she was a little bit afraid of him. Nevertheless, her stomach was quite empty. She kept glancing toward her brothers, who seemed to know their way around, and was startled when they suddenly spoke to someone.

"Good morning, Mr Collins," Thomas ventured. "Are we too early for breakfast?"

"Not at all, Master Thomas. Please come this way."

"Thank you."

Penny brought up the rear of this foursome, her eyes taking in statues and paintings that were far above her head.

"Here you are," Mr Collins offered once they were in a room with a large table. Thomas directed Penny to a seat. James sat next to her, and Thomas sat across the table.

"Breakfast will be served momentarily," Mr Collins informed them before leaving.

Penny waited only until he exited the room to fix her dress. She had sat on it awkwardly, and the neck was choking her. Putting a small glass figurine on the table, she shifted until she was comfortable.

"Oh, Penny," James chided, sounding aggrieved. "You didn't bring Mr Pat with you."

The little girl looked upset as she took it back in her hand.

"Will Mr Jennings be angry?"

"No, but there's no place for it at the breakfast table. You should have left it in the room."

"Put it in your pocket," Thomas suggested, not wanting James and Penny to argue.

Penny did so, her eyes large and sober. James looked her way and felt bad.

"It's all right, Penny. I just don't want us to make a mistake and get booted out of here. I don't know where we would go."

"Is that going to happen, Thomas?" Penny asked.

"No, Penny, I don't think so, but Father would want us to be on our best behavior."

Penny nodded, looking as lost and little as she felt.

Relief, however, was on the way. Not aware that they were up already, Jennings did not join them, but platters of food began to arrive, and in little time all hunger was forgotten.

The report back to Cook that the three children were good eaters made that woman's day. She started baking cookies, four different varieties, with plans to get word to the children that they were to visit her in the kitchen and have samples as often as they liked.

"I think this is the door," Thomas said as he led his siblings toward the back of the house and outside a short time after breakfast. Once the door was shut behind them, they stood and took in a high-walled garden, quite large and overflowing with flowers. It was nothing like the rolling hillsides at home, but the fresh air was nice, and the flowers in William Jennings' yard were beautiful.

"Stay on the path," Thomas directed when Penny started forward.

That little girl was careful to obey, and when she came to a stone bench, she sat down, noticing that it was just her size. Thomas and James moved to look at the lattice work on a trellis, and that was where Jennings found them.

"Good morning, Thomas. Good morning, James. How was your night's rest?"

"Very good, sir. Thank you."

"And breakfast? Did you have enough to eat?"

"Plenty, sir. Should we know the times for meals, Mr Jennings? Were we too early this morning?"

"Not at all. Why don't you tell me when you like to eat, and I'll see to it that Mr Collins alerts the staff." Remembering again that he was going to have to give the boys time, he mentioned tactfully, "I'm often out in the evenings, but maybe we could breakfast or lunch together."

"Thank you, sir. We would enjoy that."

"Is this a sundial?" James asked, having been distracted by the instrument high on the stone wall. He'd never seen one that didn't sit on a pedestal or base on the ground.

"Yes, it is. I found that at an auction a few years ago and thought I had a good spot for it. What do you think, James?"

"I think it's a perfect spot. I've read about these but have never seen one. Our father had a sundial in the yard, but the base broke which tipped it slightly. After that it was never correct."

"I bought this trellis at the same time," Jennings went on to add, walking over to put his hand on it. "Did you happen to notice it?"

"Yes. It looks heavy."

"It's very heavy. It was too large to come through the house, and they had quite the time getting it over the wall."

"Is there no door in the wall?" Thomas asked, wishing all of this was as normal as it must have looked.

"There is, but it's too small." The gentleman went on speaking about various things in the garden, but Penny did not join the other three. When she had heard the door open, she scooted off the bench and behind a bush. She could see her brothers from where she was, but at the moment they didn't look for her. Penny listened to their conversation and relaxed a little when she realized their host had not come to boot them out. Even though she heard the calm, quiet sound of Mr Jennings' voice and did not find him as scary as she remembered, Penny hoped her brothers would not miss her until he had gone back inside.

Chapter Two

Jennings didn't want to think about how his staff would view his actions late that night, so he kept his movements quiet in the upstairs hallway. The lantern was turned low as he walked from his room toward the door of the children's bedroom. He opened the portal quietly, went in, and shut it behind him.

That evening he'd had dinner out with an old friend. The meal had all the makings of a wonderful time, but he couldn't get the boys from his mind, so it fell a bit flat.

Now, moving almost silently across the carpet, he approached the bed and looked down where the boys slept, their faces even younger when relaxed in sleep. His heart filled with an unrecognizable emotion as he gazed down at them, and he stood for a time with a smile on his face.

Almost as an afterthought, he remembered to look at the other bed. Dark curls surrounded an adorable face that was as peacefully asleep as her brothers'. Looking at her, Jennings had to admit that she was indeed a very pretty little girl, but he hadn't the slightest idea what to do with her. As he turned to exit the room, the realization came that he didn't have to do anything with her. She could live with him until it was time for her to come out, and then he would marry her to some suitable man.

In a complete state of naïveté Jennings exited the room, wondering how long he would have to wait before he began working with the boys.

≈ ≈ ≈

It didn't take too many days for the children to find a routine. Life at home had become topsy-turvy after their father's death, and much as they missed him, it was a comfort to find themselves in a routine that seemed to fit who they were. They breakfasted together, played in the garden, lunched together, spent time reading from Jennings' remarkable library or the daily news, had dinner, and were always ready for bed at an early hour. This routine didn't start to show signs of upset until their eighth day in the house.

Jennings joined them for breakfast, and as soon as they finished, he asked the boys to go horseback riding in the park.

"You boys do ride?"

"Yes, sir, we do, but I'm not sure if we should leave Penny on her own."

Once again Jennings had lost track of the little girl. At the moment she was sitting quietly, finishing her toast. She gave no indication of having heard any of the conversation.

"Why don't you go, Thomas," James suggested. "I'll stay with Penny."

Thomas looked down at him. He knew that James loved to ride as much as he did. He thought it most kind of him to offer.

"Are you certain, James?"

"Yes. Maybe I can go next time."

Jennings was very impressed by the grown-up way they handled this, but it was not what he wanted. He wanted both boys to accompany him because he wanted to examine the boys' horse-management skills at one time, but he carefully kept this thought to himself.

"Well, then," Jennings said quietly, "in about an hour, Thomas?"

"Yes, sir. I'll be ready."

As Jennings went on his way, Thomas glanced at his siblings to see if they had caught any underlying current of displeasure, but they both acted as though all was normal. And by the time Thomas was astride a fine mount and headed toward the park with Jennings, he thought all was normal too. His cousin was a well-educated man and interested in most everything. With tremendous courtesy he told Thomas where they were, explaining the history of some homes and buildings and generally directing the conversation in a most congenial way.

James and Penny came to mind several times, and Thomas wondered if his concern for them was needless. There had been nothing in the house to indicate that any of them were in danger, but never before had he felt such a weight of responsibility. He knew his father would not wish him to shoulder more than his rightful share, but he felt his father's loss keenly and was most committed to doing as his father would have wished.

Thomas snapped out of his thoughts in time to see an open coach passing. The women inside seemed rather intent on Jennings. Both turned to watch him as the coach moved along. Thomas looked to that man to see if he acknowledged them and found that the older Jennings did not seem to notice their attention.

Questions about how old he was, if he'd ever married, and what his place in London might be suddenly popped into Thomas' mind, but Jennings chose that moment to tell Thomas about the various schools in the area. Thomas would never have been so rude as to voice any of his musings, but the change in subject put them completely from his mind. Penny and James, however, lingered. Thomas was enjoying his ride, but he couldn't help but wonder what his brother and sister were up to.

∾ ∾ ∾

"Look at this flower!" Penny said as she ran to James in the garden.

"Penny!" her brother gasped. "You can't pick them!"

"I didn't. It was on the ground."

"Oh." This stopped James for a moment. "Maybe you should put it back where you found it."

Penny didn't argue, and as soon as she turned, James went back to his book. Reading was becoming more comfortable now, and this was his own volume, a gift from his father, one he felt free to bring out of doors.

"James!" Penny suddenly cried in very real distress. The ten-year-old rushed to find her caught on a rosebush. He was reaching to help her when she jerked and tore the fabric of her dress. Penny was frightened that the tear might put her in very real trouble, and tears were not long in coming.

Mr Collins came on the scene almost immediately, but even so the children did not realize how closely the staff was keeping an eye on them.

"Is there a problem, Mr James?"

James was relieved to have Mr Collins on the scene, but Penny hung her head in embarrassment.

"Penny has torn her dress."

"Shall I look?" Mr Collins' voice was extremely solicitous, but Penny was still ashamed.

"I think Cook might be able to help us with this, Miss Penny. Shall we go ask her?"

Penny nodded, barely holding a fresh rush of tears.

"Very good," Mr Collins said as he led off down the path. "I think there might even be cookies fresh from the oven."

The children followed quietly, James feeling half sorry for his sister and half irritated that she was crying about torn clothing. The smell of the kitchen, however, soon swept away all negative thoughts. Spices and vanilla assailed his nose even before the door was opened, and James' small mouth began to water.

"What's this?" Cook asked, always looking a bit sterner than she was. Having just handed a warm cookie to each child, she stood looking down at Penny. "Oh, it's nothing but a tiny tear. We'll have Megan mending that in no time. Here, both of you take another one of these cookies and don't cry anymore."

"Thank you," Penny said, following James' lead and not feeling quite so sorry for herself.

Megan, the head housekeeper, worked all over the house. Unlike Cook, she was rail thin, and the children had never seen her idle. She could be seen in any room of the large home and at all times of the day, giving orders to the other housemaids and taking notes on a paper pad she carried in her apron pocket.

"What have we here?" she asked as she bent to see the small tear. She straightened and smiled down at Penny. "I can mend that for you. I'll just find my sewing box and a length of sheeting."

Not until Penny was swathed in the sheet did she realize Megan's intention. Modest in the white covering, Penny watched as Megan drew forth needle and thread. Cook pulled a chair close so the little girl could sit down, and after James joined her, she gave them glasses of milk.

"What did you catch your dress on, Miss Penny?" Megan asked, intending to soothe the worried lines she saw on Penny's small forehead.

"On a rosebush."

"They can be tricky," Megan said with compassion.

And that was only the beginning. With Cook, Megan, and even Mr Collins working together, the children were made to feel quite at ease, and the dress was repaired without fuss or bother.

"Lunch is in two hours," Cook told them when Penny was finally back in her clothing, ribbons tied and in place. "But don't forget to stop for cookies this afternoon."

"Thank you," James said in a very grown-up manner to the adults who had helped them and been so kind. "Come along, Penny," he said quietly to his sister as he led her away. "I think we should play in our room for a time."

∼ ∼ ∼

Jennings was growing weary. Thomas' company was not overly taxing; indeed, the lad had a soothing way about him, but he'd not had much sleep the night before, and after leading the conversation for the better part of two hours, he felt a little worn.

That was when he spotted her, or rather them. Five women in dark clothing, pushing prams or with children at their sides. Jennings stared at the nannies in the park as though he had never seen the like.

Why such a solution had never occurred to him he did not know, but he realized quite suddenly that his problems with Penny were over. He would hire a nanny. He and his sister had had one for years, and they'd gotten along just fine.

"Shall we head back?" Jennings suggested, seeing no need to mention his thoughts to his young charge. He was a man used to suiting his own needs and being in charge of his own destiny. Asked about it, he would have said it was the Jennings' way.

"Certainly, sir. I thank you for inviting me."

"Not at all, Thomas. We'll have to come again soon."

It was on Thomas' mind to ask if James could go the next time, but he didn't wish to appear presumptuous. It occurred to him for the first time what an awkward feeling it was to be a guest. He wasn't at home, and he wasn't visiting. Until Jennings took it upon himself to boot them to the curb, London was where they would stay, but would it ever feel like home? The question nagged Thomas all the way back to Aydon, the grand home on Rumney Street.

~ ~ ~

"Did you find it?" Penny asked, looking very excited as James walked around their bedroom.

"Not yet," James replied, lying to spare her. At times he was harsh with his sister, even knowing how wrong it was, but not now, not since their father died. In the past he would not have hesitated to tell her that her hiding place was ridiculous, but not this time. He had spotted the marble she hid some three minutes past but continued to look for it in an effort to entertain her.

"Am I close?" he tried, having to avert his eyes or see the shiny, dark sphere near the fireplace.

"Very close!" Penny said, all but dancing in excitement.

"Found it!" James cried, managing to sound surprised.

"Will you hide it for me, James? I want to look."

James remembered to keep it easy. He stood for a time, not hiding the marble or moving, just missing his father and Thomas.

"Is it time?" came Penny's muffled voice; she was hiding her face against the bed.

"Almost," he said and forced himself to hide the marble.

It took Penny a while to locate it, and that was fine with James. He had wandered to the windows that overlooked the street and watched a man walk past. With marble in hand, Penny joined her brother at the window.

"When is Thomas coming back?"

"I don't know."

"Where did they go?"

"To a park."

"Do you think we can go, James, do you think?"

"No, Penny. I don't know where the park is."

Outside the window, another man walked by. He had a dog on a leash.

"Who is he?"

"I don't know," James said, his voice growing a bit testy.

Penny turned to frown at him, and both children heard the door. Still in his riding togs, Thomas entered.

"Here you are," Thomas said. "I thought you might be in the yard."

"We were," James began and then told the story.

Thomas was just as tempted as James had been to react to Penny's crying over a torn dress, but he kept the thoughts to himself.

"Where did you ride, Thomas?" James wished to know, and both the younger Jenningses sat quietly while Thomas explained his outing.

"Will James ride sometime?" Penny asked.

"I don't know, Pen. I hope so."

"Did Mr Jennings say anything about my riding, Thomas?"

"No, but he seems a fair man, James," Thomas told him, hoping it was true. "I think he'll invite you sometime."

Thomas slipped into the dressing room to change from his riding clothes, his young heart trying to deal with all the changes while still in the midst of mourning.

"Oh, Papa," he whispered ever so softly, "I miss you so."

"This is Mrs Smith," Jennings said for the second time just two days later. The first introduction had been to Bates and Mr Collins. Now the children were meeting Penny's nanny.

"She's going to stay with you, Penny, and be your nanny."

James' face showed his surprise, Thomas' expression was utterly unreadable, and Penny was frozen with fear. She had had a nanny at home, but that lady, a Mrs Beesley, had been rosy-cheeked and smiling. This woman was serious. Mrs Beesley had been young. The bun at the back of Mrs Smith's head was iron gray.

"You'll be moving into the nursery, Penny, and Mrs Smith will have the room that adjoins yours." Jennings turned to the boys with a smile, completely missing the children's response. "You boys will have the bedroom all to yourselves."

Thomas waited for their cousin to ask how that sounded, or if everyone thought this a grand idea, but no question was voiced.

"Come along, Penny," Mrs Smith said calmly, and Thomas tried to relax. She didn't sound shrewish and could have been anyone's grandmother, but Penny's face was hard to ignore. She did as she was told, but Thomas' last glimpse of his sister told him she was afraid.

"Well, now, boys," Jennings said, wasting no time. "I have some things to show you in my study. Do you like maps?"

The boys loved maps—they were captivated by them, just as their father had been. James wondered if such an interest could run in the family. As for Thomas, questions about where Mrs Smith had come from and what their sister's schedule would look like were voiced only in his mind. With a chance for little more than a glance toward the stairs where they'd last seen their sister and her new nanny, the boys followed Jennings into the study, where he shut the door on the rest of the house.

~ ~ ~

"Now, Penny," Mrs Smith said in her quiet voice—they had just arrived in the nursery, a room Penny had not known existed—"I don't like noisy little children. Do you know how to be a quiet little girl?"

Penny nodded, her eyes huge and sober.

"I'm so glad," Mrs Smith praised her. "I don't want to be forced to punish you."

Penny couldn't stop the trembling that started in her limbs, but she made no sound.

"I'm going into my room to get settled. You stay in here and play, and I'll check on you later. Do you understand?"

Penny nodded.

"Answer me, Penny."

"Yes, ma'am," the little girl managed in a very soft voice.

Mrs Smith turned away, a contented smile on her face. She was too old to chase unruly children, but she needed this job. The fear she'd seen on her charge's small face told her this little girl would be no trouble to control. And that worked just fine for Mrs Smith's achy back and legs.

≈ ≈ ≈

"I feel funny about Penny," James admitted to his brother when they climbed into separate beds that night.

"Yes, I do too."

"Why didn't we see her at dinner or lunch?"

"I don't know. I don't even know where the nursery is, but if you remember, Mrs Beesley often ate with us in our nursery."

"Do you think Penny will be in the garden in the morning?"

"I don't know, James. I don't even know if we'll be in the garden in the morning. Try to sleep."

The room was quiet for a time, but James did not sleep. After several minutes, he spoke again.

"I'm afraid, Thomas."

"Of what?"

"I'm afraid Mr Jennings will make us leave."

"Why would he do that?"

"What if we don't do as he says? What if he decides he doesn't like us?"

Thomas had no answer. It didn't seem as though Mr Jennings had hard feelings toward them; indeed, he seemed to accept them into his home with amazing ease. But it was also very clear that he was a man who liked having his own way. Thomas had no desire to be uncharitable in his assessment. After all, Jennings had given them a home almost sight unseen, but something was not right in this situation, and Thomas had yet to place his finger on it.

"Try to sleep, James," Thomas said again, not sure what answer to give his brother. He was so tired of feeling like a parent when at twelve he so desperately needed one himself.

"I will, Thomas, but I think we need to do everything Mr Jennings says. I think we need to obey at all times, so he doesn't boot us out."

Thomas did not attempt to reply to this. As he'd been doing every night before he fell asleep, he prayed and asked God to help him. But this night's prayers for himself were brief. His sister heavy on his mind, he prayed that Penny would be all right and not missing them too much.

"Where are you going, Penny?" Mrs Smith asked the next morning, causing the little girl to jump and turn in surprise. Penny backed against the door she'd been reaching for but didn't answer her nanny.

"Come here, Penny," Mrs Smith said, her voice not as nice or soft.

Penny told herself to move but couldn't quite manage the act. She wanted to speak, but Mrs Smith's face had begun to look cross.

"Come here, Penny," she ordered, and this time Penny managed to move. It must not have been fast enough, however, since Mrs Smith covered the distance and took her upper arm in a harsh grip. Squeezing hard and holding Penny's arm at an awkward angle, she marched her back into the middle of the room before giving her a hard shake.

"You will come when I tell you, and you will leave the nursery when I tell you. Not before. Do I make myself clear?"

Penny nodded, but Mrs Smith shook her again.

"Answer me!"

"Yes, ma'am."

Finally released, Penny stood looking up at her nanny, afraid to speak or move.

"Come now." Mrs Smith's voice was soft again. "You must eat your breakfast."

Tears filled Penny's eyes. She was supposed to eat in the dining room with Thomas and James. Didn't Mrs Smith know that?

"What's the matter?" Mrs Smith, seeing the tears, inquired. Her voice didn't sound angry, but with more strength than necessary she took Penny's arm again and marched her to the small table by the window.

"Sit here. I'll bring your food."

Penny rubbed her arm as her nanny went toward the tray, but she didn't speak or try to go toward the nursery door again. A noise from the street pulled her attention to the window, and she looked that way. She watched a man and lady walking together under an umbrella. They had a little dog. Penny looked down at the pup. He was cute, but not even the sight of him could take her mind from the pain of her arm.

~ ~ ~

"Do they go out at all?" Cook asked Megan, her brow lowered in irritation. The dough she was working on was taking a severe beating.

"Not that I know of," Megan replied, working on a cup of tea and some biscuits. "How many days has it been?"

"Three! She's not even friendly when she comes down here, and I haven't seen so much as a peek of Miss Penny! Doesn't the old bat know that little girls need fresh air?"

"Clearly not. I told her Miss Penny was welcome in the kitchen and that you had a cookie for her, but I was told that Miss Penny had had enough sweets."

Cook snorted in anger. "With the spread of that old girl's hips, she's probably eatin' both puddings!"

"I wouldn't doubt it."

The kitchen was silent for a time, save for the pounding of Cook's fists and the soft clatter of Megan's cup on the saucer. The silence lasted for some time. In fact, Megan was pouring herself another cup when Cook suddenly joined her at the table.

"I'll tell you what," Cook said, her voice dropping in a conspiratorial manner, but before she could continue, Mr Collins came on the scene.

"Cook, Mr Jennings would like the dinner hour moved. He and the boys have gone riding and will be returning late."

"What time?" Cook said, rising to check her bread dough.

As Mr Collins gave the updated time, Megan went back to her duties. She hadn't heard what Cook's plan had been concerning Penny and Mrs Smith, but that was probably for the best. They both enjoyed working for Mr Jennings, and neither one wanted to lose her job.

Chapter Three

"I have something to show you boys," Jennings said.

The boys had come to expect these words, as nearly every day began the same way. Had it not been for the fact that they hadn't seen Penny in five days, it might have been idyllic. Mr Jennings kept them so busy they barely had time to miss their father. They went horseback riding, visited the London Botanical Gardens and the Compt Museum, and shopped in elite stores where the boys were outfitted in several new suits of clothing, bought stylish hats, and were even given riding crops by their new benefactor.

"This," Jennings proclaimed with pride, "is a pocket globe."

"Look, Thomas!" James exclaimed.

Thomas needed no urging. The pocket globe, just three inches in size, was captivating in detail, closing inside a small round case that showed the constellations of the stars inside. Jennings allowed the boys to hold it and look to their hearts' content. They smiled in delight as they located Africa, the United States, and of course, England.

"Where did you find it?" James wished to know.

"In a novelty shop on Bond Street. We'll have to visit there sometime. I think you might find it interesting. Thomas, what did we do with the map we studied yesterday, the small one?"

"It's in my room. Shall I get it?"

"Please do. This tiny globe was copied from that, and I want you to see the details so you can compare them."

Thomas was off just a moment later, taking the stairs two at a time on long, youthful legs. He went directly to his room, to the table near his bed, and found the map. When he turned back he was surprised to see his sister a few feet inside the room.

"Penny!" he said with great pleasure as he approached her. "Look at your hair! Mrs Smith made it look very pretty." This said, Thomas took a chair near the door. "What are you doing?" he asked, his heart so glad to see her.

"Mrs Smith said I could walk in the hallway," she said quietly and then abruptly announced, "I have to go." With that the little girl began to move away.

"Wait, Penny," Thomas said, a small measure of amusement in his voice. Did his sister think she would be in trouble if she spoke to him?

But Penny didn't stop. She moved away from her older brother, who put his hand around her upper arm to stop her.

"Oh, please, Thomas—" Penny turned in obvious pain, shocking him in the process. "Please don't touch my arm. It already hurts."

"Why does your arm hurt?" Thomas asked, letting go at the same time.

"I have to go," Penny said, looking well and truly panicked now.

Coming to his feet, Thomas took his sister by the shoulders, feeling her flinch again, and moved her to the chair he'd just vacated.

"Sit down."

Jennings chose that moment to investigate what had become of Thomas. He walked through the doorway unannounced.

"Thomas, what's keeping you?" he asked, his voice tinged with irritation.

"I need to see my sister," Thomas said, facing him squarely.

"Can't that wait?"

"No," Thomas stopped the man by answering firmly. "James," Thomas went on when that little boy appeared in the doorway, "come in here. I wish to see you and Penny."

"Thomas," James asked in fear as he walked toward his siblings, having seen the thundercloud on his brother's face, "what are you doing?"

"Come in, James," he said without answering.

"Thomas," James was ready to panic now. "Mr Jennings is going to throw us out."

"That is certainly his prerogative," Thomas stated, his voice resolved but at the same time missing the shock on Jennings' face as he turned on James' words. "And that goes for Mrs Smith too," Thomas added when that lady made an appearance in the doorway. "I'm going to spend some time with my brother and sister."

Her face expressionless, Mrs Smith nodded and bowed her way back out the door. Jennings looked at Thomas' set features and spoke quietly.

"Is there something you need, Thomas?"

The young man took a breath. "It has occurred to me that too many days have passed since the three of us have been together. Much as we appreciate your training and time with us, I would wish to take a break at this time and be with Penny and James."

"Of course, Thomas," Jennings said with compassion, seeing that Thomas was most sincere and upset. "Take all the time you need."

"Thank you."

Jennings left without another word, and the moment they were alone, Thomas shut the door.

"Thomas," James tried again. "What have you done?"

"Hush, James. Come here, Penny," her older brother ordered. There was a small sofa set at an angle to the left of the window. Thomas sat on it and pointed to the seat beside him. Penny joined him, her eyes sober, and James sat in the chair across from them.

"Why does your arm hurt, Penny?"

The little girl rubbed her arm and looked at her shoes.

"You can tell me, Penny."

"I have to be very quiet for Mrs Smith. She wants me to be quiet."

"What does that have to do with your arm?"

Penny looked at him. "She pulled on it."

Feeling as though he could be quite ill, Thomas' eyes slid shut. He had not seen this. He had not understood what might be happening. He opened his eyes to find both of his siblings staring at him. Penny's face was pale; James was as grave as Thomas had ever seen him.

Father, we need you. How could you leave us this way?

A sob broke in Thomas' throat as he motioned to Penny. Once she stood before him, he helped her out of her dress. He took in the dark marks on her shoulders and upper arms in horror. Wordlessly he went to the basin to splash cold water on his face and willed his breakfast to stay in place.

After a moment he dried his face very slowly, the situation suddenly becoming clear to him. William Jennings wanted nothing to do with Penny. She had been an inconvenience to him from the start. Had he even known this Mrs Smith, or was she brought into the house on a moment's thought or whim? Not that it mattered right now. All that mattered was that they get away.

Thomas returned to his sister and helped her into her dress. He smoothed her hair and then started to explain.

"We need to leave here."

"Where will we go?"

"I don't know right now, but we can't stay here."

James began to cry.

"I'm sorry, James, I know you feel safe here, but we can't stay."

"It's not that," he wept. "Why would Mrs Smith hurt Penny?"

"I don't know, but we're not going to let it go on."

Thomas stood and paced the room. His head was beginning to hurt, but he knew this was his job. Penny was helpless, and Jennings didn't care about her welfare.

"I've got it." Thomas stopped and faced James. "You and I will wake early tomorrow, pack our things, and then get Penny. We'll sneak out early in the morning and have all day to find a place to stay."

"Do you suppose Mr Jennings' sister lives in London? He mentioned her one time. Do you think we could find her?"

"Father never talked about her either, James. I just don't know."

"I want to stay with you," Penny said quietly, and mourning for the pesky little sister she could be at times, Thomas simply looked at her. Right now she looked worn and worried, and much too young to live through such hurt.

"We'll spend the day together," Thomas suddenly said, knowing he was following the whim of the moment. "We'll act as normal as possible and not even think about tomorrow until we have to. You can keep a secret, can't you, Penny?"

"I can, Thomas."

"Good girl. We'll just play outside and enjoy the day like we did last week, and we'll go to bed early like we used to."

"I want to sleep in here with you," Penny sobbed, and Thomas went to her.

"I'll see what I can do," Thomas assured her, thinking it would make it hard to get her clothing if she stayed with them, but not sure he'd sleep a wink if she was in Mrs Smith's care a moment longer.

"Okay," Thomas said, pushing all thoughts of their dark future away and coming back to the moment. "Let's head to the garden."

The three trooped down the stairs together, all three of them surprised to find Jennings at the bottom.

"Here you are," he said, seeming pleased, and James relaxed. Penny hung back some, but Thomas, holding her hand, went forward, looking more confident than he felt.

"Can we continue with our lesson now, gentlemen?"

"I think not, sir," Thomas said, his voice not sounding confident at all. "We're going outside for a time, and then we plan to spend the day together."

It was on the tip of Jennings' tongue to remind this young man that he was a guest in this home, but then he realized he didn't want him to feel that way. He wanted him to see this as home. Glancing down at Penny, Jennings believed yet again that she was the fly in this ointment.

"Is Penny not going back to Mrs Smith right now?" Jennings asked, having to work to keep his voice light.

"I'm not sure that Mrs Smith is right for Penny," Thomas tried.

"Come now, Thomas," Jennings said with a mild shake of his head before making the mistake of adding, "all children have days when they don't like their nannies."

Thomas' mind was more than made up. If they had to walk out this instant to keep Penny safe, they would.

"It's been many days," Thomas began, unaware of how young and hurt he looked, "since the three of us have had time together. We want to spend today together, and we want to start in the garden."

Jennings did not do a good job of hiding the fact that he was put out. He bowed abruptly, turned on his heel, and strode into his study. The children watched the door shut and then looked at each other.

Thomas continued to lead the way outside, part of his heart in turmoil and part in peace, thinking that whatever happened, they'd made the step, the job was done. They'd burned their boats behind them, but it didn't matter—they'd be gone by this time tomorrow morning.

≈ ≈ ≈

Jennings looked at the stack of correspondence on his desk, his jaw bunched in anger. Did those boys not know that he'd put his life on hold for them? Did they not realize he was willing to be a father to them? How ungrateful could they be? They could not expect to spend all their time with their sister! At their ages it was a ridiculous notion. What did they plan on doing when the fall term started for school?

Amid this mental rampage, Jennings spotted a letter peeking from the stack. Even without seeing the entire envelope, he knew the pale blue stationery to be his sister's. Surprisingly, a calm flooded him. There was a time when he loved to be with his sister. Very protective of her, he would have done just as Thomas was doing if she'd been even a little bit unhappy.

"I've been too hard on the boy," Jennings said to the empty room. "This is a good thing. They need to be together some days. I'll simply work that into the schedule. I'll leave them on their own today, but I'll tell them about it tomorrow."

Regardless of the warm feelings he'd experienced a moment earlier, Jennings did not open his sister's letter. He pulled his other correspondence across the desk, determined not to waste the day.

≈ ≈ ≈

With Thomas holding Penny and one of the bags and James grasping two others, the threesome were able to gain the front door of Mr Jennings' home and make a very quiet exit. The street lamps were still lit, but it would be full light in close to an hour. Walking a good block from the house before setting Penny on her feet, Thomas took her hand as soon as her feet were on the ground.

Tears she would never be able to explain streamed down her face. She was frightened and relieved and excited and terrified all at the same time. And on top of that, she'd forgotten to excuse herself before they left.

"What's the matter, Penny?" James asked when he heard her sniff.

"I have to be excused," she said for lack of a better answer.

"Can you wait until we get to the park?" Thomas asked, not slowing or even looking down. "I'll find a place for you there."

"Is that where we're going, to the park?" James was surprised.

"Yes."

"But won't that be the first place Mr Jennings looks?" James argued.

"Why would he look for us, James? He'll probably be heartily relieved to be rid of us."

On that dark note, the three walked on. The morning was cool but showed signs of being muggy and close before the day ended. Thomas forced himself not to think about it. Where would they be by the end of the day? A vision of him and James being placed into a boys' home and Penny being shipped off to an orphanage sent such a tremor through him that his grip tightened on Penny's small hand. She wiggled it in discomfort, and Thomas forced his hand to relax.

Please, Lord, Thomas prayed as he had been praying for hours. *Please help us. I feel I did the right thing. I couldn't let her be hurt. Please take care of us, just as Papa taught us that You would. We need You right now. Please guide our way.*

And working hard in his twelve-year-old heart to believe that God would take care of them, Thomas Jennings, the self-appointed guardian of the family, took his siblings almost three miles away to a park that Mr Jennings had taken the boys to visit only once. After taking care of Penny's needs, they sat on a bench that Thomas had spotted in a small alcove of bushes and trees. After passing out the biscuits he'd spirited away from the dinner table the night before, Thomas sat very still, his siblings on either side of him, and closed his eyes to think.

Jennings knew that a person could completely disappear in London, but this was not one person, it was three, and the oldest of the group, competent though he might be, was not overly familiar with the area.

His horse moving in perfect rhythm to his commands, Jennings combed each and every park they'd ever visited. He thought it highly unlikely that they'd go as far afield as Lincoln Park, and on top of that it was small, but he was going to leave no stone unturned. He would learn firsthand why the hospitality and kindness he'd offered had been rejected and thrown in his face.

Nevertheless, some of his anger did cool when he finally spotted them. He didn't expect both James and Penny to look so small, or to see Penny's small head pillowed on Thomas' shoulder, her face very dejected indeed. Not that it stayed that way for long. The moment Thomas spotted Jennings, he came to his feet, causing Penny to sit upright on the bench, her eyes huge. As Jennings came off of his mount, James also came to his feet, his face showing fear as well.

"We're not coming back," Thomas said boldly, even as Jennings approached.

"Well, I'm glad to hear it," Jennings said calmly. "It was going to be rather hard for me to offer more hospitality after you'd thrown the first in my face."

Thomas dropped his eyes in shame for several moments before going on.

"We do so appreciate your kindness, Mr Jennings, and we are sorry about leaving so abruptly. Thank you for everything you did."

Jennings waited for more, but nothing came. For a time the four stood in awkward silence.

"And that's to be the end of it, Thomas?" Jennings asked at last. "No explanation for your behavior?"

"It's not going to work, sir. I wish that it could, but—" Thomas hesitated, searching for words, but only finished with "I'm sorry."

Jennings knew nothing but frustration. What had Godwin Jennings taught these boys? Did they not realize that young men had a different role than girls? It was the way life was, and nothing would change that.

"I don't know if the world you're looking for exists, boys," Jennings said, his voice still quiet. "I know you wish to be with Penny more than you have been, but what of the fall? What of when you return to school?"

"We'll have to find something suitable," Thomas said, even as he wondered how that could possibly be.

Jennings' hands came up in confusion. "I thought you were enjoying our time, boys. I know it hasn't been easy. I know you're still in mourning, but you seemed so pleased with our activities."

"But we can't let her be hurt!" James blurted, tears pooled in his eyes. "We can't like maps and going riding so Penny is harmed!"

The young lad's sentence was a mess, but Jennings understood his every word. His heart filling with dread over the images in his mind, he walked to the bench. Penny scooted as far behind Thomas as she could get, but Jennings still sat down in the midst of them.

"Here, Thomas," he said, "sit down by me, please."

The kindness he heard in Mr Jennings' voice caused him to obey. He sat next to this older cousin, his whole frame tense. He felt Penny crowd in close beside him and shifted to make room for her.

Jennings looked over to James, who was still standing, their faces at eye level, and thought, *He's so young. He's just a little boy, and Thomas isn't much older.* Jennings' gaze moved to Penny. She looked away when their eyes met, and he read very real fear in her face.

"Mrs Smith is hurting Penny?"

"Yes," Thomas answered quietly. "She has bruises on her shoulders and arms."

"And you didn't come to me for what reason?"

"Begging your pardon, sir," Thomas said, his eyes forward and not on the man beside him. "It seems to me that Penny is bothersome to you. I was not certain you would stop Mrs Smith. I felt I had to."

Jennings knew he deserved this and more. The way he had behaved, the boys had every right to feel this way.

"Come here, Penny," Jennings said to her and watched as she came slowly off the bench. When she looked up at him, her eyes were those of a wounded animal. Jennings spoke when she stood before him.

"Mrs Smith hurt you?"

The little girl nodded.

"Where did she hurt you?"

Penny rubbed her arm.

"She pulled your arm?"

"Yes."

"Where else?"

"She pinched," Penny said, her small hand going to her shoulder.

Just barely holding the rage inside of him, Jennings went on to ask, "Did she say why she did this?"

"She likes quiet little girls."

"And she thought you were noisy?"

Penny looked confused but then said, "I wanted to go out the door."

"The nursery door?"

Penny nodded. "I wanted to eat breakfast with James and Thomas."

"Listen to me, Penny," Jennings said, reaching down to take one of her little hands in his. "No one is going to hurt you anymore. No one. Not even Mrs Smith."

"I was scared in the nursery."

"With Mrs Smith gone, the nursery will be a very fun place for you to play," Jennings said, even as memory surfaced of his own happy hours in that room. "But you may sleep wherever you wish."

"With Thomas and James?"

"With Thomas and James."

Jennings' heart squeezed almost painfully in his chest when she smiled a very small smile, some of the tension leaving her small brow. How anyone could harm this child was beyond him. But then hadn't he done his share of harm? He hadn't left marks on her skin, but he'd ignored her needs in selfish pursuit of his own wishes.

For the first time in his life William Jennings wanted to hug a child. He wanted to take her in his arms, hold her close, and tell her once again that he would never let her be harmed, but he knew better than anyone that he had not earned this privilege. However, he could still make things right. He could still repair the damage he'd caused.

"I'd like you to come back with me," Jennings invited the children. "I hope you will. I promise you that nothing like this will happen again."

The boys exchanged a look, and James nodded, his face anxious and hopeful.

"We thank you, sir," Thomas said. "And again, I'm sorry we left and didn't speak with you first."

"I know why you did it, Thomas, and you need not apologize again."

In the minutes that followed, the children's bags were loaded onto Jennings' horse so the four of them could walk unimpeded.

"Can you walk all the way, Penny? Can you make it?" Jennings asked.

She looked uncertain, so Thomas tried.

"You can walk, can't you, Penny?"

"I have to be excused," she whispered in embarrassment, and Thomas took her away as a matter of course.

Waiting with James, Jennings decided to hail a coach even as he was reminded how far in over his head he was with children in general, and especially with this little girl. Nevertheless, he would shirk his responsibility no longer. He would return to Aydon, deal with Mrs Smith, and then figure out how to be a proper guardian to these children—all three of them.

What Jennings didn't count on was Mrs Smith knowing just why the children had run. By the time the children and Jennings walked into the house on Rumney Street, that lady had departed with bag and baggage.

Chapter Four

"Send for a constable," Jennings told Bates grimly, not at all happy with this latest turn of events. If he'd been determined to have the children answer for their departure, he was nearly mad with resolve to have Mrs Smith explain her actions. "And since no one saw her departure, check the rooms for missing valuables."

"Right away, sir. Do you wish for me to ask Megan to see to the children?"

Because the children were not with him at the moment and he'd already spelled out in detail the morning's events, he now spoke plainly to the man who had been his faithful servant for more years than he could remember.

"Bates, is the staff kind to the children?"

"Yes, sir," Bates said, not bothering to hide his surprise. "Extremely so."

"Do they tolerate them or enjoy them?"

Bates smiled. "Even Cook cried when the children were discovered missing, sir."

"Good, good," Jennings said softly. He knew he was going to need more help, but at least this was a start. He couldn't overburden the staff with the care of the children along with their other duties, but something had been working before Mrs Smith arrived, and he must find out what it was. At least he assumed it was working, as the children had given no indication of fleeing.

A moment of panic rushed through Jennings when he thought about their leaving again. He couldn't watch the doors at all hours of the day, nor did he want to live like that. The thought, however, of their going and his not being able to find them was very disquieting indeed.

"And, Bates," Jennings called to his man before he could fully exit the room. "Tell Cook to prepare an early lunch, a sumptuous one."

"Yes, sir. Right away, sir."

Left on his own, Jennings sat pensively behind his desk, his mind running with the events of the day and his desire to find Mrs Smith and bring her to justice. Thinking the children might need him, he kept the study door open so he could keep an eye on the stairs, but at least for the moment he was on his own. That was when he spotted it again: the latest letter from his sister.

Usually such missives were dropped into a file drawer, unopened and unheeded, but today, for the first time in more years than he could recall, he opened the letter from Mrs Frank Palmer.

Dear Jennings, it began.

> *I hope this finds you well. How is London's weather just now? We're growing warmer by the day, and the flowers must be loving it as they are in full bloom. Does your own garden still give you pleasure?*
>
> *Did you hear from our cousin Godwin Jennings' solicitor? I don't recall that I ever met Godwin, at least not for years, but I was saddened to hear of his death. Palmer and I have wondered what must have become of the children. Did you hear anything? I can't help but wonder if they match any of the ages of our four.*

Jennings could not keep reading. The last he knew his sister had two children. To learn that he'd been this far out of touch was very upsetting. His dealings with children of late, and now this reminder, helped him to see what a selfish creature he'd become.

Rising slowly from his desk, he went in search of Bates. He wanted to know how Cook was coming with lunch, as he planned to join the children.

~ ~ ~

Thomas' heart burgeoned at the efforts of their benefactor. He'd come in just after they'd sat down to lunch and asked if he could join them. The boys, fairly comfortable with Mr Jennings, had no qualms. Penny, however, had shrunken in her chair a little. Jennings was not put off. He glanced her way several times and eventually ventured forth.

"Do you have enough milk, Penny? Would you like a little more?"

"Yes, please."

Forgetting herself for the moment, Penny put Mr Pat on the table so she could reach for her glass.

"What is this?" Jennings asked, his voice showing real interest.

Penny nearly upset her milk in her swift effort to put the glass down and take the porcelain figure from the tabletop. She bit her lip in fear, her hands holding the figurine in her lap.

"You can show it to Mr Jennings, Penny," Thomas encouraged. "He'd like to see it."

Reluctance showing in every move, her look guarded, Penny gently placed a small bunny dressed in a dapper blue coat on the table next to her plate.

"It's a rabbit wearing a coat."

"Mr Pat," Penny said softly.

"His name is Mr Pat?"

"He was my mother's."

Jennings smiled at her. "I'm glad you have something that belonged to her, Penny. I'm sure she would be pleased to know you enjoy it."

Penny smiled shyly, and in order to rescue her, Jennings went back to his lunch. He ate calmly until he found Thomas' eyes on him.

"They're not as frightening as you first thought, are they, sir?" the young man asked.

"What aren't, Thomas?"

"Little girls."

Jennings laughed, the first laugh the children had ever heard from him.

"No, they aren't, Thomas," he had to agree. "No, indeed."

≈ ≈ ≈

"See to it that the children have plenty to wear and have any of their favorite belongings packed as well," Jennings told Bates much later that same day. He'd added this last order since Mr Pat had also been in attendance at the dinner table. "If all goes according to plan, I'll be sending for the staff, but for now, have Collins keep things busy here."

He'd finally made it back to the study and finished his sister's letter. He'd read it through twice. Not having received a reply in all these years did not seem to have put her off. His sister's letter was sanguine and caring. And the note at the bottom was one he could not ignore.

I know how busy you must be, Jennings, but should you ever have time to write or stop in, it would be lovely to see you or hear from you.

Much as William Jennings knew that he did not deserve a sister such as he had, he was not going to ignore this offer. If he'd had more time, he would have gone back and read all his sister's letters, but right now he just wanted to see her. He wanted to talk with her and Frank Palmer, and share with them this event that had happened in his life. Even knowing that his not calling on them until he had a need was a selfish act, he hoped they would forgive him for the children's sake.

"We'll be off just after breakfast tomorrow."

"Very well, sir," Bates said, all the while making notes. "Do you wish Megan or one of the other housemaids to go along to make Miss Penny more comfortable?"

"I think we can manage," Jennings said. "She's quite content with her brothers, and they deal with her needs most competently."

Bates was taking more notes when there came a soft knock on the doorframe. The men looked to see Thomas standing just outside.

"Did you wish to see me, sir?"

"Yes, Thomas. Come in. That will be all, Bates."

"Yes, sir."

"Sit down, Thomas. I wish to ask you a question." Jennings waited only until Thomas was comfortable in one of the large leather armchairs to begin. "I'm trying to understand something, Thomas. It might seem obvious to you, but I need a little help."

"Yes, sir."

"Before Mrs Smith came, were you hoping to get away from Aydon?"

"No, sir."

"I repeat, this might seem clear to you, but I need to ask, why?"

"Because Penny was safe then, and we were able to see her."

"So if I had insisted that you come on rides with me or come in here for a lesson of some sort that would have excluded Penny, would you have tried to leave?"

"I would have been most uncomfortable leaving Penny on her own, but I don't think I would have taken such action if she was not being harmed. If she was upset and lonely, I would have tried refusing you, if not—" Thomas finished with a shrug since he didn't honestly know what course he would have chosen.

But Jennings had heard enough. He had suspected as much, and now Thomas confirmed it. It shouldn't have been such a mystery to him, but it had been.

"Thank you for explaining to me, Thomas. Now, I need to tell you that we're leaving in the morning."

Thomas nodded.

"My sister and her family live near Collingbourne. We'll be leaving after breakfast, quite possibly for an extended stay."

"All of us, sir?"

"Yes. I told Bates that we did not need one of the women for Penny, but if you'd rather she have someone along, he can arrange that."

"Will Penny be with us the entire time?"

"Yes, certainly."

"James and I can take care of her, sir."

"I felt confident you could."

A high-pitched shriek sailed through the doorway just then, and Jennings came half out of his seat.

"Was that Penny?"

"Yes, sir."

"Should we see to her?"

"No," Thomas said with a smile. "She and James are playing in the nursery. Would you like me to tell them to quiet down?"

"No," Jennings said slowly, his face thoughtful. "They don't need to quiet down at all." He was quiet himself for a moment before adding, "My sister and I used to play in that nursery."

Thomas nodded and watched the older man for a moment. Something had certainly changed in him that day.

Just twenty-four hours earlier, Thomas was ready never to see him again, but the young man could now see that Mr Jennings had been completely unaware of Penny's needs. He had not been malicious, just inattentive.

It gave Thomas no end of comfort to know that his father had been right: God would never leave them or fail to see to their needs.

≈ ≈ ≈

"Breakfast is served," Mr Collins said to James when he opened the door of the bedroom.

"Thank you," James said before turning to the other two occupants, letting the door fall open in the process, and adding, "I told you."

"Well, go and eat!" Thomas said impatiently. "We'll come as swiftly as we can."

"Ouch! That hurts," Penny cried, her brow lowered in anger and pain.

"If you'll recall, Penelope Jennings," her brother said ruthlessly, "I wanted to braid this last night and you wouldn't let me, so now you have snarls."

Watching them bicker but knowing that breakfast was ready, James stood in indecision before heading down the hallway. Mr Collins had gone on his way. Megan was needed and without delay. Thomas was still struggling with his sister's dark, curly mane when the head housekeeper came to the door.

"Why, Miss Penny," she called, entering without invitation, "I think you must have the kindest brother in all of England to help you with your hair."

Penny didn't look quite so mulish with Megan in the room, and in fact her heart smarted over how cross she had been to Thomas.

"May I help you, Master Thomas, or do you have things managed?"

"I would very much appreciate your help," Thomas replied, his voice and face showing his relief. "I can't brush it out without hurting her."

"You start from the bottom," Megan said calmly, having taken the brush in hand. "You work the lower snarls out first and then make your way to the top."

"Oh, I see." Thomas watched in amazement at the difference Megan's deft hand movements had already made.

"Why don't you go and have some breakfast, Master Thomas? I'll have Penny to you in no time."

"Thank you, Megan," Thomas said before making his way from the room. Head down, knowing they were running late, he all but collided with Jennings in the hallway.

"Problems, Thomas?" he asked calmly, although he was eager to get under way.

"My sister has enough hair for three six-year-olds!"

Jennings' hand came to his mouth. He didn't think he'd seen Thomas frustrated with Penny and found it amusing.

"Are things under control?"

"Megan is seeing to her."

"I'll go along in and escort her down when she's ready. Go and eat."

Thomas gladly went on his way, and Jennings slipped into the children's room. Megan was well along in her efforts, but still Jennings took a nearby chair to watch.

"How is it coming, Megan?"

"Just fine, sir. She won't be long now."

Jennings sat quietly and watched the process. He also watched Penny watching him back and knew he should say something. He opted for the first thing that came to mind.

"You have very pretty hair, Penny."

"It's long," she said, her face apologetic and a bit grim.

"That's true. Has it ever been cut?"

"No."

"So it's been growing for six years," Jennings figured quietly.

"It has?" Penny asked, her face showing surprise.

Jennings smiled a little. If she stayed as pretty in later years as she was today, he'd have no trouble at all finding a man to marry her. The thought had no more materialized when he realized it wouldn't be that simple. If he didn't find a man that would care for her, he wouldn't want her to leave the safety of his home. It was not something he'd considered before but was now quite certain of.

"All set!" Megan said triumphantly, interrupting his premature musings.

"What do we say, Penny?" Jennings encouraged, remembering the way his nanny had reminded him.

"Thank you."

"You're welcome, Miss Penny."

"Do you have Mr Pat?" Jennings stood and asked.

The little girl nodded.

"Then let's be off to breakfast and on our way."

Not certain if he should take her hand or not, Jennings opted to let her walk on her own. Dressed, hair in place, and with someplace specific to go, Penny didn't seem at all threatening to the thirty-three-year-old bachelor, but if the truth be told, most of the time he had not a clue as to what to do with this adorable little girl.

After staying overnight in Newbury, the small group made much of the rest of their journey in silence. Sometimes, however, there was nonstop talking as Jennings explained points of interest to the children or they asked questions.

Jennings could feel a tenseness coming over him the closer the carriage drew to Tipton, Frank and Lydia Palmer's home. Would they welcome him after so many years? Would they take one look at him toting three children to their door and promptly slam the portal in his face? Jennings didn't wish for the children to know his angst over the matter, but he thought he caught Thomas' gaze on him from time to time. It was a cheeky move, his coming like this, and he knew it. His pride was on the line—that was all too evident—but right now he thought it worth the risk.

"Are we near, Mr Jennings?" James suddenly asked.

"We are, James. How is that book coming?"

"I've read it before," James told him kindly, wondering at the fact that the older man had already asked him that question.

"Has it been some time since you've seen your sister, Mr Jennings?" This came from Thomas.

"As a matter of fact, it has," Jennings felt relieved to admit. "I didn't send word ahead, and now I rather wish I had."

Thomas nodded and looked out the window. Had Mr Jennings been his father and not a guardian, he would have asked all sorts of questions, such as where they would stay, whether this family had children, and so on. As it was, he felt it best to take his cue from the older Jennings and keep silent when he was silent.

"There's Tipton now," Mr Jennings said at last, and the children vied for position at the window to see a grand home in a picturesque setting.

"They have a pond!" James noticed.

"Let me see," Penny said, but both boys were in the way.

"Look at the size of that tree," Thomas said in awe.

"I can't see," Penny tried again.

"Come here, Penny." Jennings was happy to rescue her and take his mind from the imminent meeting. He was so distracted by seeing his sister that he didn't actually take note of the fact that Penny allowed herself to be lifted into his lap so she could see out his window. The carriage was pulling up the long drive before they both noticed where she was. Penny moved to the seat next to him, looked up into his face, and then quickly looked down again in embarrassment.

Jennings thought about patting her little knee or making some gesture but was uncertain what to do. On top of that, he was out of time. The carriage was coming to a halt and Thomas was turning to him.

"May we see the pond, sir?"

"Yes, Thomas, but do keep a close eye on Penny."

Jennings allowed the children to scramble from the carriage and head to the pond.

"Keep well back now!" he called to them as he emerged from the coach and then stood by while they went near the water, Penny's small hand tucked into Thomas'. He knew the edge was not deep but still kept watch for a few minutes.

Jennings' head eventually tipped back, and he looked up at the cloudless blue sky. It had been a long time since he'd been in this part of the country, and he had forgotten its beauty. His eyes were taking in the familiar details, the rolling hills and valleys, when he realized he was being watched.

Not far outside the front door stood his sister. Jennings glanced at the children before turning fully to cover the distance to his only sibling.

"Jennings," Lydia said when he neared, tears standing in her eyes.

"Liddy." Jennings' voice was just as quiet with emotion as he came forward to hug her and kiss her cheek. Lydia gladly returned the embrace and then looked up at him when he stepped back, his hands still on her arms.

"You look well, Liddy."

"As do you, Jennings," she said before glancing toward the pond. "Godwin's children?"

"Yes."

"They came to you." Her voice held all the wonder she felt.

"Over a fortnight ago."

"Palmer and I have spoken of them many times. We received the solicitor's letter and thought you might be in line as guardian, but it seemed too fantastic to be real." Lydia caught herself babbling and took a breath. "How are they doing, Jennings?"

"Holding their own, no thanks to me."

Lydia's brow knit with confusion.

"I'm not very good at this type of thing," the proud man admitted.

Lydia smiled in relief, glad that nothing serious was wrong. "I hope you've come so we can keep you here for a time and get to know these children."

"As a matter of fact, I have. I seem to find plenty to visit with the boys about, but six-year-old girls have proved to be quite a puzzle to me."

Lydia couldn't hold her laughter.

"Jennings!" Palmer's voice came from behind the couple, and the two men shook hands as soon as Lydia's husband was near. "Welcome to Tipton. It's been much too long."

"I agree with you, Palmer. I hope I'm welcome."

"Very welcome. Now, tell me if my eyes deceive me, or have you become a guardian?"

"It's all too true," he said soberly. The other man was instantly alert.

"I take it you've done this unwillingly," Palmer said, keeping his voice low.

"Not at all, but I made a mess of things when I hired a cruel nanny for Penny."

"Oh, Jennings," Lydia said, a hand to her mouth, her eyes large with shock and hurt over what she saw in his face. "Is the girl all right?"

"Yes, and I plan to keep her that way." There was no missing the determination in his voice.

"Methinks," Palmer said, a smile coming to his lips, "that before us stands a man with a mission."

Jennings had no choice but to agree, a reluctant smile twisting his own mouth.

"How old are they?" Lydia wished to know.

"Thomas is twelve, James is ten, and Penelope, who goes by Penny, is six."

"How did Godwin die?" Palmer asked next, glancing at the children. They had found a pile of small sticks and were throwing them into the water. Palmer didn't notice his brother-in-law's lack of response until he looked back at the man.

Standing very still, his eyes on Palmer but not actually seeing him, Jennings looked stunned. He stared down at his sister as well, his mind racing.

"What is it, Jennings?" Lydia pressed.

"I never asked them," the prodigal brother admitted, his face turning away from them in pain and astonishment over his own lack. "They landed at my door so suddenly. The letter warning me of their coming was lost. I had no word. We just began life together. I can't explain beyond that."

Lydia felt a rescue was needed. She spoke kindly and sincerely when her brother finally looked back at her.

"We're so pleased that you came to gain help with this little girl, Jennings, but could it be that the boys might benefit from this visit as well?"

Again, William Jennings had no choice but to agree.

The children had tired of the game and were headed their way. Jennings was grateful he'd realized these things in the presence of his sister. Lost as he felt just now, he watched the warm, gentle way in which she welcomed Thomas, James, and Penny to Tipton and somehow knew that everything would be all right.

Chapter Five

"Thomas, James, Penny," Lydia said as soon as she had taken the children indoors, "I'm so sorry for your loss."

"Thank you," Thomas replied, feeling very real comfort from the warmth in her soft, feminine voice, and the tender way she touched Penny's small head.

"Our children are on an outing just now, but they'll be returning soon. Would you like to see your rooms?"

Penny had moved in rather closely to Thomas on this question, and Jennings took note of it.

"Is there a room that would accommodate all three children, Liddy?"

"There is," she told him before looking back to the children. "You boys don't mind sharing a bed?"

"No, ma'am," James answered, his little face serious. "We need Penny near us."

"I'm so glad you told me, James, and you must go on telling me anything you need. Come this way now, and we'll see you all settled."

Through a spacious entryway and to the foot of a wide staircase, the children followed their hostess. The house was spacious but still felt homey. The sweeping stairway led to a wide hall and rooms that at a swift glance appeared to be roomy as well.

The children took it all in, seeing things familiar to them and others that were new and thus intriguing. Their room held two beds and all the normal amenities, but the views from the windows were new, as was a large painting of a ship and a detailed map of the area.

"How will this be?" Lydia asked, her face wreathed in smiles and her heart feeling pleased that the children could meet them a little at a time. Her own children were well mannered, but at home they were a boisterous group, and Lydia did not want these new members of the family over-whelmed.

"Did you need me, mum?" A female voice brought all eyes to the door.

"Yes, Judith. I want the children to come back down-stairs with me. Would you be so kind as to settle their things?"

"Of course, mum," the servant said with a smile. "And who are these fine children?"

Lydia's smile matched hers.

"These are my young cousins. Here is Thomas, then James, and the young lady is Penny. Children, this is Judith, and she takes very good care of us. Should you need any-thing, Judith can help you."

"Indeed, I can, and I'm going to start by making this room your very own. When you return, all your things will be tucked away, and you'll have the fun of finding them."

They smiled at her, drawn to her bubbly welcome. Lydia, however, didn't linger. She shepherded the children down to the large drawing room, where Jennings and Palmer were talking.

"Ah, here you are," Palmer welcomed. "Did you like your room?"

"Yes, thank you, sir," Thomas said with feeling. "We will be most comfortable."

"Good, good. Did Mrs Palmer tell you that our children will be home soon?"

"She did, yes."

"And did she also tell you that you are alike in age? Our Frank is twelve, Walt is ten, Emma is seven, and Lizzy is soon to be five."

"And before I forget," Lydia put in, noting that Jennings was sitting very quietly during this exchange and taking it all in, "I must get your birthdays, children. Why don't you give them to me right now?" she asked as she moved to find paper at the small writing desk.

"You've done something to make them laugh," Palmer said, and Lydia turned to find the children smiling hugely.

"What did I say?" she turned to them, glancing at Jennings and wishing he wasn't quite so inscrutable.

"We share a birthday, Mrs Palmer, and it's always a bit funny when others discover that."

Lydia came to a complete halt.

"The three of you? You all have the same birthday?"

"Yes, ma'am."

"When is it?"

"Twenty-one July," James informed her.

"Why, James, that's only about a month away."

"Yes, ma'am," Thomas answered, taking charge again. "I will be thirteen, James will be eleven, and Penny seven."

"And all on twenty-one July?"

The children nodded, the boys still smiling greatly at her reaction. Penny had grown distracted with the pattern on the carpet. Lydia turned to the other adults in the room, but only Palmer was having a good time with this. Jennings looked more strained than ever.

"Well, just let me write that down, and then you children can go and play for a time. How does that sound?"

It had been Lydia's plan to speak with the children for a time—she knew that Palmer wanted that too—but she couldn't ignore her brother's demeanor. And Lydia wasn't the only one to notice. The children had no more left, having been given instructions on finding the nursery, when Palmer spoke to his wife's brother.

"What's troubling you, Jennings?"

Jennings came abruptly to his feet. He strode to the window, back straight with dread, and stood looking out. The Palmers waited. At last he turned to them, his features set.

"I'm not sure we can stay."

"Why, Jennings?" Palmer asked, even as he sensed his wife tensing.

Jennings shook his head, unable to find the words. After several more seconds, he spoke.

"It has occurred to me that I've grown myopic in recent years."

"In what way?" Palmer questioned him.

"I'm centered on my own interests and no one else's," Jennings answered as he began to move about, this time in agitation. "I didn't even remember until I'd walked into this room and saw the Bible on the table why I'd broken contact with you in the first place, and now the children's birthdays!" he fumed quietly, his sentences running together. "I didn't even think to ask them such a thing. I wanted those boys the moment I saw them. I was relieved to have them without having to deal with a wife, but I never intended for Penny to be harmed, and I won't stand for it! But not until just now did I realize that by coming to you for help, I'll be opening myself up to hearing all sorts of nonsense about God, things I don't wish to hear. At the same time, I know I can't do this alone. I've got to have help with these children, so it would seem I have no choice."

Jennings had kept his voice quiet during the entire tirade, but it had gone from passionate to thoughtful. He did not expect to turn and find his sister's hand over her mouth, her eyes filled with merriment.

"Lydia, do not tell me you are amused by this!"

"But, Jennings," she said as a soft laugh escaped, unable
to help herself, "You are too funny. You insult us and then
tell us you need us. On top of that, I don't know when I've
heard such passion from you on any subject."

Though still not able to laugh at himself, Jennings
relaxed some and even sat down again. He looked to his
brother-in-law and found him slightly amused as well.

"Remind me, Jennings," Palmer asked calmly, "what did
we do those many years ago that caused you to run?"

Looking at them now, still the kind, warm people he
remembered from many years back, Jennings drew a blank.
They sat a moment, silence surrounding the three of them,
before full memory returned to Jennings.

"Are you still attending that church where Pastor Hurst
tells people about their sin?"

"Yes, we are," Palmer said without apology.

"And how many followers does he have now?"

"Pastor Hurst? He hasn't any. We're following Jesus
Christ."

It was the very thing he expected them to say, the very
thing that had made him so dreadfully uncomfortable before,
but this time there was a difference. They had already welcomed him and the children, and he didn't believe they'd
done this with a hidden agenda.

"I guess the first thing I should ask," Jennings started
again, "is whether we're still welcome now that I've insulted
you?"

"For as long as you like," Palmer said, his voice and
manner still mild. "But I must warn you, as soon as the
cousins meet, no matter how uncomfortable you feel, you'll
not escape easily at all."

"I hadn't thought of that," Jennings admitted, remembering how shocked he was to hear that his sister had four
children.

After thinking for a moment, Jennings made up his mind. He might disagree wholeheartedly with his sister and Pastor Hurst, but he would not separate from his family again. He wanted to know his only nieces and nephews, and he wanted his young charges to know them. But even beyond that, one fact was glaringly evident: He hadn't the slightest idea how to be a parent, and for the sake of the three children now entrusted to him, he would stay.

≈ ≈ ≈

"What do you think of them?" Thomas asked of James when they'd found the nursery and settled in. The room's furnishings were a bit on the young side for Thomas, but he was happy to do nothing for a time and to do it in a place that felt safe.

"They're nice. Does Mrs Palmer remind you of Aunt Fanny?"

"She wasn't really our aunt, James—just a neighbor."

"I know, but her voice is like Aunt Fanny's, and she was very kind."

"Yes, she was," Thomas agreed softly, and if James had been looking at him just then, he might have asked about the speculative look on his older brother's face. Had Thomas shared, he would have asked how Mrs Palmer could be so kind when her brother seemed so aloof. He knew some of it was the difference between men and women, but his heart sensed that there was more to it.

"I can't get it out." Penny's voice floated into Thomas' musings, and he watched as James dislodged a block from inside the large dollhouse.

"Thomas," Penny asked when she had the block in hand, "what did Mrs Palmer say her daughters were named?"

"I think it was Emily and Lizzy."

"No, it was Emma and Lizzy," James corrected as he dumped a puzzle on the floor.

"That's right. And they're your age, Penny."

Penny nodded but didn't comment. She went back to the dollhouse, her face pensive. Thomas could have asked her if she was upset, but he thought he knew. It was nice to feel safe, and it would be fun to gain new playmates their own age, but not all the toys and friends in the world would take away the ache they felt to see their father one more time.

~ ~ ~

The Palmer children were on an outing with their neighbor, Miss Marianne Walker. She was too young to be their mother but old enough to be responsible for them. A young aunt was how she'd described herself one time, but the children still thought of her as an older sister.

Young Frank Palmer, oldest of the Palmer children, not overly distracted by the flowers his sisters were picking, was enjoying his time by the stream. The small fish were active at this time of year. He found them fascinating and wondered at the fact that they never seemed to bump into each other. The occasional rub alongside could be seen, but rarely was there a head-on encounter, even in the midst of panic. That, along with the splendid rocks he was finding, made him feel he could sit in this spot all day.

"What did you find, Frank?" Walter Palmer, Walt to family and friends alike, asked as he approached.

"An interesting rock. Look at the shape."

"It looks like a fish."

"I think so too."

"You should see the fish a little way down the stream, Frank. Come and see them."

"Look right here, Walt," Frank invited. "They're very active here too."

"Oh, yes, but there's more down where I was."

That was all Frank needed to hear. He accompanied his brother down the shore and sure enough, they stumbled on roughly twice the fish as had been in Frank's area.

Across the small wooden bridge, knee-deep in wildflowers, stood their escort. Beside Marianne were Emma and Lizzy Palmer.

"Look at this one, Marianne," Lizzy directed, showing her a small yellow bloom.

"Isn't it pretty?" Marianne agreed as she shifted the basket to include it.

"Where did the pink one go?" the youngest girl now asked.

"With all the other pink ones," Emma explained, her brow raised in surprise that this had not been more obvious to her sibling.

"But I wanted that one," Lizzy said, her face sincere.

"Here." Marianne crouched down to her level and let her look into the basket. "See if you can find it."

"Oh, Lizzy," Emma said with a laugh like her mother's, "you'll never spot it."

"I will, Emma. I know just the one."

Marianne remained quiet as Lizzy examined the flowers. Lizzy's small brow was earnestly wrinkled as she searched, and Marianne couldn't stop her smile. The almost-five-year-old was such a perfect combination of her parents, with her father's dark curls and her mother's blue eyes.

"This is it," Lizzy said, her face lighting up.

Marianne hugged her.

"I'm so pleased you found it."

"It's pretty."

"Yes, it is—just like the little girl holding it."

Lizzy smiled at her and moved in for another hug.

"Marianne," Walt called to her when she came to her feet; he was still near the stream. "Are we moving on now?"

"Are you ready?"

A yes came from both boys, and the girls began to gather their things. The five of them walked back to the waiting carriage and driver, towing along their rocks and flowers.

"Are your hands muddy, Liz?" Frank asked of his sister before he would allow her to climb into the carriage.

"Just a little," she said as she displayed them.

Marianne came from behind them and offered her hand-kerchief. "Here, use this, Lizzy."

"Thank you," the little girl said, remembering her manners. But it did little good. The handkerchief ended up as dirty as the small hands, which didn't look as though they'd been cleaned at all.

"It's all right, Lizzy. You can wash before we have lunch. Mildred is always ready for you," Marianne said, referring to the head housekeeper at her parents' home.

"Are we having lunch at your house, Marianne?"

"Yes, Walt. I wanted to show you my new book."

"The one on pyramids?"

"Yes. It arrived yesterday."

With that they were off. No one ever declined a meal at Blackburn Manor—it was much too fun for that. Blackburn Manor was Tipton's nearest neighbor. Set in a fair glen at the base of the foothills, it was picturesque and inviting.

When the coach stopped in the wide courtyard, a footman held the door while the five explorers emerged from the carriage.

"Here you are!" Mildred exclaimed with delight as she met them just inside the front door. To Marianne she said, "Your mother is on her way."

"I'm here," Mrs Walker proclaimed as she entered the spacious foyer not many steps behind Mildred, a smile in her voice and on her face. "How was the outing?"

"Splendid, but we're all quite famished," Marianne responded with familial ease as she kissed her mother's cheek.

"How are you, children?" Mrs Walker greeted. She listened to their tales of the morning's adventure before Mildred whisked them away for a swift wash before convening for an early lunch.

Around the table just ten minutes later, Mr Walker also in attendance, the children continued to tell of their exploits.

"What color flowers did you girls find?" Mr Walker asked of Lizzy and Emma.

"Some yellow, some pink, and some muddy."

The table enjoyed this description from the youngest member of the group.

This covered, Frank wished to know if Mr Walker knew anything of fish and their swimming habits. Mr Walker, Frank, and Walt then had a long discussion on the subject.

Not until the meal began to wind down did Marianne say they would be having pudding on the lawn. Thrilled with this news, the children happily moved outdoors from the comfort of the dining room and the delicious meal that had been prepared. Remembering to express their thanks, they trailed after Marianne as though she were blowing a flute.

"Are you coming, Papa, Mama?" Marianne paused to ask.

"You go ahead," her father answered, sending her off with a wave. A moment later the room was once again peaceful.

"No wonder she's not interested in marriage," Mrs Walker commented, her face and voice thoughtful. "She has Lydia's four to raise and enjoy."

"And aren't they blessed?" her husband said mildly, barely glancing up from his own dish of sorbet.

"As are you, Mr Walker," she accused. "You're not fooling me a bit."

"Why would I try, Mrs Walker? The day Marianne falls in love, I'll post the banns myself."

Mrs Walker had nothing to say to this. Her entire family knew that she was more talk than anything else, but she did wish for her youngest child to find happiness in marriage. At age twenty and four, the title of spinster was already being liberally applied.

Her own sweet in front of her but ignored, Mrs Walker watched her daughter on the lawn. Marianne laughed with the children and even threw a ball to Walt, the sound of her sweet laughter floating inside to her parents.

"You're worrying again, Mrs Walker," the man across from her stated, and this time his gaze was full on her.

"I am," she admitted. "When Elinore was married, I never dreamed that Marianne would be years behind her."

"What is it that worries you?"

"That she'll be alone and uncared for."

"And how could that happen with James to take the estate and Henry after him?"

Mrs Walker stared at him for a moment. He certainly had a good point. James and Henry both adored their youngest sister. Should anything become of Mr Walker, they would see she came to no harm.

"You're right, of course. I'm just anxious."

"Why are you?" Mr Walker pursued in genuine caring.

Mrs Walker stared at him, loath to admit the truth. Mr Walker's brows rose as he waited.

"Some days I feel my own mortality most keenly. Lately I've been feeling old."

"And if you're not here to take care of Marianne, the job won't get done."

"Put like that you make me feel a fool, but that is the way I feel right now."

"Your four older children would cry in outrage—you know that, don't you?"

Mrs Walker smiled at the thought, knowing he was right. Mr Walker smiled back. They did not continue to speak of it, but it was good to have such thoughts on the table. If the truth be told, Mr Walker struggled with his own brand of protectiveness toward his youngest child. In a directly opposite manner, he feared that Marianne would marry too soon, that it would be to the wrong man, and that she would be unhappy for the rest of her life. Nevertheless, the bottom line was clear: Neither one of Marianne's parents were trusting God in the way they'd taught her to do. And she would probably laugh at them had she been able to overhear their conversation.

"Come quick!" Walt burst into the room, his eyes huge as he called to the Walkers. "Marianne is hurt!"

No further words were needed to bring husband and wife to their feet. Their child was hurt. There wasn't a moment to lose.

Chapter Six

All three of the children looked up when Jennings entered the nursery at Tipton. Thomas came to his feet, as did James, but Penny stayed behind the large dollhouse, her small face peeking out.

"How are you doing?" Jennings asked, sitting in one of the rocking chairs and waving the boys back to their seats.

"Fine, sir," Thomas answered for all of them, not adding that they were a bit hungry, even though they'd just been speaking of it.

"Have you been outside of this room? Are you getting to know the house and grounds?"

James looked to Thomas. He had wanted to go exploring, but his older brother had thought better of it.

"I wasn't sure if we should," Thomas admitted without embarrassment.

"I should have been more specific," Jennings said. "You'll find my sister's family very welcoming. Come and go as you please."

"Thank you, sir. We'll plan on that."

"Are you getting hungry?" Jennings asked next.

"Yes," James spoke up, and even Penny came to her feet.

"Well, lunch is about ready. By the time we get downstairs, it should be on."

The children needed no other urging, and Jennings was reminded yet again of how much care was involved in parenting. Part of him wanted to tell Lydia to take over and that he would follow her lead, but if he did that, would the children's view of him be altered? And that question begged one more: What *was* the children's view of him?

With a mental start, Jennings realized all three children were standing and waiting for him.

"Shall we go?" he asked, working to keep his voice calm, all the while thinking that he would have to pull himself together.

Thomas, James, and Penny filed out in front of him and proceeded down the stairs. Lydia met them at the bottom, stopping short of saying she was just headed to check their progress. Her brother had his inscrutable look again, and she wondered if something had gone wrong.

"Did you enjoy the nursery?" Lydia asked, leading the way to the small dining room.

"Yes, thank you," Thomas answered.

Lydia's attention turned to Penny. "What did you play with, Penny?"

"The dollhouse," she said quietly, her eyes taking in Lydia's face and hair. Penny had not spent much time in the company of ladies and was captivated by what she saw. She wanted to touch Lydia Palmer's light blue dress but knew she must not.

Lydia caught the little girl's eyes on her but didn't comment. She wondered how long the child's mother had been gone and forced herself not to dwell on how alone the Jennings children were at this time.

"We have some lovely things to eat today. Are you all hungry?" Lydia asked.

The children smiled as they answered in the affirmative, and Palmer, who had watched them come in, felt his heart turn over.

If Jennings leaves and takes these children away from us, Lord, it will be many days before I stop thinking about them.

To cover this sudden rush of emotions, Palmer invited James to sit on one side of him and Thomas on the other.

"You take a seat by Mrs Palmer, all right, Penny?"

That little girl bit her lip but still managed to have a seat. As they'd come to expect, Jennings was quiet. He was seated next to James and across from Penny. It wasn't normally considered protocol to give deference to children when an adult was in the group, but Palmer hoped that Jennings would understand this one time.

"We always pray before we eat, children, so if you'll bow your heads," Palmer said, letting the sentence hang and noticing that the children had a completely comfortable reaction to this, their eyes closing as their heads bowed over their plates.

"What a joy, Father, to have Jennings, Thomas, James, and Penny with us. We thank You for them, for this food, and for all You provide each day. Amen."

"Amen," the children chorused softly, and Palmer and Lydia exchanged a swift look.

It was obvious to the host couple that someone had been working with these children. Jennings also noticed it, and to his surprise, no negative feelings came to mind. These children had been exceptionally well behaved, and maybe some sort of faith in God was the reason.

Jennings almost shook his head over his own musings. Where that thought had emerged from, he would never know.

"So tell me, Thomas," Palmer prompted, "what schools have you and James been attending?"

"We are both at Wimley Banks, in Bristol."

"I know the one. A fine school."

"Our father attended."

"And you carried on the tradition. I think that's very fine."

"Is it a large school?" Lydia wished to know.

Thomas did the honors, filling the adults in before going back to his meal.

"How was the weather in London when you left, Jennings?" Palmer worked to include him, and this seemed to do the trick. Jennings was more talkative as the meal progressed.

"I think we'll take a turn through the grounds," Jennings suggested when he could see the children were finished. "How does that sound?"

The children were amenable, so after thanking their host and hostess, they left with Jennings. He hadn't trooped around the property for many years and was eager to explore as well. As soon as they emerged from the house, they headed for the stables.

"Do the Palmers have many horses?" James asked, having spied the building.

"They do, yes—some fine stock."

The foursome continued to head that way, taking in the grounds as they walked. A long gravel drive led to the stable area. They passed sweeping lawns and manicured gardens ablaze with color. Penny was preoccupied with the flowers she saw but didn't wish to be scolded for lagging behind. If she could have stated her opinion just then, she'd have told someone that she was tired and wanted to be read to, but no one had asked her.

Nevertheless, some of her fatigue fell away as they entered the large barn and saw several horses, beautiful animals with proud heads, long manes, and gleaming coats. The group walked through the building, looking their fill and discussing different aspects of the stock and stable.

James made a comment about the haymow, which drew all eyes that way. It was on the tip of Jennings' tongue to launch into an explanation and turn this outing into a learning experience, but Penny chose that moment to yawn. The boys, although not looking tired, both had sudden looks of vulnerability on their young faces. Putting his own wants aside, Jennings spied some iron benches in the distance, beyond the barn a piece, and took the children that way.

"Let's sit here," he suggested as they approached, and the boys did. Penny had found some flowers just off the path and was looking to her heart's content.

It took a moment for Jennings to find his nerve, but at last he admitted to his cousin's sons, "I should have asked you before about the way your father died. Would it be too difficult for you to tell me now?"

"Do you think it would be all right if Penny went into the field just there and picked flowers?" Thomas asked unexpectedly.

"Certainly," Jennings said, hiding his surprise. "I think that would be fine."

"Here, Penny," Thomas said, gaining her attention for the first time. "Mr Jennings wants to speak with James and me. You go ahead into the field and pick some flowers."

Penny looked in the direction he was pointing.

"I can pick them to keep?"

"Yes. Not too many, but some."

"What if I find a snake?"

"If you see any snakes, just return here to the bench and tell us."

The little girl needed no other urging. Even Jennings turned to watch her wade through the tall wildflowers, her progress impeded because the grasses were up to her waist.

"Is she not afraid of snakes?"

"No, not unless they take her by surprise, and then she's only startled."

They watched Penny for a few minutes longer, and then Thomas explained. "Penny doesn't know the details of our father's death. She can be timid about some things, such as strangers, but she's never shown any fear of horses, and my father wouldn't want her to."

"But that's how your father died?"

"Yes," Thomas said, knowing how ironic it all was and amazed at how fresh the pain felt. "A snake came across the horse's path, and the animal reared so violently that they both went down. The horse landed on my father, who had been thrown against the ground, and Father was killed instantly."

James' eyes were averted, but there was no missing the tears. Thomas was very brave, and Jennings almost wished the boy could cry—it might make him feel better.

"Thank you for telling me."

"May I ask you a question, sir?"

"Yes."

"Do you know what's being done with our father's estate? Is that all settled?"

"The instructions in Mr Willoughby's letter were not overly detailed. He requested that I contact him. I didn't want to do that until I'd spoken to you."

Thomas nodded, his face thoughtful. Jennings continued, wanting the boys to know all the facts.

"I didn't explain to you at the time, but the solicitor's letter was mislaid. I was handed the letter and learned of your arrival at the same moment."

Both boys showed surprise over this, and James even blurted, "So that's why you hired that awful Mrs Smith."

Jennings couldn't stop his smile over this youthful insight.

"I'm afraid it's a little more complicated than that, James, but you are partly right. Tell me, boys, what do you recall hearing about the estate?"

"That William Jennings would be in charge; that William Jennings would handle it."

"And I shall," Jennings assured them. "Who was left to care for your home when you came to me?"

"I know Murch was staying on." Thomas took this question. "He and Mrs Murch will see to things."

"Were they seeing to things before your father's accident?"

"Yes, along with Chauncy. He did the gardening."

Jennings thought a moment. Now that he'd spoken with the boys there were several ways he could handle this, and one in particular was looking the most favorable.

"A bee!" came a small cry from the field.

Thomas stood. "Do not panic, Penelope! Walk back to us. Don't run."

The little girl did as she was told, and during her progress, Jennings revealed his plan.

"I shall be in touch with your father's solicitor and clarify the details with him. Once I have all the information, we'll plan a trip to Morehouse and see everything settled. Does that suit you?"

"Yes, sir. Thank you, sir."

"I should like to see home again," James admitted quietly.

"And so you shall, James," Jennings found it felt very good to be able to tell him.

Penny had almost arrived back. The three watched her approach. When she stood before them, her small hand clutching a bunch of wildflowers, they saw that her cheeks were red and a single tear had escaped.

Not able to help himself, Jennings hunkered down very close in front of her for the first time.

"Were you stung?"

"No," she said, tears very near.

"But you were frightened?"

"He was on a flower I wanted," she explained, and another tear slid down.

Jennings didn't even try to stop himself. A smile tugging at his firm mouth, he pulled a snowy white handkerchief from his pocket and gently mopped her face.

"Do you need the other flower?" he asked her.

Looking a little less miserable and remembering what she'd been told about being thankful, Penny forced herself to say, "I have enough."

"Mr Jennings was offering to take you back, Penny. You need to thank him."

"Thank you," Penny said, having more eye contact with him than she'd ever attempted.

"You're welcome."

Unfortunately for both of them, the older Jennings was out of words. He came somewhat awkwardly to his feet, stuffed the handkerchief back into his pocket, and suggested they explore a bit longer.

"So what do you think, Palmer?" Lydia asked the question she'd been wanting to ask since her brother arrived.

"I think he's utterly lost. I mean, he always has been, but this time it's obvious even to him. He was so certain that if he could have offspring under his own terms, life would be perfect." Palmer chuckled a little. "It's almost amusing to watch him learn otherwise."

Lydia shook her head in wry agreement. "I want them to stay. I want it very much."

"As do I, but we'll have to wait and see. We can't have Jennings upsetting our own household in his attempt to find himself and his parenting skills."

"Yes, Palmer, but will Thomas, James, and Penny survive the process?"

"I think they're stronger than we give them credit for. There's a peace in the boys that tells me someone has been teaching them the Way."

"I sense it too. I hope they get on with our children. It could so help during this painful time."

"When are they due back?"

"They were going to lunch at Blackburn Manor, so probably midafternoon."

"Good. They'll all have the rest of the day to get acquainted, and we'll keep the next few days uneventful."

Lydia nodded, pleased that her husband had a plan. It was on the tip of her tongue to admit to him that she wanted to keep the children for her own, but she kept quiet. God had a plan in place, and right now it included Jennings. If the need ever arose for those children to become her own, she wouldn't need to tell anyone how she felt—it would be written all over her face.

≈ ≈ ≈

"Frank!" his mother said with some surprise when she looked up from her writing desk about an hour later to find her oldest child in the doorway. "I didn't realize you'd returned." Even as she said this, she knew something was amiss. "What is it, Frank?" she asked as she stood. "You look upset."

"We tried to get Marianne to stay home, but she insisted on bringing us back."

"Why would you want her to remain at home?"

"We were playing ball in the yard, and she got hit in the eye."

"Oh, no. Where is she?"

"In the carriage if you wish to see her."

Lydia very much wanted to see her. She followed Frank's progress back outside and found her other three children crowded around the door of the carriage, laughing and smiling.

"Here, children," Lydia said firmly, "let me past."

Lydia stuck her head in the coach to find a smiling Marianne.

"Hello, Liddy."

"Marianne! What have you done?" Lydia said, not able to hold her laugh. The older woman's friend had a black eye that looked as if it had been painted on. A perfect curve had appeared beneath her left eye, giving her a rather roguish look.

"Aren't I a sight?"

"Please tell me my children had nothing to do with this."

"Oh, come now, Liddy, we were playing, that's all."

Lydia sighed and smiled. "Will you come in?"

"No!" Marianne looked horrified at the thought. "I'm taking myself home to seclusion until I look presentable again, but I knew if the children only told you and you didn't see me, you would think it worse than it was."

"You're probably right. I'll come and see you soon, shall I?"

"Please do."

Lydia leaned a little closer into the carriage and lowered her voice.

"Before you go, I've got to tell you that my brother is here."

"Jennings?" Marianne said in amazement.

"Yes. I'm dying to tell you all about it, but it will have to wait."

"All right. Come soon, however. I want to hear."

"I will. How were the children?"

"Wonderful as always. A little mud here and there, but we had a smashing time."

"Good. Give me a hug and get yourself home."

The five Palmers waved Marianne's carriage off, and before they could even turn to the house, Palmer joined them.

"Did Mari not want to come in?" he asked.

"No, she had a blackened eye and is headed home to seclude herself."

"Do you children have anything to tell us?"

"It was all quite innocent, Father," Frank put in, not afraid to admit the truth even though their friend was harmed. "Marianne turned to say something to Lizzy just as Walt threw the ball back to her."

Palmer looked down at his younger son's face. He looked sober and sad.

"So you're the culprit, Walt?"

"Yes, sir. And her eye blackened so swiftly, almost as we watched."

Palmer put a hand on his shoulder.

"It's like that sometimes. You spoke with her, Lydia?"

"Yes, and she's very well. She plans to stay away from the public eye for now, but she is in great spirits."

"All right. You'll have to call on her, Liddy."

"Yes. She asked me to."

"And in the midst of all this, I don't suppose you were able to tell the children our news."

"No, I wasn't."

Knowing better than to ask, the children looked to their father expectantly.

"Your Uncle Jennings has arrived, and with him are your three cousins."

"From Mother's side?" Frank asked, knowing how thin the Jennings' family line had become.

"Yes. They're distant relations, but still your cousins, and your ages into the bargain."

"Are there girls?" Emma asked, her hand tugging on her father's coat.

"One little girl. Her name is Penny, and she's soon to be seven."

The little girls exchanged smiles of excitement.

"And the boys?" Walt asked.

"Thomas is onto thirteen very soon, and James will be eleven."

"They all share a birthday," Lydia put in, still amazed by this.

"They were all born the same day?" Frank clarified.

"Yes, twenty-one July."

"We should have a great party."

"I think so too."

"When can we meet them?" Walt wished to know.

"They're on an outing with your Uncle Jennings, so as soon as they return."

The family at last made their way inside, the children still full of questions about the new family members.

"We don't know a lot," Palmer finally settled them down enough to say. They had gone into the green salon, a place where they spent many contented evenings. "I believe that their mother has been gone for some time, but they just recently lost their father."

"And now they live with Uncle Jennings?" Frank asked.

"Yes."

"I remember him," Walt put in.

"Do you, Walt? What do you recall?"

"That he's tall with dark hair."

"That's right. There's a little gray at his temples now, but that about describes him."

"How long will they stay?" Emma wished to know. Having another little girl her age right in the house was as good as visiting at Blackburn Manor when Marianne's sisters were there, with all their children.

"We're not sure. They have chosen to be in one room— the big one across from you, Walt—and I can tell you they are fine-mannered, sweet children who have been through a painful ordeal."

"Anything you can do to make their stay pleasant would be very helpful," Lydia added.

"But could they stay a long time?" Emma pressed.

"They might. We might even get to see them in London."

This was met with rave reviews, and in the midst of this babble, Jennings' voice was heard at the door.

"It looks as though we're in time for introductions," he said with more calm than he felt. These were his own nieces and nephews, handsome children that he should have known very well, but they were like strangers.

"Come in, Jennings," Palmer invited, and in a matter of moments, the introductions were made; first, the children to their uncle and then to their new cousins.

Palmer and Lydia's children waited only for Jennings to make a remark to Palmer, which they saw as a sign to speak with their cousins. In a matter of minutes, all seven children were grouped off and talking. Thomas and Frank even went so far as to ask to be excused so Frank could show this new member of the family the atlas in the library. Walt and James had their heads together over the pocket globe that Jennings had given the boys, and all three little girls had dolls out on the window seat, teacups and all.

"You certainly had this one pegged, didn't you, Palmer?" Jennings said quietly.

"About the children getting on? Yes, I suspected as much."

"You have fine children, Lydia," Jennings felt a need to tell his sister.

"Thank you, Jennings. Walt was saying that he remembers you. He even described you."

Jennings fell quiet. He certainly remembered Walt and young Frank, and it was still painful to think of all he had missed. His eyes went to the window seat, and he smiled at the three little girls who had taken no time at all becoming friends.

"Do tell us you'll stay, Jennings," Lydia put in, knowing she should probably keep her mouth shut but just not wanting to.

Jennings looked to her.

"I'll have some business to attend to concerning Godwin's estate, and I can't be away from home forever, Lydia, but I will tell you this, I'll not go as I did before."

Lydia's relief was so great that she turned slightly to blink tears away. When that didn't work, she stood and rang for tea. Anything to get her mind from the wonderful news so she wouldn't sob all over the room.

Jennings, more pleased than he would have imagined at being there, understood just how she felt. If he'd been forced to sum up his feelings of the moment, he would have said that leaving was the last thing on his mind.

Chapter Seven

"Are they all right?" Jennings asked the moment Lydia slipped into the hallway.

"They're fine. Go in and wish them a good night."

Jennings looked momentarily nonplussed before nodding slightly and reaching for the door handle. He entered the quiet, dark room and realized he didn't know who occupied which bed.

"Are you sleeping?" he asked quietly from his place just inside the door.

Both James and Thomas told him no.

"Who's in this bed?" he asked as he moved to the foot of one.

"It's me," Penny said, her voice very small.

"Are you comfortable, Penny?"

"Yes."

"Are you warm enough?"

"Yes."

"Do you have Mr Pat with you?"

Jennings heard the bedcovers rustling.

"Right here."

"Good. You'll sleep fine now. Where are you, James?"

"Here, sir."

Jennings went toward the voice.

"Are you all settled for the night?"

"Yes, sir."

"Good. Did you have a good time with Walt?"

"Yes, sir. He has his own horse."

"I heard about that. Did you go to see it?"

"Yes, sir, we did." He sounded awed, and Jennings smiled.

"I'm glad."

Jennings then moved to the other side of the bed. "You must be over here, Thomas."

"Yes, sir. May I ask you a question, sir?"

"You certainly may, Thomas," Jennings said, and went so far as to sit on the edge of Thomas' side of the bed.

"Are we staying for a time, Mr Jennings?"

"What would you like us to do? Would you like to stay?"

"We would, yes." Thomas sounded calm and grown up, but in truth he knew great relief at being able to answer this question. For the first time since their father died, he felt safe—truly safe. He was in no hurry to leave this home that seemed the ideal of every dream he'd ever had. He would give much to turn back the hands of time and have his father return, but their home had not had a mother, and Lydia Palmer was one of the kindest women he'd ever met.

"Well, we shall be here for a time, Thomas, so I'm glad it suits you. I take it you had a good time getting to know Frank?"

"Yes, a very fine time."

"I'm glad," Jennings said as he stood. "Sleep well, all of you. I'll see you in the morning."

Soft "goodnights" came from the three of them, and when Jennings found himself back in the hall, he simply stood for a time. Feelings that were foreign and almost frightening washed over him. Was it possible to become so attached so quickly? It took knowing that Penny had been hurt for his feelings to turn toward her, but already his heart was completely involved with all three children.

The temptation to go back inside and check on them one last time was strong, but he fought it. *Palmer and Lydia seem to enjoy their children but still have a life of their own,*

Jennings thought to himself as he finally moved down the hallway. He continued to ponder this as he walked downstairs to join them for the remainder of the evening.

≈ ≈ ≈

Blackburn Manor

"Oh, my," Lydia said the moment she walked into Marianne's room the next morning. The sun was shining through the large windows, giving the older woman a very clear view of the ball's damage. Tinged with yellow and dark purple, the black eye was darker than ever.

"Does it hurt?" Lydia asked once they'd hugged.

"Only if I press on it."

"No headache?"

"A slight headache last night, but it's gone this morning."

"Walt sent these to you," Lydia said, setting down a small basket of flowers.

"Is he feeling terrible?"

"Not too bad, but he did pray for you for a long time last night."

"He is so sweet."

"Yes, he is, but when I left him he was already contentedly playing with his cousin James."

Marianne searched her friend's face and then scooted forward on her seat.

"So Godwin's children did go to Jennings?"

"Yes," Lydia answered, her voice breathless with excitement. "I can hardly take it in, Mari. He showed up without a word of warning and with three children."

"How are the children doing?"

"I think they're all right," Lydia said in thoughtful pleasure, her eyes going to the window before she turned back to Marianne with a smile. "You're going to fall in love with them. They're so sweet, and they look like family."

"Tell me about them."

"Well, ironically they all share a birthday in July, so the ages I give you will change soon, but presently Thomas is twelve, James is ten, and Penny is six."

"And your children are having the time of their lives," Marianne guessed.

"They are. The only thing that compares is when your nieces and nephews visit."

Marianne smiled. "And your brother, Liddy? How is he doing with all of this?"

Lydia's face grew thoughtful again. "I can't always tell. He wants to take care of the children, but he doesn't know how. He's so analytical in his thinking that I suspect he sees them as small projects. He doesn't relate well to them as people, and of course in light of their recent loss, they need that more than ever."

"How did their father die?"

"A riding accident, Jennings told us last night, but even that subject emphasizes my point. He didn't ask the children what happened until yesterday, and only then because that was one of the first questions Palmer asked of him."

"So what do you think brought him to you?"

"Palmer and I talked about it last night for a long time. We think Jennings has been somewhat humbled by this whole ordeal. He genuinely needs help raising these children and came to us almost without thinking."

"How do you know that?"

Lydia laughed. "Because he said he'd forgotten how much gibberish he was going to have to hear about God."

Marianne laughed so hard her eye hurt.

"Don't tell me any more, Liddy," the younger woman gasped. "My eye can't take it. Did he really say that?"

"Yes," Lydia said dryly. "He wanted to know if Pastor Hurst was still preaching that man sins."

Marianne shook her head, still highly amused.

"But, Mari, I almost forgot to tell you, Palmer and I think the children have had some Bible training. They were very comfortable with prayer, and when Palmer read out of the big Bible just before bedtime, they listened with tremendous ease."

"How about Jennings?"

"His face was very intent, but he made no comment."

Marianne sat back with a sigh. "Did you ever dream, Liddy, that your life could take such a turn in just one day?"

"No. I've prayed for Jennings for years, but I never imagined this."

"Isn't it lovely that God understands what frail and weak creatures we are?" Marianne asked, thinking about Jennings and her own life. "Yet He still provided a way of repentance for us."

"It is lovely, Mari, and I need to thank Him for it more and more."

The good friends, as close as sisters after all these years, talked for the next hour and would have gone on, but Lydia wanted to check on the troops at home. They had gone from two adults and four children to three adults and seven children all in the course of one day. Life at Tipton might be something of a madhouse in the weeks to come, Lydia reflected, but she was determined to enjoy every moment.

Tipton

"Uncle Jennings," Walt said as he and James approached; the families had been combined for nearly a week. "Do you know where Frank and Thomas have gone?"

"I think they said something about the stables. Have you tried there?"

"Yes, but we didn't find them."

"Do they want to be found?" Palmer asked as he entered the room, having heard enough of the conversation.

Walt smiled at his father, who smiled right back.

"Why wouldn't they wish to be found?" James asked in real confusion.

"Well, James," Palmer began, "they're a few years older and may wish for some time for their own pursuits. Does that make sense?"

"Yes."

"Is there something we can do for you?" Jennings offered, not realizing he was already making strides in dealing with the children.

"We want to play croquet and need four to make it interesting."

"You could try the girls," Palmer suggested. Walt's look became comical.

"Why don't you keep looking for Frank and Thomas?" Jennings recommended, honestly not wanting to go outside just then.

"What if we still can't find them?" Walt asked.

"Choose another game," his father said with just enough emphasis to close the matter.

"We head to church tomorrow morning, Jennings," Palmer mentioned when the boys had gone on their way. "Will you and the children be joining us?"

Jennings looked across at his brother-in-law. His hospitality and help had been beyond value, but Jennings wasn't sure he could sit through a sermon from a man who he believed to be totally in error.

"Have I put you on the spot?"

"No, I'm just thinking through some things."

"And coming up with what?"

"Questions."

"Try asking me."

Jennings stared at the other man, knowing he could be honest, before saying, "How do I sit and listen to a man I think is foolish?"

"Why do you think he's foolish?"

"His ideas, Palmer! They're outrageous."

"Tell me something, Jennings. Do you honestly think they're his ideas?"

"Yes. He's taken some of the verses in the Bible and completely twisted them around."

"So you've studied the verses for yourself?" Palmer asked.

Jennings' eyes narrowed dangerously at that point, and Palmer put his hand up.

"Before you grow cross, Jennings, hear me out."

The other man nodded, so Palmer tried again.

"You're nearly an expert with maps and charts. Why? Because you've studied and been taught on the subject. Pastor Hurst's area of expertise is God's Word. For years he has spent long hours studying Scripture and interacting with other men in the congregation, such as myself, who have studied to make sure his interpretation and application are biblical."

Jennings' face had relaxed during this explanation, and he now admitted that Palmer had a point.

"We'll probably go with you," Jennings said after a moment's quiet.

"I'm glad."

"I sense the children would wish it."

"I think you must be right."

Jennings nodded, glad it was settled, but still asked himself what he was in for.

Subtly observing the other man's face, Palmer had all he could do not to smile. He found himself praying for his brother-in-law, hoping he would soon see how much God loved him, knowing that God was well accustomed to dealing with skeptics and doubters.

~ ~ ~

Lydia stood very still, listening intently. Something was wrong. The girls had been playing, but it had grown very quiet. From the distance, Lydia thought she heard a small cry. She didn't think it was one of her girls, which left only one choice: Penny. She hurried in the direction of the small salon and was nearly at the door when her own Emma came rushing out.

"Oh, Mama! We can't find Mr Pat, and Penny is terribly upset!"

"All right, I'm coming."

"Do you need me, mum?" Judith asked; she had also come at the sound of Emma's distressed tone.

"We've a small crisis, Judith. Penny—" Lydia began as soon as she was in the room. "It's all right, dear. Don't cry," she said as she took her in her arms. "We'll find Mr Pat."

But it wasn't that simple. Penny wasn't sobbing or even crying loudly. Indeed she was nearly frozen with her distress, the occasional tear falling from her eyes.

"Do you know where you last had him?"

"I don't know. I need Mr Pat."

"We'll find him," Lydia said optimistically, even as she prayed that Thomas or James would make an appearance. She had seen very early in the visit that Penny was attached to her brothers and believed they could help in any situation. Instead, she got the next best thing. Her own brother appeared, Palmer at his side, and went directly to Penny.

"What is it, Penny?" Jennings asked, taking a seat to be on her level. "Are you hurt?"

"No, I need Mr Pat."

"Where is he?"

"I don't know."

"Well, let's think a moment. Did you have him at breakfast?"

Penny nodded, looking miserable.

"Could he still be in the dining room?"

"No." Emma shared this news. "He was here just a little while ago."

"And you've played right here the whole time?" Lydia asked.

"We went to the garden to get some flowers," Lizzy told her mother, "but we came right back."

"Which means he could be many places," Jennings said quietly.

Before Penny could look too stricken, Palmer gave an order. "All right, girls, spread out and start looking."

"Come on, Penny," Lizzy, the youngest of the group, said as she took her hand. "We'll help you find him."

Companionable as ever, the girls began their search. It did not escape Jennings' notice that Palmer and Lydia did not join in. He had been ready to help but then stood in indecision.

"Is it not a good idea to help them?" he asked as soon as the little girls headed back toward the garden and out of earshot.

Palmer answered, "It's not being uncaring, Jennings, but if they can work this out for themselves, that would be best."

Jennings looked skeptical, and Lydia questioned him. "You don't agree, Jennings?"

"I don't know. Mr Pat is not just any toy. He belonged to her mother."

Jennings found the Palmers smiling at him.

"You find it amusing?" he asked, a slight edge to his voice.

"Not in the least. We've just never seen you so concerned about anyone."

Jennings turned to see Penny outside.

"I do see your point, Palmer, but Penny has had enough losses," he said quietly before calmly moving to join the search.

~ ~ ~

"I lost Mr Pat today," Penny said quietly to Thomas that night. The girls had invited her to sleep in their room—they did this every night—and Penny had wanted to, but not tonight. Tonight she needed to tell Thomas about her day.

Thomas, who had been readying for bed and thought Penny was already asleep, went to her side.

"But you had him at dinner, Penny."

"Yes, we found him, but he was lost."

Thomas heard the quiver in her voice and reached to smooth her small brow.

"Mr Jennings found him for me. He was on a wall in the garden."

"I'm glad, Penny. Did you thank him?"

Penny bit her lip. She only remembered wanting to cry harder than ever when at last she felt the figurine in her hand.

Thomas suddenly wondered if it was wrong for her to be so attached to a small porcelain figure. He believed his father could have given him an answer, but he didn't let his mind wander too far that way. Thomas was still wrestling with the idea when Mr Jennings knocked and entered.

"Everyone settled in?" he asked, his eyes scanning the occupants of the room with just one lantern turned low.

"Almost," Thomas said as he stood, taking a moment to look back at Penny. "You can thank him now if you need to."

Penny's dark head nodded against the white pillow.

"Mr Jennings? she said quietly.

"Yes, Penny." He came that way.

"Thank you for finding Mr Pat."

"You're welcome. He isn't broken, is he?"

"No. His ear broke one time, and Papa fixed it."

Jennings had no clue what to say to this, so he only smiled and stood.

Penny, not able to see his face in the dim light, just watched as he moved away. For some reason she wanted to cry again. She couldn't have said why, but she watched with great relief as Mr Jennings quietly left and the room finally became dark. She turned her face into the pillow and cried tears that had long been delayed.

≈ ≈ ≈

"I want you to pay special attention to verse seventeen," Pastor Hurst said the next morning. "Jesus is at it again. He doesn't give direct answers, but He asks questions. The young ruler here is not coming in humility and need, and Jesus is about to uncover this."

A borrowed Bible open in his hands, Jennings searched to find where the Bible said this man was a ruler. He finally gave up and whispered the question to Palmer.

"That's in the parallel passage in Luke 18. There is also an account in Mark 10."

Immediately Jennings wondered how they could know which account was true but then was distracted when he felt eyes on him. He glanced over to find James studying him intently. The older man leaned close.

"What is it, James?"

"Are you well, Mr Jennings?"

"I am, thank you for asking."

James smiled up at him for a moment and then shifted his eyes to the front. Jennings also began to pay attention, but not before he wondered what he must have looked like that James would ask such a thing.

"This young man is very sure of himself," Pastor said next. "He's come with every kind of preconceived notion. What he doesn't understand is whom he's talking to. He has no clue that the Man standing before him knows every inch of his heart.

"Tell me, friends, how often do you go to God with your mind made up? Oh, your plan is an honorable one. You're praying for the needs of your neighbor or the salvation of a friend, but that friend is as godless as they come, and you don't really believe God can save and rescue his kind."

The pastor stopped and smiled.

"I've done this myself, and if I don't keep careful watch on my heart, I'll do it again. I go to God in prayer, but then I make the mistake of deciding ahead of time what I want His answer to be."

Pastor Hurst kept on, but Jennings didn't hear a lot of it. He wasn't thinking so much about what the Bible passage had said as the way the pastor had just admitted his own weakness. Had he talked that way before? Jennings honestly couldn't remember, but this time the man seemed a little less arrogant, a little less quick to condemn.

The service ended when Jennings wasn't looking, and when they stood to sing, he knew a moment of panic. They had not arrived early enough to speak with anyone, but now people would be moving around and talking. Jennings wasn't sure he was up to talking with anyone. He determined to busy himself with the children, but that was before Palmer rescued him.

Not leaving his side for a moment, Palmer engaged his brother-in-law in general conversation, feeling a sense of contentment when the guarded look dropped from Jennings' face altogether.

~ ~ ~

Lydia walked from the church steps and immediately spotted her younger son; he was standing on his own. She watched as he looked into the distance and approached him quietly.

"Hello."

Walt turned to her.

"Hello."

"You seem to be looking for someone."

"I thought she would come."

Lydia moved so she could tip Walt's chin up and meet his eyes.

"Marianne is fine, but blackened eyes take time to lose their color. That's the only reason she's not here."

Walt looked up at her, wanting to believe.

"You saw her two days ago, dear, and you know how well she's doing. She would not wish you to worry."

"No, she wouldn't. She tells me I worry too much already."

Lydia smiled and caught James hovering in the background.

"Hello, James."

"Does Walt wish to play?" the other boy asked.

"I think Walt could use a little cheering up right now, James. Can you help him with that?"

James smiled a little shyly, his head dipping as Walt came toward him.

"Come on, James," Walt offered. "I'll show you the spring."

Lydia watched them walk away, still shaking her head in wonder that James, his siblings, and Jennings were in their lives at all.

Chapter Eight

Tipton

Jennings was on an outing with the four boys when the missive arrived. A horseman brought the news, his mount stirring dust for half a mile, and Palmer slipped him a coin before sending him on his way.

"What is it, Palmer?" Lydia asked when he came back inside; she was waiting in the foyer.

"It's for Jennings, from London."

"Shall we try to find him?"

Palmer consulted his pocket watch.

"They've been gone several hours. I think he'll be returning soon."

Palmer was right. Less than an hour later Jennings and the boys trooped back, eyes bright with adventure, and all proclaiming to be starved. Food, however, was the last thing on Jennings' mind once he'd read the letter.

"Mrs Smith has been located," Jennings informed Palmer and his sister.

"Is she the nanny you hired?"

"Yes. I'll leave tonight. May I leave the children, Lydia?"

"Of course."

"Talk to them, Jennings," Palmer advised. "They're old enough to understand what you're about."

Jennings nodded, and just ten minutes later he and the children were sequestered in the small salon.

"I've a letter from my man in London," he told the children without delay. "The authorities have located Mrs Smith."

Penny moved in a little closer to James, who stood next to her, something Jennings did not miss.

"Come here, Penny," he said gently. "Do you remember what I told you in London?"

The little girl bit her lip, looking more uncertain than ever.

"I told you I wouldn't let anyone hurt you again, and I meant that."

Penny nodded, her small face sober.

"You will remain here, but I'm going to leave shortly."

"If we don't have to see Mrs Smith again," James asked, "why are you going back, sir?"

"Because she must answer for the way she treated Penny and the way she misrepresented herself to me."

"What will happen to her?" Thomas asked.

"I don't know. The courts will have to decide."

"But Penny won't need to see her?"

"No. I'll see to that."

And with that the children would have to be satisfied. Jennings told them he would return as soon as possible and not to worry. The whole family saw him off and stood waving until his head disappeared inside the carriage.

Jennings finally sat back against the plush seat, his heart troubled by the timing of this trip. He'd been having a splendid time with the boys. They had all talked freely to him and not been afraid to speak to each other in his presence. There was something very guileless and open about all seven of these children, and Jennings was most eager to know them better. He'd been contemplating an outing with the little girls as soon as he could think of a plan, and now this.

Closing his eyes in hopes of gaining some extra sleep, he knew he would have to put all of his plans aside until a certain woman was made to answer for her deeds.

∾ ∾ ∾

"Marianne!" Walt cried in delight on Tuesday morning when the children arrived at the breakfast table to find her waiting for them.

"Hello. Did you ever think you'd see me out again?"

Walt was too busy hugging her to answer.

Thomas, James, and Penny watched as Emma and Lizzy went for their hugs, and even as Frank went over to kiss Marianne's cheek and greet her.

"I think some introductions are in order," Lydia said when things settled down. "Marianne, this is Thomas Jennings, James Jennings, and Penelope Jennings, better known as Penny.

"Children, this is Miss Marianne Walker."

"It's a pleasure to meet you, Miss Walker."

"Oh, that won't do," Frank said comically to Thomas. "Marianne is family. She won't even answer us if we call her Miss Walker."

Both Thomas and James smiled greatly over this when Marianne grinned and winked at them. Penny was quiet, but her young eyes were watchful.

"Shall we eat?" Lydia suggested. The children needed no other urging. A merry feast ensued, during which time plans unfolded for the day.

"Who's up for gathering wildflowers in the fields?" Marianne asked.

Lizzy and Emma were enthusiastic, but the boys were on the quiet side.

"Not interested?" Lydia asked them.

"We were rather hoping to go riding, Mother," Frank admitted, sending an apologetic smile in Marianne's direction.

"All four of you?"

"Yes."

Lydia looked more than a little skeptical over this.

"What if Father went with us?" Walt suggested.

"I think that would be fine, Walt, but I can't answer for him. He had a meeting this morning, and I'm not sure how long he'll be."

"When did he leave?"

"Rather early."

"Then he could be back anytime."

Lydia smiled at her son's optimism and let the matter drop.

"All right, ladies," Marianne said to just the little girls. "It looks like it's the four of us. When you're done, gather baskets and bonnets and we'll be off."

The girls moved to leave, but Lydia stopped them.

"The flowers aren't going anywhere. You need to finish eating."

Emma looked as though she would protest, but with a glance at Penny she sat back and finished her meal.

Unbeknownst to Penny, Lydia and Marianne were keeping an eye on her as well. It wasn't long before all the children were ready to leave the table, and when they did, Lydia wasted no time.

"Did you notice the way Penny watched you?"

"How could I miss it?" Marianne asked right back. "Do you think she had enough to eat?"

"Probably not. She seemed completely distracted by you."

"Do you have any idea what she could be thinking?"

"I only wish I did. She's a fascinating little child," Lydia said thoughtfully, still staring at the place where Penny had been sitting. "One minute she's playing along, doing fine, and then another minute she's looking worried but won't talk about it to anyone but her brothers."

"She's been through so much in the last few months. The person she needs most isn't here. It's not hard to understand why she seems so unsettled."

The older woman agreed with her, neither one of them knowing that in the next two hours Marianne would need to muster every drop of patience she could manage. Penny came along willingly to the fields to pick flowers, but after picking only a few, she stood staring at Marianne. Whenever Marianne would turn to her, Penny would drop her eyes in embarrassment. If Marianne tried to engage her in conversation, Penny kept her answers to a nod or shake of the head. Marianne exchanged glances with Lizzy and Emma on several occasions, and those little girls tried to include Penny, but at the moment, Penny was clearly in a world of her own. Marianne was beginning to think she would have to give up when a small matter came up.

"Tell her," Marianne heard Emma say to Penny.

"Will you?"

"No, just tell Marianne. She'll take care of you."

Thinking she might need to step in, Marianne watched Penny hesitate, but then she surprised her by coming close and whispering, "I have to be excused."

Marianne smiled.

"Shall we show her our secret place, girls?"

Emma and Lizzy nodded, eyes coming alive with mirth and excitement, before Marianne took Penny's hand and began to lead her to the woods.

"I must tell you, Miss Penny," Marianne began in a conspiratorial tone, "that when we just can't make ourselves walk back to the house, we sneak this way to our secret place."

Penny's little eyes were huge as they looked up at the woman who was holding her hand, but she said not a word.

Walking with direct purpose, Marianne took the girls into the woods on a short path before cutting off and slipping into a secluded spot. The branches had done a work on everyone's hair, but once inside the small cove formed by the bushes, Penny couldn't help but notice it was spacious, completely surrounded by bushes and trees. It was also completely private.

"Here we are!" Marianne proclaimed in delight, and Penny found herself smiling.

"You can go right over here, Penny," Lizzy directed, and suddenly everyone had the giggles.

By the time they left the secret spot, walls had come down. When Marianne knelt down once again to pick flowers, Penny was right beside her. That little girl handed her a small, delicate purple bloom.

"Oh, isn't that pretty, Penny! Are there more of those?"

"It's for you," Penny told her, having missed the question in her fascination with this woman.

Marianne smiled into her eyes before putting her arms around her and giving her a gentle hug. To her immense pleasure, Penny returned the embrace.

"Thank you. It's so pretty. Just like you."

"I think you're beautiful."

"Well, thank you, Penny."

The two smiled at each other before Lizzy—who was just a tad jealous—came to join them.

Just twenty minutes later they were ready to head for the house and show Lydia their bouquets. A very different foursome returned to the house, Penny's small hand tucked into Marianne's larger one as she chimed in on the conversation all the way back.

~ ~ ~

London

"Where is this child?" the magistrate, Judge Lucas, asked of Jennings. Mrs Smith was being held in the next room.

"She's with my sister right now."

"How am I supposed to accuse this Smith woman if I can't see the marks she left on the child?" Mr Lucas asked, his voice not giving Jennings much hope.

"It's been several weeks now, sir," Jennings answered, keeping his voice respectful. "Even if Penny were here, the marks would have faded. I have one of my maids with me, however. Megan saw Penelope's bruises and is willing to attest to that."

"What's her full name?" the magistrate asked, searching the papers before him.

"Megan Cornell."

"Where is she?"

Megan stepped forward, not at all cowed by the judge's scowl. She knew that if he would just look at her, he would realize who she was.

The scowling visage finally looked up from the papers, and Jennings watched in amazement as the judge's face lit with pleasure.

"Why, Meggie, is that you?" the man asked, using her name from childhood.

"It's me, sir."

"Working as a maid, are you?"

"Yes, Mr Lucas," she said again, not bothering to mention that she'd been a maid for years.

"Are you treated well?"

"Very well, thank you, sir."

"Your mum's foot is right again. I'm having breakfast the way I like."

Megan, whose mother had cooked for Mr Lucas for many years, only smiled at him.

"Tell me about this woman and the little girl, Meggie."

Megan gave a swift rundown, not leaving any facts out, telling how the children arrived with almost no warning and how Mrs Smith kept Penny in her room all day.

"And you saw the marks?"

"I did, sir."

"Did it look as though she'd struck her?"

"No, more like pinch marks from strong fingers."

"And the child? Was she difficult?"

Megan's eyes softened. "Not in the least, sir. She's the sweetest child you'll ever hope to meet."

"Very well. I'll hold Smith over for trial." The gavel came down. "Next case."

But before Jennings and Megan could walk away, Judge Lucas called her back. He bent over and told her something that made her smile. Jennings waited with surprising patience for her to be done. Once in the carriage, he questioned her.

"You knew that magistrate?"

"Yes, my mum is his cook."

"I think you might have won that battle for us, Megan."

"I hope so, sir. I hope they put that wicked Mrs Smith away where she can't hurt anyone else."

Jennings hoped for the same thing, but he mostly hoped that this distasteful business would wrap up soon and he could get back to Tipton.

Tipton

"Tell me something, Thomas," Palmer questioned the young man when they had a moment alone. "You seem very comfortable when I read from the Word and when we go to church. Did your father do those things with you?"

"Yes, sir. Our father taught us the Scriptures from the time we were very small."

"That's wonderful, Thomas. Has that been a help during this time?"

Tears came to Thomas' eyes.

"I don't know if I would have made it otherwise, sir."

Palmer put a hand on the boy's shoulder.

"You're doing a fine job, Thomas. Your father would be proud."

"I hope so. I hope he knows that we remember what he taught us."

Palmer was proud of what the man had done. What father didn't hope for such a thing?

"May I ask you a question, Mr Palmer?"

"Certainly."

"We've noticed that Mr Jennings isn't comfortable at church and when you read from the big Bible in the evenings. Do you know what he believes?"

"Not specifically, I don't, but I know he has a hard time with the concept that people sin."

Thomas' brows rose.

"How could he doubt it? I mean, right now he's in London because of the way Mrs Smith treated Penny. How could he think she's not a sinner?"

"He probably does, but he wouldn't put himself in the same category."

Thomas nodded.

"That's an easy mistake to make."

Again Palmer was impressed with the boy's maturity and insight. They talked for a bit longer before some of the other children came looking for Thomas. As Palmer watched Thomas and his own Frank walk away, he determined to check with his son and make sure that his own beliefs were as sound as those of Thomas Jennings.

≈ ≈ ≈

"I don't have very good news, I'm afraid," Lydia greeted Marianne when she arrived just after breakfast on Saturday morning.

"Oh, what's wrong?"

"My girls got into the candy, and both have sick stomachs."

"Oh, no!"

"Oh, yes. I'm not very happy with them right now."

"What about Penny? Is she ill?"

"No, and I don't want her to pay for Emma's and Lizzy's foolishness. I think I'll leave them with Judith, and just Penny and I will go with you."

"Oh, that's fine."

"Penny is finishing her breakfast. I'll go in and hurry her along and tell the girls where we're going."

Thinking that Penny would only be distracted by her presence and that Lizzy and Emma would not wish for company, Marianne went to the small salon to wait. She had only just taken a seat when James and Walt wandered past.

"Hello," Marianne greeted them, and the two boys peeked in before joining her.

"Are you off to town today?" Walt asked.

"Yes. Your sisters are not well, so your mother and Penny are going with me."

"They ate too much candy," James said with a small shudder, making Walt laugh.

"James isn't too fancy on sweets."

"Is that true, James?" Marianne asked. "What do you like?"

"I like a few sweets, the occasional biscuit or cake, but not candy."

"I must admit I have quite the sweet tooth."

"Have you ever made yourself ill?" James asked.

"I might have as a child, but I can't say that I recall."

Years of training kept James from voicing his thoughts. The very idea of eating too much candy was appalling to him, but he didn't want to sound insulting. He was only glad his own sister wasn't involved. He didn't think his father would have been too pleased about that.

James knew he was doing it again. At certain moments he could almost persuade himself that his father wasn't really gone, that they were just separated from him for a time. He knew it wasn't the best way to view his father's passing, but some days he felt it was the only way he could cope.

"Are you all right, James?" Marianne asked, and that boy started.

"Yes."

Both Marianne and Walt were watching him, and James felt his face go red. When he averted his gaze, Walt looked to Marianne, who gave him a small smile of compassion. It wasn't hard for either of them to figure out why James might be distracted.

"What will you shop for in town?" Walt asked Marianne, taking a seat next to her and half wishing he could go along.

"Just odds and ends. Mother and I are planning a trip to London at the end of the summer, so anything that can wait goes onto my London list."

"My birthday is in the fall," Walt said audaciously.

"Is it now?" Marianne asked as if she hadn't known.

"I think a gift from London would be very special."

Marianne laughed, and James joined her.

"Your birthday is before Walter's, James. What are you hoping for?"

"I don't know," he admitted. "I haven't given it much thought."

"Well, you had best start a list," Walt told him.

"Why is that?"

This question so stumped Walt that he was speechless.
He always made a list for his mother for his birthday. Some
things he asked for were outrageous, and some were quite
sincere, but at any rate it had become something of a tradition.

"Do you exchange birthday gifts in your family, James?"
Marianne asked.

"Oh, yes. My father always gave us a birthday present,
but I never thought about how he knew what we wanted. I
wonder how he did."

Marianne smiled. "Maybe you gave subtle hints, and he
wrote them down."

This sounded so like his father that James smiled. "Yes,
I think you might be right."

James was on the verge of asking about gift-exchanging
in Marianne's house when Lydia and Penny joined them.

"We're ready, Marianne."

"As am I," Marianne said as she stood but then remained
still because Penny was headed over to hug her.

"You look very pretty today, Miss Penny."

"Thank you."

"Are you ready to shop?"

Instead of answering, Penny's face looked a little worried. She admitted, "I left Mr Pat by my bed so he won't be
lost."

"I think that's very wise. Do you have a shopping list, or
are you just going to look?"

"I don't shop," Penny told her, her small face still serious.

"Why don't you?"

"I'm too little," Penny told her, as though this should be
more than obvious.

Marianne and Lydia could only laugh at her.

"We'll see you later, boys," Lydia said to James and Walt,
who saw them out. They waved until the carriage was out
of sight and then stood in indecision.

"I wish I could have gone," James admitted quietly.

"You do?" Walt said in such surprise that James was embarrassed. He ducked his head and studied the toe of his shoe, his head not coming up until Walt said, "So do I!"

James laughed and said, "We missed our chance."

"I think you must be right. Although I don't know if Mother would have been too keen on the idea."

"But Marianne would have talked her around."

Walt laughed over this.

"You catch on very fast, James Jennings."

On this light note, both boys headed toward the stables. Nothing cheered either of them like a view of the horses.

Chapter Nine

"Do you have a long list?" Lydia asked of Marianne as the carriage got underway.

"Not too long, but I do want to find several items. I ordered a fan from Benwick last month, and I hope it's come in."

"What was wrong with your old one?"

"One of Father's dogs got hold of it."

"But your father's dogs don't even come into the house."

"I know. I dropped it outside and didn't find it again until it was in Rufus' mouth."

Lydia laughed over this and then glanced down. From a seat next to Marianne, her little face peeking out of her bonnet, Penny was studying the passing countryside. Lydia and Marianne were talking as they always did, and while nothing personal had been mentioned, Lydia had forgotten the little girl's presence.

"Well, Penny, will you have fun with us today?" Lydia asked.

Penny turned to her and nodded.

"Have you been to Collingbourne, Penny?" Marianne wanted to know.

"I think for church on Sunday," the little girl answered.

"Well, Penny," Lydia interjected, "our church sits on the edge of town, so I don't think you've actually been to Collingbourne itself."

Marianne smiled and touched Penny's nose.

"You're going to like it."

Penny smiled back, letting her head drop until it was resting against Marianne's arm. The little girl thought she might be willing to go anywhere if she could go with Marianne Walker.

≈ ≈ ≈

Collingbourne

A quaint village on the river Avon, Collingbourne boasted shops and businesses that hummed with patrons and customers on this busy Saturday morning. The street was fairly crowded, but Marianne's carriage driver, aware of her first stop, maneuvered the coach neatly into place before jumping down to assist with the door.

He had brought them to Benwick's, a general goods shop that boasted an inventory of infinite variety. Sundry articles such as lace, shoes, stationery supplies, sewing needs, books, candy, glassware, maps, gloves, and much more could be purchased.

Once out of the coach, the three females embarked on their outing, Marianne in the lead and Lydia holding Penny's small hand.

"You may walk around and look, Penny," Lydia instructed once they were inside. "But please don't leave the store."

Penny agreed to this, but Lydia should have known it was a waste of words. The little girl trailed after Marianne and never left her side. From her place near the younger of the two women, Penny took in the notions and wares of all types. She was delighted with some small jars and bottles in various shades of colored glass, and even spotted a handful of porcelain figures that reminded her of Mr Pat.

"Mari," Lydia asked, finding them at one point, "did your mother find some of that white ribbon she was looking for last week?"

"No."

"Benwick has some at the far counter."

"Oh, thank you. I'll add it to my list."

The women shopped for a time, working from their lists and also enjoying some spur-of-the-moment purchases. Penny, very content to be with both of them, grew more relaxed as the day wore on, and was even confident enough to walk ahead of them between stores.

"You look thoughtful," Marianne said to Lydia on one of these occasions.

"I was watching Penny and thinking of Jennings. I can't help but wonder how this whole situation will work out."

"How do you mean?"

"Well, I can't imagine he and the children will live with us forever, but I don't know how he'll do on his own."

"Are you sure he'll keep the children?"

"Oh, Mari," Lydia said with a sigh. "If you could have seen his face when he had to leave them just for this trip to London. He's trying so hard, and at times the only way I can describe his face is vulnerable. It's almost more than I can take when I look at him. It doesn't really matter that he doesn't know everything to do. He's lost his heart and probably doesn't even know it."

"And what of your heart?"

Lydia sighed again. "My heart feels like crying all the time. I've never seen Jennings like this. I know I keep saying that, but it's so amazing to me. I can't help but think that if God can soften his heart to the children, then He can also soften Jennings' heart about spiritual issues."

"We'll keep praying for that, Lydia, and keep our eyes open for God's will in the matter."

"You're certainly right about that."

The women walked in silence for a moment, and then Marianne, whose mind was also on Jennings and the children, spotted something in town.

"I've just had the most wonderful idea," Marianne suddenly said, but Penny was headed back their way, and she only finished with, "let's go into Gray's for tea, and I'll tell you there."

Lydia thought that sounded wonderful. Her feet were beginning to hurt, and her throat was dry. So with Penny seated between them, the ladies had a light tea, both of them checking through their lists to make the most of their time in town. They found the most urgent items already checked off, so that lifted some of the pressure.

"Are you finished eating, Penny?"

"Yes, ma'am," that little girl said, a few crumbs on her mouth.

"Well, let's get moving again," Marianne suggested, but as soon as they were back on the street, Lydia caught her arm.

"Oh, Marianne, I see Anne Gardiner across the street, and I didn't see her Sunday. I think I'll go over."

"All right. I'll go ahead up the street." The women shared a small smile. "Tell Anne I said hello."

"I will."

"Well, Penny," Marianne said, looking down at the little girl. "It looks as if we're on our own."

"Are you still shopping, Marianne?"

"I will be, but right now you and I are going someplace special."

"Where is it?"

"You shall see in just a moment."

Penny's hand in hers, Marianne started up the street to a minuscule storefront where an artist was painting a woman's portrait. Marianne found herself relieved. She knew if Penny could witness the process, she would be much less intimidated by the idea.

"This artist," Marianne said as they looked through the window, "specializes in miniature portraits of children. He works very fast and does a fine job. And today, I want him to paint you."

Penny's eyes grew enormous at this announcement, but she made no protest when Marianne started into the shop. The artist, a Mr Clay, was nearly finished with his present subject, and Penny was in his chair just five minutes later.

"If you care to look at frames," Mr Clay called to Marianne as he worked, "they can be found on that shelf against the back wall."

"Thank you," Marianne replied as she moved that way, thinking a frame was just the thing to finish off this gift. Had Marianne watched the painter at work even a moment longer, she might have seen that William Jennings, having just arrived from London, had spotted his charge from the window and was swiftly coming inside.

"Penny!" he said, causing that little girl to start. "Where are Thomas and James?"

Penny, thinking she was in trouble, sat very still and said, "I don't know."

"Is Lydia here with you?"

"No," Penny told him, her voice even smaller.

"Hello, Mr Jennings," Marianne suddenly spoke from his side.

Jennings turned to her.

"We thought you were in London."

Jennings looked down at the woman beside him, all sorts of questions coming to mind. Only one emerged.

"Did you?"

"Yes. Did you have a successful trip?"

"Yes."

"Marianne?" Penny was at her feet now.

"Yes, dear."

"He's all done."

"Oh, how lovely. Come and help me with the frame."

Jennings watched in amazement as Penny accompanied this woman to a shelf full of frames, and he would have gone on watching if his sister hadn't come in the door behind him.

"Well, Jennings, you're back!" She went to give him a hug. "How did it go?"

"It went well," he said in near automation. "How are things here? How are the children?"

"Doing splendidly. How did the painting turn out, Marianne?"

"See for yourself."

The small painting of Penny was exclaimed over by both ladies, and Jennings watched in some amazement as even Penny smiled in delight.

"Thank you," Marianne said to Mr Clay as she paid him for his services.

"You are most welcome."

Jennings followed a chattering threesome back outside, and not until Lydia glanced at her brother's face did she realize something was wrong. The reason for his somber expression came to her a moment later.

"Oh, Jennings, forgive us. I don't think you remember Marianne Walker, and here we are talking without you."

"Oh, Mr Jennings!" Now it was Marianne's turn. "I'm so sorry. I remembered you, but you must have wondered who had taken Penny."

"It's all right," Jennings said, but not in a manner that Marianne found convincing.

"And the portrait—" she continued, feeling she must go on, "I should have waited and checked with you. Again, I'm sorry."

"Please, Miss Walker, don't trouble yourself. It's fine."

Mentally Lydia thought it might be best if they cut their shopping a bit short. The girls did need one final item, but it was in a shop up the street and could be obtained swiftly.

"I'm going to take Penny to the next block," Lydia now began, wanting to rescue her brother. "Why don't we meet at the carriage in fifteen minutes?"

"All right," Marianne answered before Jennings could remind his sister that he had his own coach. Seeing, however, that it would be best to walk Miss Walker to her carriage and not leave her stranded on the street, he kept this to himself.

They started down the street, their pace slow, and Jennings' silence making Marianne more uncomfortable by the second. A scene across the street had arrested Jennings' attention until he was quite absorbed. Taking in his frowning features, Marianne was certain she must apologize again.

"I fear that we have offended you, Mr Jennings. I'm so sorry."

Jennings' creased brow did not immediately relax, even when he looked down at his companion, and it took a few moments for that gentleman to see that he was going to have to be very honest.

"I assure you, Miss Walker, I am not at all distressed by your outing with Penny or by the painting, and to prove it to you, I'll tell you why I was just looking so distracted. Do you see that young couple over there?"

Marianne looked in the direction he indicated.

"Yes." She studied them a moment. "It appears as though the young lady has hurt herself."

"Indeed, she has not," Jennings stated with quiet conviction, "but that young man doesn't know it. She waited until he walked a few feet past her, then grabbed her ankle and cried out in pain."

"Oh, my," Marianne said softly, wondering at the woman's charade, but also at her companion's tone.

"I abhor pretense," he went on sincerely. "Especially in women who feign injuries like sprained ankles, soot to the eyes, or pretending to have her horse run off with her in order to gain a man's attention."

Marianne nodded but didn't reply. Indeed she had nothing to say.

For a time they walked in silence, each deep in thought.

"Blackburn Manor," Jennings said very quietly when they were quite near the coach.

Marianne looked at him.

Jennings glanced sideways at her, his face softened somewhat with a self-derisive smile.

"I've been away longer than I thought," Jennings admitted. "I've only just fully realized who you are."

Marianne smiled at him.

Jennings shook his head. "I don't know when I've managed to be so rude."

"It has been a few years," Marianne said graciously, and silently Jennings agreed with her. The last time he had seen this woman she'd been about eighteen, and although not unbecoming at the time, the years had been good to her. If memory served, she was more attractive now than she was then.

"Marianne!" Penny's voice suddenly drew his thoughts, and Jennings had all he could do not to look stunned as Penny ran to hug the woman beside him.

"Not until after we'd left, Jennings," Lydia was saying as she caught up, and that man tried to attend, "did I realize you must have your own coach. Why don't you send him on to Tipton and ride with us?"

Jennings barely managed to agree. He gave instructions to his driver and joined his sister and Marianne, still trying not to gawk at the change in Penny. As he watched, she climbed into the carriage and cuddled up to Marianne, her face looking sleepy and content.

When Marianne bent and spoke to her, Jennings took a moment with his sister.

"Did I actually hear Penny call her Marianne?"

"It's our fault, Jennings," Lydia said for his ears alone. "Marianne is like a sister to our own brood. They only know her by Marianne, and your children have naturally followed suit."

Jennings was quiet. It wasn't just his sister's words about the children calling Marianne by her first name that he was mulling over, but also her reference to "his children." He hadn't thought of Thomas, James, and Penny in that light, but they were indeed his; they even bore the Jennings name.

"I hope you'll come in when we get back to Tipton, Mari."

"Oh, thank you, I will. I wonder how the girls are feeling."

"I've been wondering that myself."

"Were Emma and Lizzy sick?" Jennings wished to know.

"Too much candy," Lydia told him, feeling more compassion now than she had earlier. At the moment she was glad to be going home to them.

"What were the boys going to do today?" Jennings asked next.

"This morning they had some plans of their own, but eventually Palmer was going to give them an early tea and take them riding."

Jennings had no other comment, but he hoped the boys would be there when he arrived. The changes going on inside of him were all at once strange and a little frightening, but he wanted to be with these children; he wanted to see firsthand that they were well. Having Penny across the carriage from him, happy and obviously in good health, did much for his heart, but he couldn't completely rest until he saw Thomas and James and knew they were fine as well.

~ ~ ~

Tipton

"Can you tell us what happened in London?" Palmer asked much later that day. Marianne was still present, so Palmer had explained the situation to her, thinking nothing of her joining them.

"Yes," Jennings answered immediately, also not seeming to mind the second woman's presence. "The judge knew my maid, and based on her testimony he held Mrs Smith over for trial. They'll notify me when she goes before the judge."

"But they did keep her?" Lydia asked.

"Yes. I'm not sure what would have come up without Megan's testimony, but the judge took her word for everything."

"Why wouldn't he have taken your word?" Marianne asked.

"Because I didn't have Penny with me. I'm sure the bruises are probably gone by now, so I can't see what good it would have done, but he expected to see the child. It's lucky for me that Megan saw the bruises because the judge was willing to accept everything she said."

Lydia stopped just short of telling her brother that she had been praying the whole time. She wasn't sure he would want to hear it. She would have said something if Marianne had not been present, but she didn't want to risk embarrassing him.

The door opened while these thoughts still rolled in Lydia's mind. Emma poked her head in. Her stomach and Lizzy's were quite settled now, and because the boys had gone riding that day, they were looking for someone to take them out in one of the pony traps.

"It's going to be dark soon," Palmer explained, but his daughters' faces looked completely let down. It was certainly their own fault that they'd eaten too much candy, but in truth it hadn't been a very fun day for them.

"I'll come out with you," Jennings spoke up, surprising Palmer and Lydia.

"Oh, thank you!" Emma and Lizzy exclaimed. Penny had enjoyed a long outing that day, so her enthusiasm could not match theirs. Nevertheless, she was happy to go along, and a short time later, Jennings was giving them a ride up the drive to the stable. He thought they would have to take turns, but as little as they were, they all fit next to him on the seat.

"What pony is this?" Penny asked Emma at one point.

"I think this is Bessy."

"No," Lizzy spoke up. "Bessy has a short tail. This is Fern."

"Oh, that's right. I think this is the one that kicks sometimes."

Jennings found himself smiling at the serious voices next to him.

"Uncle Jennings," he now heard, just as he felt a small tap on his arm.

"Yes, Lizzy?"

"Where's your wife?"

Jennings smiled at how swiftly they'd gone from ponies to wives but said only, "I don't have a wife."

"How come?"

"Elisabeth!" her older sister scolded, and Lizzy dropped her eyes in embarrassment.

Jennings knew she had been impertinent, but he was tempted to tell her it was all right. Her voice had been so sweet and sincere.

With a glance to his side he caught Penny's eye. She was looking at him as though she wished for an answer too. He wasn't about to tell these three little girls his view on marriage, but he did admit to himself that suddenly having three children would have been easier if he had the help Palmer did in his sister.

"We go to church tomorrow," Lizzy said. "I have a new dress."

"It's not very new, Lizzy," Emma pointed out.

"It is, Emma," the youngest of the group insisted.

Jennings glanced their way to see if they would actually argue and this time caught Penny in a huge yawn. Knowing his nieces might protest, he turned the trap around just a few minutes later. There would be time tomorrow for more pony rides if they wished, but Penny's tired eyes and drooping shoulders were not something Jennings' heart could ignore.

"I saw Anne Gardiner in town today," Lydia told Palmer as she climbed into bed. That man was already sitting in bed, his pillow pushed against the headboard, the lantern turned high, and the paper in his hand. He set the paper aside but kept the lamp bright.

"You did? How is she?"

"Doing well. She says her father's state of mind makes it difficult at times to leave the house, so I was thankful that we had a few moments."

"Was that before or after Jennings found you?"

"Just before. Do you know," Lydia wondered as she shifted her pillow and rolled to her side to see her husband, "I never did ask him what he was doing in town. I would have thought he'd have come right to the house."

"He didn't say what he was about?"

"No. We were still in Mr Clay's shop and, well, we just didn't speak of it."

"That picture is remarkable," Palmer commented, thinking of the miniature of Penny. It was now hanging in the room she still shared with her brothers. "We should have our girls done."

"I was hoping you would say that," Lydia smiled at him. "It's been more than a year since we've had any portraits done, and children change so fast."

Palmer smiled at her and scooted down in the bed, bringing his pillow with him.

"Do you think Jennings will come to church with us in the morning?"

"He didn't say, and I can't tell what he's thinking right now."

"I hope he won't prevent the children from coming."

"I'm hearing your worrying tone."

"Oh, Palmer, it's so hard. I want everything to turn out all right."

"And by whose standards will it be all right?"

Lydia sighed and said, "You always ask questions that convict me."

Palmer laughed.

"I ask them of myself as well, love. I want Jennings and the children to stay as much as you do, but I don't want God having to pry my fingers off of them. In His sovereign way, He has the right to take them away or leave them right here. I need to be ready to agree with Him in either case."

Husband and wife stared at each other.

"Does it still feel like a miracle to you, Palmer?"

"Yes," he answered softly, "every time I look at Jennings or into the faces of those sweet children."

Lydia felt as though she could cry and knew it was time to sleep.

"I love you, Frank Palmer, but if I don't get to sleep, I'm going to be in tears."

Palmer only smiled and leaned to kiss her. He reached again for his paper once they'd said goodnight, but Lydia's breathing evened out in a matter of seconds. No surprise really—she was a mother to seven these days. The thought alone made him realize he was tired as well.

A moment later he put his paper down for the last time.

Chapter Ten

"Where's my shoe?" a sleepy Penny asked her brother on Sunday morning.

"I don't know. I'm looking for my sock."

Penny scowled at James but didn't speak. Thomas caught the interchange and almost said something, but when Penny turned away he thought the matter was over.

He was wrong. Penny complained again a few minutes later, and James snapped at her. Their voices continued to rise, and moments later Jennings opened the door.

"Problems?" he asked mildly, taking in the disheveled room and cross children.

"Penny thinks I took her shoe," James voiced in disgust. "I don't know what I would do with it!"

Thomas was on the verge of telling him to hush, but Jennings beat him to it.

"That's enough, James. Penny, where was the shoe you have on?"

"By my bed," she said, managing to frown and speak at the same time.

"Did you look under the bed for the other one?"

Penny scowled in that direction but didn't move.

Jennings, who had just happened to be walking by in the hallway when he heard the angry voices, went down on one knee next to the bed and found the shoe. James had discovered his sock by then, and after Penny's shoe was in place, they looked almost ready to leave the room.

"I think we'll try separate rooms tonight," Jennings told them, his voice carrying enough authority that no one argued. "I believe Emma and Lizzy want you in with them, Penny, and that way the boys can have this room."

The children all nodded.

"Are you ready to come to breakfast? We leave for church in an hour."

"I need Judith for my hair," Penny told him, impressing Jennings with the way she spoke up.

"I'll send her to you," Jennings said as he headed toward the door.

Thomas waited only until they were alone to let his siblings know how he felt.

"It would seem that Mr Jennings didn't realize the two of you were in the wrong just now," the oldest sibling stated, his voice low and upset. "Father would have waited for you to apologize for your treatment of each other. Well, Father's not here, but that doesn't change the fact that you need to tell each other that you are sorry."

Penny and James looked at their brother and then at each other. The apologies—started by Penny—came a moment later.

"We shouldn't have quarreled in front of him," James said, his heart bothered by this.

"We can't pretend to be perfect, James," Thomas said, his mind already on this. "But quarreling like five-year-olds is not who we are, or at least it shouldn't be."

"Does Mr Jennings know about Jesus?" Penny asked.

"We're not sure, Penny. I think we need to be thankful that we're able to attend church while we're here. If ever we don't live with the Palmers, it's hard to say if Mr Jennings will take us or not."

"I want to stay here," Penny said.

"We all do," James put in just before Judith knocked and entered, hairbrush in hand.

~ ~ ~

Blackburn Manor

"To what was Pastor Hurst referring when he mentioned the book of beginnings this morning?" Jennings asked of Palmer and their host on Sunday afternoon.

The face of James Walker, Marianne's father, was calm as he looked at the younger man. It was like watching and listening to himself at an earlier age. His heart knew keen compassion.

"He was talking about Genesis," Walker answered. "The name means beginnings."

"He said everything started there. What did he mean by that?"

"Just that, Jennings," Palmer put in, not wanting the matter to be complicated. "The earth's beginnings, man's beginning, the first family—the list is endless."

"The first family?"

"Yes. God gave Eve to Adam, and they became husband and wife. They were the first family. In fact, it's significant for us to remember that it was the last thing He made during creation week."

Jennings had to think on this. The things he was hearing and seeing at this church were different from anything he'd heard before. They were smashing all of his preconceived notions to pieces. It was almost more than he could take in.

"After church," Jennings said as he recalled, "on the way over here, I heard Thomas and James talking about eternity. Do you actually believe that ones so young can understand such things?"

"Eternity is a large subject, Jennings; I'll grant you that," Walker replied, fielding the question. "But understanding it is not a requirement to knowing that God can and will save us from our sin."

"And you believe those children sin?"

"The Bible says they're slaves to sin. Once we've surrendered to God's Son and He saves us, that's no longer true, but man is a slave to sin prior to that moment. It sounds as though Thomas and James have accepted Christ, so their sin is covered by Christ's death on the cross, but yes, I believe they were born sinners, and although forgiven, they'll sin until the day they die."

Jennings had to shake his head. Sin was not what little children did. Sins had been committed by Mrs Smith—that was obvious—but the Jennings children were not even capable of such things.

"Is there anything else I can tell you, Jennings?" Walker asked the man who now sat very quietly.

"I don't think so. Thank you, sir."

"Well, if ever you wish to discuss it some more, please come to see me."

"When did you start to believe this?" Jennings asked.

"When Palmer and Lydia did. About seven years ago there was a small revival in our area, as God called many of us and we came to Christ."

Jennings frowned.

"When we say, 'came to Christ,'" Palmer added, "we're talking about that moment when we agreed with God that we couldn't save ourselves and believed on His Son to rescue us."

Jennings nodded—that had been the question in his mind. He realized there was more he wished to know but found himself relieved when there was a knock on the door. It was Mrs Walker.

"Would you care to join us, Mr Walker? We're headed to the patio for lemonade."

"We'll be there shortly, Mrs Walker. Thank you."

The men talked a little more, and by the time they joined the ladies, the children had converged on the lemonade table. Penny was in Marianne's lap, glass in hand, looking as though she'd been there all her life.

"It's a warm day, Penny. Maybe Marianne would like to sit on her own."

"She's fine, Thomas, thank you," Marianne replied.

Watching Marianne's gentle way with Penny, Jennings was struck by how different the women at church had been from his female contacts in London. Just the day before he'd complained about a woman's behavior to gain a man's attention. He realized now that he'd seen no evidence of that type of deceit the two mornings he'd been to church.

"Mrs Walker?" Frank and Thomas had come to that lady's chair. "May we go in and play pool?"

"Of course you may, Frank. You know the way."

Frank and Thomas went toward the house, both remembering to say thanks for the lemonade. When Walt and James finished their glasses, they followed in their wake.

"It's a good thing Mari's not joining them," Walker commented, drawing a look from his wife and a small smile from his daughter.

"Do you play pool, Miss Walker?" Jennings asked, his interest piqued.

"On occasion," she said, smiling a little and wondering at her own embarrassment. Penny had climbed from her lap to play with Lizzy and Emma, and Marianne found herself wishing she had something to do with her hands.

"Come along, Mari," Lydia said as she stood. "I'll take you on in archery."

"Put the dogs away!" Walker cried in teasing as the two women left in laughter.

They walked across the lawn side by side and were well away from the back patio when Lydia spoke.

"I think your father embarrassed you, Mari. Am I right?"

"I can't think why, Liddy, but you are right," the younger woman admitted. "I've played pool for years, and now suddenly I feel foolish."

"I'm sure it was Jennings' presence."

Marianne sighed. "You're probably right. We don't know each other at all, and his face is not an easy one to read."

"That's certainly true."

The ladies had arrived at the archery table. It was set up with everything they needed. They slipped protective covers onto their left forearms and fitted the fingers of their right hands with the small leather sheaths.

"You go ahead," Marianne invited. "I have the advantage of being in my own yard."

"Very sporting of you," Lydia said with a smile, but did not decline.

By the third shot, Lydia was frowning, proclaiming that her game was off this day. She had often beat Marianne in the past, so Marianne had no choice but to agree with her. They had just started their second game when the gentlemen joined them. They sat by the table, some 30 feet to their side, to watch the show.

"You're going to make us nervous," Lydia said just as she let an arrow fly. It was a fine shot and stuck in the center circle.

"Come now, Liddy," Jennings said to her. "We know what a fine shot you are."

Lydia only sent him a look as Marianne let one fly. The arrow stuck hard in the bull's-eye.

The men clapped and cheered so Lydia was able to speak for Marianne's ears alone.

"I don't know how you managed that when you're shaking so hard."

"Why am I so nervous around Jennings?"

"He just has that effect."

"Let's have teams!" Palmer suggested, and Marianne had all she could do not to groan.

"You'll do fine," Lydia whispered as the men approached.

Marianne waited only until Jennings was at her side.

"I'm not sure you're getting the best partner, Mr Jennings."

"I witnessed your last shot, Miss Walker. I'm not worried."

Marianne was opening her mouth to repeat herself, but Jennings' whisper cut her off.

"We'll beat them."

Marianne could have said plenty to that, but the game was already underway. Jennings shot true, but it had been a while since he'd played. Palmer hit two bull's-eyes in a row, and that didn't help, but by the last game the Palmers led by only one point.

"All right, Miss Walker," Jennings said, growing more relaxed by the second. He had just bent to whisper in her ear, "Keep your shoulders relaxed on this one, and you'll do just fine."

Aware of his large presence behind her, Marianne nodded and raised the bow and arrow. She concentrated, telling herself it was all in fun and she should relax, but that didn't work. One of her poorer shots left the bow, and the Palmers ended up winning by that one point.

"I hate losing," Jennings said quietly, more to himself than anyone else, but Marianne heard it nevertheless. She didn't know if she should apologize or just let the matter drop.

After the bows and arrows had been laid down, the girls were finally given permission by Mrs Walker to join the adults. Marianne suddenly had a little girl in her arms, but she still managed to take a peek at Mr Jennings' face. She found it as unreadable as ever and still didn't know if she should apologize for her archery performance or not.

As it was, when the Palmers and Jenningses left for Tipton a short time later, Marianne still did not have her answer.

≈ ≈ ≈

About a week after spending the day with the Walkers, Jennings took a long ride on horseback. He was gone until almost noon, and when he arrived back, he and Palmer disappeared into Palmer's study, where they stayed for a few hours. Not until after two o'clock did they send for Lydia, who joined them as soon as she was able.

"Come in, dear," Palmer spoke when she poked her head in the door of his study. He didn't speak again until he'd seen his wife to a comfortable chair.

"Do you want me to fill her in, Jennings, or will you?"

"Go ahead, please."

Palmer looked back to his wife.

"Jennings wants all of the children to stay together this summer and possibly even into the fall when they go to school, so he's looking for a house in this area."

"Oh, how wonderful, Jennings. What have you found?"

"I looked at Thornton Hall this morning, and I think it suits us."

"Thornton Hall? Is that up for let?"

"Only just. When I was in town on Saturday I inquired about it and made an appointment for this morning. It's close enough that the children could ride over here with ease, but far enough away from town to give us our own space."

"It's been years since I've been in Thornton Hall, but I recall that it's lovely."

"It's very nice, and many of the furnishings are to be left. I would not have to go on a huge shopping venture."

"Will you keep your house in London?" Lydia asked, hoping he would because it had been in the family for several generations.

"Yes, I want the children to be comfortable in that city as well."

Lydia stared at her brother, her face a picture of the confusion she could not hide.

"What is it, Lydia?" her husband asked.

"I don't know if I should say it," she replied, her voice quiet.

"I think you should, Lydia," her brother commanded. "We're going to be neighbors. I need to know what's on your mind."

"I will tell you, Jennings, but I would ask that you not be angry."

"I'll do my best," he told her.

Lydia stared at him a moment and then blurted, "The changes in you are so drastic! You seem to be putting your whole life aside to make room for these children. They probably don't have any idea how blessed they actually are, but what if you find you don't wish to be a father? You've lived as a bachelor for more than thirty years, and now in such a short time your whole life has changed. What if this isn't really what you want?"

Jennings smiled a little.

"Is this your way of asking why I don't seem as selfish as I used to?"

"In a way, I guess it is," Lydia answered gratefully, glad that he understood and didn't seem upset. "You were never hateful or cruel, but neither am I used to seeing you put others first."

Jennings looked around the room, his gaze intense. After nearly a minute of silence, he turned back to the Palmers with an answer.

"I've never met a woman I felt was my equal, and while I never wanted to marry just to father children, I still wanted children. I've yearned for them at times," he said seriously. "With those facts in mind, you can well imagine my thinking that the fates had smiled upon me when I found myself a guardian to three children without having to bother with a wife."

Palmer couldn't stop his smile. Seeing it, Jennings smiled as well, although his was a bit on the sheepish side.

"As to your question, Liddy, about my deciding it's not really what I want, I guess I don't see that as an option. These children are my responsibility. The issue with Mrs Smith might have gone on indefinitely, but I saw my mistake early. As you pointed out, I've had years of living for myself; I think I can take a little time to see that these children are well."

Lydia found herself remarkably relieved that he had thought this through.

"Thank you for telling me, Jennings. And whether or not you want to hear it, I'll tell you that I'm praying for you."

"We both are," Palmer put in, "but I must also add one more thing. God's very best plan involves both a husband and a wife so that children have two parents—a mother and a father. You can raise these children on your own—clearly Godwin was doing that—but at some point you might need to stop seeing a wife as a bother and understand what a help she could be, not just to the children, but to you as well."

Jennings had no reply to this. It was one more aspect of family life that he had never considered. He knew how valuable Lydia was to Palmer—putting God in the mix had never occurred to him. In truth, Jennings was a little tired of thinking and talking about God, but some of Palmer's points could not be ignored.

"Will you speak with the children about this plan, Jennings?" Lydia asked next.

"Yes, with Thomas first and then James and Penny."

"Our children are not going to be very pleased."

"When they see what an easy ride or walk it is, they'll understand."

"How did you hear of Thornton Hall?"

"Just a bit of luck," Jennings told them confidently. "I happened to be speaking to a man in London whose brother-in-law was in charge of the details. The family's only just moved on."

Neither Palmer nor Lydia commented; they didn't even allow themselves to smile. Lydia excused herself with just a few words—it was time to check on the children—but she could have told her brother in very plain English that luck had nothing whatsoever to do with it.

Blackburn Manor

"Your sister wants you to come for a visit," Mrs Walker told Marianne, her eyes still on the letter in her hand.

"Elinore or Caroline?"

"Elinore."

"Does she say when?"

Still in their dressing gowns, the two women sat at the breakfast table, making an easy start to the day over tea and toast.

"This week if you can make it," the mother said as she studied the letter a little more and then looked at her daughter. "Just for a few days. The children miss you."

"I miss them too. Will it work for you if I leave in the morning?"

"I'm sure it will. The Markhams are coming to dinner at the end of the week, but they'll understand."

"Not to mention, if I'm not here I won't have to listen to how much her nephew wants to marry me."

"Does she still do that?"

"When she gets the chance."

Mrs Walker shook her head, but something had been on her mind for a week, and she thought this might be the opportunity to mention it.

"Did I misunderstand something, or were you rather flustered in Mr Jennings' presence a week ago Sunday?"

Marianne rolled her eyes. "I don't know what came over me, Mother. I felt like a schoolgirl."

"Is it because of the children, do you think?"

"What do you mean?"

"Only that they're so taken with you, but they're rather reserved with him."

Marianne bit her lip. "I hadn't thought of it, but you might be right. Do you suppose he knows he resents me, or hasn't he figured it out yet?"

"You misunderstand me, Mari. I don't think Mr Jennings resents you at all. I thought maybe you were feeling awkward because of the children's affection."

"Oh!" was the only word that escaped Marianne's lips on that point, even as she realized she didn't want to think about this. She had not the slightest idea why she was so flustered in Mr Jennings' company, and she also had no way of knowing what he was thinking. With so little information, any thought she put into the matter would be a waste of time.

"I know only this," Marianne now said. "I'm going to go off to Elinore's in the morning, and I'm not going to worry about it."

"And leave me here to worry on my own?" Mrs Walker teased her. "You thoughtless child."

On a laugh, Marianne rose to kiss her mother. Even if she was only leaving for a few days, she had plenty to do.

≈ ≈ ≈

Tipton

"You wanted to see me, sir?" Thomas asked as he gained Palmer's study and found Jennings on his own.

"Yes, Thomas, please come in."

When the two of them were comfortable on the red leather davenport, Jennings shifted so he could see the boy's face.

"I've found a home for us to let, Thomas. It's very near here."

"So you wish for us to stay near Collingbourne and not return to London?"

"Yes. I wouldn't want to take you from your cousins this summer, and there's time yet for plans to be made about schooling."

Thomas nodded, his face giving nothing away.

"Do you think that would work for you, James, and Penny?"

"Yes, sir. It's very kind of you to ask my opinion. I would..." he began, but stopped.

"Yes?"

Thomas looked hesitant but tried again. "I would like to ask one question if I may."

"Anything you wish."

"May James and Penny and I still attend the church where Pastor Hurst preaches?"

"Certainly you may, Thomas. I'll see to it myself, but I would like to ask you a few questions that have been on my mind."

"Yes, sir."

"Do you attend church to please your father?"

"My heavenly Father or Godwin Jennings?"

"Godwin."

"That is not why I go, sir, although I know he would be pleased."

"Why do you go?"

"The life of one who chooses to follow Christ is very challenging, sir. I can rest knowing that God is in control at all times, but I can't stop changing and growing. And to change and grow, I have to keep learning. I find Pastor Hurst to be a fine teacher."

"When did you first begin to believe this way, Thomas?"

"I was a child, a little older than Penny. My father used to say that for many years he was rather lukewarm about his faith, but then my mother died and he was forced to depend on God as he never had before. He worked hard to teach James, Penny, and me to do the same."

"Thank you for telling me."

"You're welcome, sir. Would you find me rude if I asked what you believe?"

Jennings smiled. "I don't find you rude, Thomas, but neither do I have an answer just now. When I do, I'll let you know."

The conversation didn't go on much longer. Jennings explained that he would take Thomas and his siblings to see the house in the morning. Thomas thanked him and went on his way.

The reality of it all hit the oldest Jennings child just after he exited the study and shut the door behind him. His heart overwhelmed with emotions, he sought out a place where he could be alone.

Chapter Eleven

When young Frank arrived in the salon long after the children had retired to bed that night, his father met him in the middle of the room. Lydia kept her seat, and Jennings looked on, but the conversation was hushed.

"What is it, Frank?"

"Did anyone have a moment with Thomas?"

"I'm not sure. Why?"

"He wasn't himself all evening, and I wondered if Uncle Jennings had been rather harsh on him."

"He wasn't harsh on him at all, Frank. He just told him about Thornton Hall."

Frank looked frustrated.

"Come along, Frank. Tell your mother and uncle what you've seen."

The younger Palmer did as he was told, his uncle listening closely.

"When you say he wasn't himself, Frank, what exactly do you mean?"

"He was very quiet. He played the game with us, but I could tell he was distracted."

"Did you ask him what was wrong?" Lydia asked.

"No, I didn't think he would want to share."

"I'll check on him," Jennings said, rising to do just that. However, he found Thomas sleeping soundly. He determined to check with him in the morning, but at the breakfast table he was in a fine humor, and Jennings felt it was best to let the matter drop.

~ ~ ~

"Just over this rise—" Jennings said to the three children with him an hour after breakfast. They were in an open coach, all eyes turned for a first glimpse of Thornton Hall. And they were not disappointed. A fine prospect but not overly grand, its open gardens and walled areas could be viewed from the gravel drive. A maze cut through the hedges could be glimpsed in the backyard. Fruit trees dotted the landscape. The house itself looked to be in fine shape— two stories with many windows, balustrades, and double doors that opened onto balconies.

"May we go in?" James asked, his face alight with excitement.

"Indeed we may," Jennings felt very good in telling him. Lydia had said that he was changed, and he would have to admit that he was, but what she didn't realize was how good it felt to do things for these children.

The carriage pulled abreast of the front door, and the four stepped down. A footman, still in residence with several other servants, opened the door for them.

"Hello," Jennings greeted him.

"You are most welcome, sir. Would you like for me to show you around or leave you to your own exploration?"

"I think we'll do fine on our own. We'll call if we've a need."

"Very well, sir. There is always someone nearby."

Thomas could have wept with relief. It was nothing like Morehead. That had been his greatest fear. A new "home" with this new "father" he could manage, but the same type of home without Godwin Jennings was simply more than his heart could take.

They stood in a huge foyer, stairs to the right and doors in every direction. Jennings showed them the large parlor, small parlors, very spacious library, dining room, and stairs to the servants' quarters—all before taking them upstairs to show them their rooms.

"We'll start with you, Penny," Jennings said as he opened one of the first doors. "How does this suit?"

"Oh," that little girl managed when she was given a view of a room done in every shade of pink. It was so feminine and inviting that she could only turn in a circle and stare.

"Look around, Penny, and if you need us, we'll be just down the hall."

James' room was done in browns, and Thomas' room was all green. Both were spacious and well laid out. The boys seemed as delighted as their sister.

All the rooms had views of the yard and land to the rear of the house, and Penny's was especially good for looking down into the maze.

Jennings' own room looked to the front of the mansion. It had been done in black and gray—not his first choice—but in time he would have that redone.

"Mr Jennings," that man heard at his open doorway. He turned to see Penny standing just inside.

"Yes, Penny?"

"Where is the mother at this house?"

Jennings came to her in the doorway and knelt down to her level.

"What are you looking for, Penny?"

"A mother, like Aunt Lydia. Is she here?"

Jennings was stunned but knew he must be honest.

"In order for there to be a mother here, Penny, I must be married, and I am not married."

A slightly guarded look filled the little girl's eyes, but she still faced him.

"Is there a nanny?"

"No, there is no nanny. Megan and Cook will be coming from London later today. They'll get things all ready for us so we can move in. If sometime after that we find we need a nanny, we'll pick that woman together. Do you understand?"

Penny nodded, and only then did Jennings see that the boys were standing in the hall listening.

"Thank you, sir," Thomas said to him for more than one reason.

Jennings came to full height.

"I think it's time you started calling me Jennings," he said, his gaze taking in all three of them. "I don't need to be Mr to you; I think Jennings will be just fine."

"Mr Jennings," Penny said, having immediately forgotten what he had said.

"Yes, Penny?"

"Can we show Marianne our new house?"

"Yes, we can."

"Today? Can we show her today?"

"*May* we," Thomas corrected her, "and no, Penny, Marianne is on a trip to see her sister."

"Oh."

Jennings didn't know what it was about that "oh," but the word along with Penny's solemn little face did things to his heart.

"We'll have Marianne come just as soon as she is able. Will that be satisfactory?"

Penny nodded but didn't say anything.

"Penny," James prompted her.

"Thank you," she added, her eyes having grown a bit.

Jennings smiled, thinking again of how proud their father would have been of them.

"I think there are acres of grounds to explore! Shall we see some of them?"

The children were all for this, and Jennings let them lead the way. He couldn't remember the last time his heart was so light. He would need to recall it at bedtime the very evening they moved in, however, because the scene that night would not be lighthearted in the least.

Tipton

"How do you think they're doing?" Lydia asked Palmer. With their children in bed, they were alone in the small parlor for the first time in a very long while.

"I think fine. The children were excited, and Jennings seemed very content."

Side by side they sat quietly for a time, Lydia gazing across the room, Palmer watching Lydia.

"You're worrying," he accused her.

"How do you know that?"

"Because I've kissed your neck twice and you haven't noticed."

Lydia turned to look at him.

"Have you?"

"Yes." Palmer was amused now.

Lydia turned her gaze back to the room.

"All right. Do it again. This time I'll pay attention."

A smile lighting his eyes, Palmer leaned and kissed her ear and then her shoulder.

"That was nice," Lydia said.

"I was hoping you would think so."

Mrs Palmer turned to look at him, working to appear as innocent as possible.

"I was worrying, so I think we'd better do something to get my mind off of Jennings and the children."

"A game of whist?" Palmer asked, his eyes as serious as he could manage.

Lydia laughed and put her arms around him. Palmer held her right back. The last thing they needed at the moment was a card game.

≈ ≈ ≈

Thornton Hall

"Let me have her," Jennings directed Thomas, who was holding his sobbing sister far past her bedtime. He had been holding her for close to an hour, and Jennings knew it had to stop.

"No, no," Penny cried as the exchange was made, but Jennings ignored her.

"Head to bed, Thomas. I'll see you in the morning."

The young man took one more look at his inconsolable sister, nodded, and went on his way. Jennings was just behind him, but he turned in the hallway to head downstairs, his arms full of a fighting, crying child.

"Thomas, Thomas, I need Thomas!"

"No, Penny." Jennings kept his voice calm with an effort. He was tired as well.

She continued to cry and beg for her older brother, but Jennings said nothing until he was in a large chair before the fire in the blue salon. A few servants hovered nearby, but Penny seemed unaware of anything but her misery.

"Penny," Jennings spoke at last, his deep voice low. "I need to tell you something."

"I need Thomas," she sobbed miserably.

"Thomas needs his sleep. You don't want him to get so tired that he grows ill, do you?"

The little girl sniffed and sobbed but said nothing.

"I'll tell you what. So that James and Thomas can sleep, you and I will sit here together until you feel tired enough to go to bed."

Again no answer. Jennings's brain scrambled for things to say.

"What day shall we have Emma and Lizzy over to spend the night with you in your pink room?"

"I don't know."

"Well, we'll have to plan it. We left Tipton sooner than I thought possible, and you're sure to miss them, so we'll have to plan many days when you can play together."

Jennings looked down now to see that he was being watched.

"Do you have Mr Pat with you?"

Penny raised the hand that clutched the rabbit.

"How long have you had Mr Pat?"

"Since I was a little girl."

"That's a long time," Jennings said, managing only a slight smile in his voice.

A great yawn escaped Penny, followed by several slow blinks; nevertheless, she opened her eyes wide and continued to stare up at Jennings.

"Are you getting tired?" Jennings thought it safe to ask.

"My room is scary," Penny said, a distinct quiver in her voice.

"It is? What's scary about it?"

"It's just scary."

"Well, you know what we're going to do?" Jennings said as he stood, Penny still in his arms. "We're going to go back up to your room, turn the lantern high, and see if everything is all right. Then if it is, you can lie in the bed and I'll sit in the chair until you fall asleep."

Penny didn't say anything, but Jennings believed with all his heart this plan would work. Megan had even delivered a glass of milk to Penny's bedside table, but not two feet into the room she was inconsolable once again.

This time there was no talking to her. She cried herself to sleep in Jennings' arms, as that man asked himself what he could possibly do next.

≈ ≈ ≈

"All right, Penny," Jennings said the next afternoon, having come up with another plan. The sun was shining full into her windows, and both her brothers were present.

"Lie on the bed and tell me what part of the room scares you."

She looked terribly uncertain but did as she was asked. As soon as she lay back, Jennings watched her eyes go immediately to the large wardrobe across from the foot of her bed.

"Let's open these doors and see what's in here."

Penny sat up when he did this.

"Oh, look, your dresses hang in here. James," Jennings directed, shifting them out of the way, "come climb in here and make sure the walls are solid."

Thomas smiled. This was the first Mr Jennings he'd met, the problem solver, the analytical mind that liked a challenge. It wasn't hard to see why little girls were beyond his reach.

Jennings and James were still poking around in the wardrobe when Penny let out a shriek. All eyes flew to her as she pointed to a large bee near her window. As they watched, the bee landed and was quiet, but buzzing could still be heard.

"We have a hive outside that window," Jennings said quietly on his way to the window, "and they're finding their way indoors." With that Jennings smiled at Penny. "Thank you, Penny. Our mystery is solved."

"You're going to make the bees go away?" She had already come off the bed and was near the door.

"Yes, I am."

And Penny soon learned that he meant it. Two groundskeepers were stung in the process, and many hands were needed, both inside and out, to get the second-floor job done, but by bedtime that night, the hive and bees were gone. Penny was still a bit tense, but Jennings sat with her until she fell asleep.

He was able to do this with relative patience because his pocket still held the missive from his sister. The note invited all three children to come the next morning and spend the day. Jennings had swiftly sent an affirmative reply. He found he could use a day on his own.

~ ~ ~

In the late afternoon on Saturday, Marianne Walker sat very still at the edge of the woods, calling herself every type of fool. She had only just arrived back from her sister's that morning. The carriage ride had been long, and at the time a walk had sounded like such a fine idea.

The sound of a horse's approach caught her ears a moment later, and Marianne turned her head swiftly with plans to call out to whoever was passing. Her heart sank when she saw Mr Jennings ride into view.

"Well, Miss Walker," he said pleasantly, bringing his mount a bit closer and swinging from the saddle. "The children told me you were away."

"I arrived back just this morning," she said, feeling awkward about not standing but knowing it was impossible.

Jennings smiled at her before his eyes shifted to the view of the valley below them.

"Well, you certainly picked a good spot for a rest. The view here is beyond compare."

"Yes, it is," Marianne agreed, taking note for the first time.

"Well, I'd best leave you to your solitude," Jennings now said, a bit loath to leave.

"Oh, don't leave on my account, Mr Jennings."

"Are you sure?"

"Very sure," she said graciously and smiled when he sank to the grass some ten feet away and joined her. "Will you be moving to Thornton Hall soon?"

"We moved this week."

"So soon?"

"Yes. I hadn't planned to rush it, but my people came from London and got right to work. They sent word to Tipton that the house was ready on Wednesday. It took the better part of the day, but we moved Thursday."

"And how are you settling in?"

"It's had its rough points, but I think the children like it."

And you? Marianne wanted to ask but feared it was too personal. *How are you doing?*

"Penny had bees in her room."

"Oh, no!"

"She was a bit panicked, but we got rid of them."

"I think I would panic as well," Marianne said and a moment later saw that he was watching her.

"I don't think you're the panicky type, Miss Walker."

Marianne laughed. "With bees in my room, I might surprise you."

They were quiet for a time, and suddenly Jennings noticed that the wind had picked up.

"I think it's going to cool off rather swiftly this evening. May I see you back, Miss Walker?"

This took Marianne by surprise, but she still recovered nicely.

"I believe I'll sit for a time, Mr Jennings. Please don't let me keep you."

"Are you certain? I hate to rush off, but I told the girls we would take the pony trap out when I got back."

"Thank you for your concern, but I think I just want to sit for a time."

Jennings wasn't too sure he wanted to leave her, but he reminded himself that she had been alone when he found her. He also knew that this section of forest and valley was a part of her father's land. He bowed graciously and started off. The view along the path was much the same, but in his haste to return to the children, he didn't take as much notice this time.

Tipton was in sight when it hit him. Bringing his horse to a halt, he thought about the fact that Miss Walker hadn't even stood to bid him goodbye. Something was wrong.

Hoping he had miscalculated but strongly suspecting he hadn't, Jennings turned his mount and heeled him in the direction from which he'd just come.

Marianne was a picture of serenity as she looked out over the valley, but in truth her mind rushed with options. Walking home was out of the question, but waiting for her family to notice she'd been gone too long was not at all comforting. And Jennings was right, the wind was picking up. In less than an hour she would be very cold.

She didn't know if she was relieved or not when she watched Jennings ride back into view. Her ears had caught the sound of his horse, so she was turned and looking at him when he approached. He left his horse much as he had before, but this time he walked with purpose until he stood directly before her.

"You're hurt, are you not?" he wasted no time in asking.

"Why would you ask that, Mr Jennings?" Marianne hedged.

With a shake of his head, Jennings dropped to one knee.

"It wasn't hard to figure. I told you my view on deceit and women who feign injuries."

Marianne looked away. As if the ankle wasn't painful enough, she'd now been caught feigning in another way.

Jennings did not touch her but continued to kneel and watch her. Marianne could feel his gaze and knew she would have to admit the truth.

"As a matter of fact, my ankle is rather uncomfortable right now."

Jennings studied her profile until she looked his way. His gaze a bit stern, he held her eyes for a few seconds.

"Let's have a look," he said, his tone so matter-of-fact that Marianne couldn't object, but neither could she stop the gasp that escaped her when he placed his hand beneath her ankle.

"What did you do?"

"My foot found a hole, and the ankle twisted at an odd angle."

"I don't believe it's broken, but it's already swelling," Jennings said quietly, his face bent over her foot as he carefully probed the bone.

Marianne looked at him until he glanced into her eyes. Then she dropped her own.

"Well," Jennings continued, his voice still congenial. "We'd best get you back. Come along now, put your arm around me, and I'll lift you onto my horse."

Marianne saw no hope for it. She placed her arm around his neck as he scooped her up, one arm at her back and another supporting her knees. His hold was gentle yet sure, but Marianne kept her eyes down in embarrassment. She would have kept them down through the entire ordeal, but once Mr Jennings lifted her into his arms, he stood very still, just holding her. Purely out of curiosity, Marianne looked up to find him watching her.

"For future reference, Miss Walker, I don't believe you
capable of any type of deceit."

Marianne looked away, "How can you say that when I
just tried to hide my hurt ankle?"

To her surprise, he laughed. She was so taken by the
sound that she was sitting on his horse and on the way
home before she realized he hadn't answered.

∽ ∽ ∽

Blackburn Manor

"Is he gone?" Marianne asked when her mother entered
her room.

"Yes. He said he would tell Lydia and the family what
happened and asked that you take care of yourself."

Marianne shook her head. "I don't know what's come
over me."

"It's interesting," Mrs Walker agreed. "A black eye just a
few weeks ago and now a twisted ankle." The older lady sat
on the edge of her daughter's bed. "If I didn't know better,
I'd say you were in love."

"Why, Mother? Do you get clumsy when you're in love?"

"Your mother did," Walker confirmed as he joined them.
"I'm surprised I lived to actually marry her. She tried to scald
me with hot tea and I don't know what else."

"Oh, Walker," his wife said, trying not to laugh. "Stop
telling her such tales."

"How are you?" Walker kissed his daughter's brow and
took a nearby chair.

"I feel foolish, and I don't think I'll be on this ankle for
several days, but other than that, I'm fine."

"Well, at least this didn't happen at Elinore's and leave
you stranded away from home."

"I'm just glad Mr Jennings stumbled across you," Mrs Walker put in. "Who knows how long you would have been out there."

"I tried not to think of that at the time. I even wondered if I'd twisted my ankle in a snake hole!"

Marianne's look of horror was so amusing that her parents laughed. Walker was soon on his way, but Mrs Walker stayed to find out what special treat her daughter wanted for supper.

In truth, Marianne wasn't all that hungry, but she gave an answer to please her mother. Once alone, however, her thoughts went back to her rescuer, and there they stayed.

Chapter Twelve

Tipton

Lizzy had not come down to breakfast. Lydia and Judith were busy with the meal and Walt's pants—he'd torn a seam—so Palmer did the honors. He climbed the stairs at a fast pace and took the hallway at a near trot, but the sight of his daughter, a solitary figure by the window, caused all his movements to cease.

After a moment Palmer entered, and only then did the youngest Palmer turn her head from her contemplation out the window.

"Hey, Princess," her father said softly. "Are you coming down to eat?"

Lizzy turned fully to him, the light from the window silhouetting her hair, and admitted, "I miss Penny."

Palmer took a seat on a nearby bed and leaned toward her.

"So do I."

Lizzy brightened.

"Can she come back?"

"To live here?"

"Yes! Right in this room."

"I'm afraid that's not going to work. She needs to be with Uncle Jennings and her brothers."

"She likes it here," Lizzy tried to convince him.

Palmer took her in his arms.

"You don't need to say this to Penny, but you need to remember that both of Penny's parents are gone."

Lizzy looked up at him.

"We need to be very thankful that Uncle Jennings is taking care of Penny and the boys, and that she has such a wonderful home of her own."

Lizzy frowned a bit.

"What's the matter?"

"Whenever I have to be thankful, it's because I can't have something."

Palmer bit his lip to keep from laughing but still managed to reply, "No, it's a reminder of all the things you already have because God is so good to us."

Father's and daughter's eyes met. Palmer smiled and Lizzy smiled back.

"Come along, dear. Come and eat breakfast, or we'll be late for church."

≈ ≈ ≈

"Pride is such an ugly thing, my friends, and most of what we've talked about today would not be an issue if hearts were humble," Pastor Hurst said near the end of the sermon. "The book of Proverbs even says that God detests pride. It's abominable to Him. And yet many of us live day in and day out thinking we're just fine."

The pastor held up his Bible. "We say things such as, 'I don't have to agree with that Book.' Or, 'Who are you to tell me that I have to change and do things God's way?' Well, friend," he continued, placing the Bible back on the podium. "I'm just a man. Anything I've told you, I've told you with the Bible as my standard. You also need to make the Bible your standard. You can't do that unless you read and meditate on this Book for yourself.

"Turn with me to one more passage," the pastor said as though he'd had a last-minute thought. "This time to Psalms. Psalm 121 reads, 'I will lift up mine eyes unto the hills, from whence cometh my help. My help cometh from the Lord, who made heaven and earth. He will not suffer thy foot to be moved; he that keepeth thee will not slumber. Behold, he who keepeth Israel shall neither slumber nor sleep.'

"Did you hear that? This God who wants us to know His Word and live for Him never needs to sleep. He's willing to watch over us at all times, keeping our feet on the path. Are there sacrifices to living a life for Christ? Yes! Is it always easy and fun? Of course not, but keep in mind that the God we serve is unlike anyone you've ever known or will know. He's great and powerful, and if we treat sin lightly, He is not amused. But for the heart that is humble before Him, He is a mighty saving God in whom we can abide from this day forward and into eternity." Pastor paused and smiled at the group before him. "Let's pray and thank God for all His benefits."

The people in the service began to stand and visit almost as soon as Pastor spoke his last word. Palmer and Lydia began to discuss something, and Jennings stood close by and listened as Lydia asked her husband about a particular verse.

While Jennings listened to Palmer's explanation and the importance of thankfulness in all situations, he happened to glance up to find a young woman's eyes on him. As soon as she'd been found out, she dropped her eyes and turned back to the group of other young women. It was not the first time it had happened, and again Jennings was reminded of how different the people in this church were than his contacts in London. This time, however, he also realized that his sister never pushed him to meet or show interest in any of the women. It occurred to him that at one time she'd been something of a matchmaker, but he'd seen no sign of that this time.

"Are you coming to the house, Jennings?" he suddenly found Lydia asking.

"I believe we will, Lydia, but not until we stop and see how Marianne Walker is faring. The children, Penny especially, were concerned when they heard about her ankle, so we'll stop to see if she's up to company."

"Give her our best," Palmer said before Lydia could open her mouth to ask if they could join them.

"Certainly," Jennings agreed, never having noticed the way his sister opened her mouth, closed it, and then gave her husband a questioning look.

"What happened just now?" Lydia asked when they were alone, her face confused.

Palmer took her hand. "It's good to have Jennings making this step. It's excellent that he's willing to go and visit Marianne just because the children are concerned. Doing those things on his own shows tremendous growth. It's also nice that his children can visit Marianne without having to share her with our children."

"Good point," Lydia agreed, even as she saw that Lizzy, Penny, and Emma were headed in their direction, determined looks on their small faces. She could see what they were going to ask and knew what Palmer's answer would be.

After the reply, all three faces reflected the same confusion that Lydia's had, but they were not given the explanation she'd been afforded. Jennings came looking for Penny just a few minutes later, and that was the end of that.

∾ ∾ ∾

Blackburn Manor

"Mr Jennings and the children are here," Mrs Walker told Marianne. "Are you up to a visit?"

"Yes," Marianne said with great pleasure, setting her Bible aside, her hands going to her hair until she realized what she was doing and stopped.

Just a few moments later, Jennings and the children were shown into the library where Marianne was comfortably situated on one of the settees. Spotting her, Penny wasted no time. That little girl scurried over to Marianne's side and into the arms that were waiting. The boys followed at a slower pace, but smiles lit their faces when Marianne greeted them.

"Isn't this a lovely surprise! Please sit down. Have you just been to church?" Marianne asked.

"Yes."

"How was everyone?"

"Fine," Thomas answered for the group.

Marianne glanced at Jennings just then, who asked, "How is the ankle?"

Marianne rolled her eyes. "I shall be a lady of leisure for several days."

"Still swollen?"

"I'm afraid so."

"Walt said you were having a tough go of it this month," James put in. "A blackened eye and now a twisted ankle. He said your guardian angels must be worn out."

Marianne found this highly amusing, and James smiled at her mirth.

"I brought you a flower," Penny said.

"Did you?"

Penny nodded but said nothing else.

Marianne looked to Jennings for help.

"It was sat upon in the carriage," Jennings informed her dryly, his own gaze amused.

Marianne had all she could do not to laugh again. Nearly all of what Marianne knew of Jennings was through his sister. At times Lydia had described him in myriad fashions: hard, difficult, uncommunicative, vulnerable, lost, needing help. But just now the only impression Marianne received was of a man who had been parenting for a long time. He was relaxed and comfortable with the children, and they seemed more comfortable around him than ever before.

"Tell me about your house," Marianne invited, and the children took turns describing their rooms.

"We have a maze," James said.

"I've heard of the maze at Thornton Hall," Marianne said. "Is it fun?"

"We haven't ventured very far, but if someone will stand at Penny's window, they can see directly down."

"That's a comfort. You won't be afraid to get lost if you can look up and find someone guiding you."

Her words, innocently said, had the most profound effect on Jennings' heart. In those days before they'd left London, when Penny had been hurt and he knew it had been his own fault, Jennings had felt very afraid. Having come to Lydia and her family and found guidance had made all the difference in the world.

And I haven't told her, Jennings realized silently. *I haven't said anything to Liddy or Palmer, and they've done so much.*

"Sea bathing!" Marianne's words startled Jennings back to the conversation. "Where did you do that?"

"At Weston-super-Mare. Our father took us each year."

"It wasn't far from our home," Thomas put in quietly.

"How fun for you! Would you stay for a time, or did you live close enough to go home the same day?"

"We would stay one or two nights."

"Was the water cold?"

All three children nodded yes over this question, their eyes growing large as they remembered. Marianne could see that the recollection was a fond one.

"When did you all learn to swim?"

"When we were little," Penny told her, causing her brothers to react. Thomas smiled, but James said, "You're still little."

"Not as little," Penny told him, looking hurt. "I meant littler."

"You knew what she meant, didn't you, James?" Jennings put in, his voice hinting of a quiet reprimand.

James admitted that he had.

"Marianne," Penny spoke up.

"Yes, dear?"

"Will you teach me to shoot with the bow and arrow?"

Marianne had not been expecting this.

"Well, dear," she answered, feeling a bit awkward and keeping her eyes down or on Penny's sweet face. "I think Mr Jennings might be more suited to teach you."

"On the contrary, Miss Walker," Jennings put in kindly. "I've seen you shoot. I'm sure you could teach Penny very well."

Marianne felt herself blush. After they had lost to the Palmers, she'd assumed he found her incompetent.

"I would be happy to teach you, Penny. Anytime you'd like."

"It looks as if the boys will need to head back to school before Penny does, so maybe we should schedule those lessons for later in the summer when Penny and I are looking for things to do."

"That would be fine. I'll plan on that."

For the first time Jennings noticed Marianne's red face and wondered at the cause. Glancing toward her feet, which were under a light coverlet, he remembered what she'd been through the day before. It was on the tip of his tongue to ask if she had gained a bit of a fever from the experience, but he thought it might be time to draw this visit to a close.

"Is there anything we can get for you, Miss Walker?"

"No, I'm quite comfortable, thank you."

"Well, children, I think then that we need to give Miss Walker some peace."

"Thank you for coming," Marianne told them sincerely and smiled when Penny gave her a hug.

With lots of smiles and waves, the foursome bid the con-
valescing woman goodbye and made their way to the carriage.

"Just so you know, Thomas," Jennings said almost as
soon as the carriage was underway, "I haven't forgotten
about the trip to see your home. We'll go sometime after
your birthdays."

This was such good news that Thomas could not keep
the tears from his eyes. Knowing that Jennings saw the dis-
play of emotion, he was terribly embarrassed and only too
glad when that man made no comment.

"Can Marianne come with us?" Penny asked.

"I don't see why not," Jennings said calmly, "if she would
like to."

"What about our birthday party?" James wished to know.
"May we invite Marianne to our party?"

"Certainly."

"When we go to Morehouse," James asked also, "will
there be time to go on to Weston-super-Mare?"

"We can make time. How would that be?"

"That would be very nice," the young man said with a
sigh. "Thank you."

By then Thomas had composed himself. He stared at
Jennings until that man's eyes met his.

"Thank you" was all Thomas said, his voice quiet. Jennings nodded. He had been reminded again how fresh their
grief was. Most of the time they did so well that it slipped to
the back of his mind. But more amazing to him than anything else was how wonderful it felt to do things for these
children.

To the children's delight and surprise, Jennings did not
take them to Thornton Hall but to Tipton. Always ready to

see Frank, Walt, Emma, and Lizzy, the three Jennings children piled from the carriage, the Palmer children meeting them as they stepped down, talking almost as soon as their feet were on the ground.

Lydia had some refreshments ready, and while the children settled on the veranda, the adults took the salon.

"How was Marianne?" Lydia wished to know.

"I think doing well. By the time we left I thought she looked a bit flushed and wondered if her injury might have affected her rather severely, but I didn't question her in front of the children."

Palmer looked quite concerned about this, but Lydia had an inkling that Marianne's flushed face had little to do with her ankle. Knowing she would never be able to explain his effect on women to her brother, Lydia kept her mouth closed. Palmer, on the other hand, caught the look on his wife's face.

"So what does your week look like, Jennings? Are you and the children busy?"

"Somewhat, but Penny seems a bit tired at night and is still crying easily."

"Of all the rooms to have bees coming in at the window, it had to be hers. But I wouldn't worry, Jennings; she'll adjust," Palmer said confidently. "It's tough being both mother and father, but you're doing a fine job."

Jennings barely nodded to this, and Lydia wondered what was on his mind. She thought she might have a chance to ask until just an hour later when Jennings called for the children and said they must be on their way.

"Get in children," he instructed his charges when they were at the carriage on the drive. "I'll be right with you."

After saying this he turned Lydia aside and spoke to her.

"I haven't told you, Lydia, how much I appreciate everything you and Palmer have done."

Lydia stared up at him.

"And I'm sorry," Jennings went on. "I should never have separated from you for all those years. It was foolish of me."

Jennings then kissed his sister's cheek and went on his way. Lydia waved when the carriage pulled from their yard, but she did so without thought.

"Is everything all right?" Palmer asked when he joined her.

Lydia related what her brother had said and ended with, "Something is happening, Palmer. Something is happening in Jennings' heart, and I don't know if he even recognizes it."

"I think you must be right, Lydia. He's changed from even the first day he arrived here."

Lydia did not answer, but after a moment nodded and began to turn away.

"Liddy," her husband called her back. "When we were inside, you had something on your mind when Marianne's name was mentioned. Do you recall what it was?"

Lydia did.

"I think Marianne is having a normal female reaction to Jennings, so when he mentioned her red face, I was feeling pity for her."

"What is a normal female reaction to your brother?"

"Oh, you know, Palmer."

"No, Liddy, I don't."

Lydia cast about for the right words.

"Jennings is very tall and dark, and his good looks draw women to him. On top of that, there's a cynical unapproachability that women find fascinating."

Palmer could have said he was fascinated himself, but it was with his wife's explanation of his brother–in–law, not the man himself.

"Are you trying to tell me that Marianne is falling for Jennings?"

"No," Lydia said with conviction. "She's much too level-headed for that, but his nearness does affect her. She's not as comfortable with him as she is with the other men in her life, and I'm sure that was the blushing Jennings witnessed."

Palmer didn't comment. These were new thoughts to him, and he was working to decide if he agreed. He prayed for Marianne. The younger woman was blessed with common sense but not immune to emotions. Palmer asked God to help her remember that she belonged to Him, and that only a marriage built in Him was to be considered.

Thornton Hall

Thursday night, a week after they moved to Thornton Hall, Penny went to sleep for the first time without mishap. If anything, this should have made Jennings more confident than ever, but the idea that had sprung on him during the weekend would not be put aside.

He sat alone before the fireplace in his bedroom, a small fire taking the chill from the air, much the way he'd done in London when he needed time to think. And think he did. His mind dwelt on the subject until he took himself to bed and slept. The idea greeted him the moment he awoke. He was distracted over breakfast, not even realizing he was, and just an hour after that meal, decided to act on his plan.

William Jennings did not believe himself to be an impetuous man. He believed he'd thought this through. So after seeing that the children were happily playing at Tipton, Jennings made his way to Blackburn Manor to call on Marianne Walker.

"You are up and about," Jennings said when he was given entrance to the salon and Marianne greeted him while standing.

"Only just," she told him. "I awoke this morning, and the swelling was completely gone, and I could stand without pain."

"I'm glad to hear it," Jennings told her, and then found himself determined to speak of the business at hand. "I hope I haven't caught you at a poor time, Miss Walker, but in truth I've come on business."

"Not at all, Mr Jennings. Please sit down."

Feeling none of the emotional pull that would normally accompany such a visit, Jennings faced his hostess squarely and presented his case.

"I'm here today, Miss Walker, to ask you to become my wife. I've seen how attached the children are to you, and I think you would make them a fine mother. You and I don't know each other very well, but it wouldn't be a normal marriage in that sense because I assume you would be spending most of your time with the children. I'll understand if you would like to think about it and speak with your father, but you would do me a great honor if you would marry me and become mother to Thomas, James, and Penny."

As he was speaking, color rushed to Marianne's face before draining away swiftly. She didn't know when she'd been so astounded, and in fact had to clear her throat before she could utter a sound.

"You pay me a great compliment, Mr Jennings," she began quietly. "Motherhood is a most serious matter, and I am very fond of Thomas, James, and Penny, but in truth I'm not certain that my marrying you is the best thing." Marianne kept her voice very gentle, working hard to be kind, but she could hear the tremor. "Young as Penny is, it's not that many years before she will be a wife herself, or, at the very least, not in need of mothering. In less than ten years you would be stuck with a wife you no longer needed."

Jennings' face was expressionless over this, his eyes intent as he listened.

"But I must be very honest with you, Mr Jennings, and tell you that the main reason I must decline is the difference in our beliefs. I think we respect each other, but we do not agree in a matter I find most weighty, and that is a serious enough reason for me that I fear I must refuse.

"I hope this will not alter my being able to see the children. I do think so much of them."

"Of course," Jennings said civilly, only now seeing that he had not thought through every aspect of this union. "You must see the children. They think the world of you."

He stood, and Marianne also came to her feet.

"I thank you for seeing me, Miss Walker. I shall take my leave now."

"Thank you again, Mr Jennings."

Jennings nodded seriously, placed his hat on his head, and turned on his way.

Save for the shaking she could not control, Marianne stood completely still as he left. Her ankle was completely free of pain, but there was an ache in the region of her heart that was unlike anything she'd ever known.

Chapter Thirteen

Tipton

Jennings found the Palmers in the study. Palmer had been working on his books, and Lydia had paid him a visit.

"Well, you weren't gone very long," Palmer commented.

"No," Jennings replied a bit testily. "It didn't take long for the lady to say no."

"What lady?" Lydia asked, realizing only then that she had no idea where her brother had gone.

"Miss Walker," Jennings said as he dropped hard into a chair.

"What did you ask?"

"I asked her to marry me, to become a mother to the children."

"Jennings." Lydia's voice was all at once breathless. "Tell me you did not do this."

"Do what?" Jennings demanded, coming back to his feet. "What crime have I committed that you look so stricken? I'm more than able to provide for the lady in question. I know she cares for the children. She mentioned the differences in our beliefs, but I sensed there was more to her rejection than that matter."

"Calm down, Jennings," Palmer ordered. "If this was strictly for the children, why is your pride sticking out a mile?"

"I can't think what you mean," Jennings said coldly.

"You've taken this personally. It's written all over you."

"And why wouldn't I? She says my beliefs don't measure up."

"That's the way she put it?" Lydia asked in disbelief, her face so upset that Jennings knew he was going to have to calm down.

"No," he said, quieting. He walked slowly back and made himself sit down again. "She didn't say it that way, but I can't tell you that I'm pleased with her reasons, no matter how she put it."

For the space of several seconds, the room was quiet. A large clock ticked on the wall as all three inhabitants of the room gathered their thoughts and attempted to calm pounding hearts.

"Jennings," Lydia started again, "please tell me why you did this. What plan did you have?"

"Palmer has said it himself, Lydia—children need both parents. Marianne is fond of the children, and you know how they feel about her. It was only logical to me."

Lydia sat down very slowly, her face looking more stricken than before. Seeing it, Jennings felt irritated all over again.

"Come now, Lydia. You act as though I insulted the woman by asking her! I meant no such thing. If she was insulted, then she read something wrong."

"It's not that," Lydia said, just above a whisper, her eyes on the carpet. "Marianne Walker is the closest friend I have. She doesn't make insensitive remarks. She doesn't have cruel comments in mind waiting to be pulled out and thrown at others. She would not have wanted to say no to you because she does love the children. And she would have wanted to be as kind to you as she could possibly manage. I can't stand the thought of her heart in pain as she chose to be obedient to God and not marry someone who doesn't share her faith."

For the first time, Jennings thought about Marianne's feelings. His mind went back over the scene. She had looked well enough, quite lovely actually, when he'd come into the room, but she had looked rather pale when answering him, and he'd caught just a hint of moisture in her eyes. But that didn't settle all of Jennings' questions.

"What is this obedience to God you spoke of, Liddy?"

Palmer did the answering. "Scripture is very clear about marriage, Jennings. If both parties do not embrace Jesus Christ, and Him crucified, it's called an unequal yoke."

Jennings did not grow angry over this, but he did feel tired of it all. In some way he was told he wasn't good enough every Sunday. At one time in his life he would have pushed all such thoughts aside, but lately he'd begun to think about the issue of sin and found the thinking process rather draining.

Long before this vital conversation should have ended, Judith was at the door. A messenger had come from Thornton Hall, attempting to deliver a message to Jennings, a message that had arrived from London. Mrs Smith's trial would be coming up in three days.

Within the next hour Jennings made plans for his trip and for the children to stay at Tipton. Mrs Smith once again consuming his mind and Megan sitting silently across from him in the carriage, Jennings left for London without giving Marianne Walker another thought.

≈ ≈ ≈

Blackburn Manor

"Are you busy, Father?" Marianne asked from the doorway of her father's study.

"Never too busy for you," he said lovingly. Marianne was glad she'd cried all the tears out in the privacy of her room. She came forward and took a seat, her head full of pain and confusion, almost wishing her father had been present when Jennings asked the question so she wouldn't have to explain.

"What is it, Mari?" Walker said when he saw her face.

"I've done the most foolish thing possible."

Such statements were not normal for his daughter, so Walker gently asked, "Can it be as bad as all that?"

Marianne told him what had transpired with Mr Jennings.

"But, Marianne, you did the right thing," Walker said the moment she was through. "What can be foolish in this?"

"The foolishness is that I think I have feelings for this man," she admitted, her heart so torn she felt ill. "I know I can't have him—his rejection of Christ is complete—but to hear him ask the question that under other circumstances would be sweet to hear was almost more than I could bear."

"There, there, Mari; it's all right." Her father came around the front of his desk and gently kissed her brow. Tears had started again, just a few this time, and Mr Walker handed over his handkerchief. When Marianne was somewhat composed, her eyes focused on the window, Walker spoke.

"What if he believed, Mari? Would you have accepted then?"

Marianne looked to him in surprise.

"I think not, Mari," he continued. "You don't want to be married for the sole reason of seeing to his children. You're not a woman who wants to be in love alone."

Again Marianne stared at him.

"You see, my dear, it's more complicated than it first sounds. Not only does the man need to love Christ, but he needs to love you as well. It certainly complicates matters that your heart has become involved, but it's not that surprising. We don't have any eligible men at the church, or you would have married long ago. Now Mr Jennings comes along, handsome and polite, with three children you can love, and you find yourself flustered in his presence. I can see how you would think that was love, but if you look closely, you may find that it's not."

"What do you mean?"

"What has light to do with darkness, Marianne? What has Satan to do with God? Those are questions that Second Corinthians asks us and that you must ask yourself. You're a special being because Christ indwells you. I don't care how charming or handsome Mr Jennings is, you're not alike in the way that truly counts."

It was the best thing anyone could have said to Marianne. She didn't think it would make all the pain go away, but her father was right. She needed to examine her feelings in this light and not be carried away by emotions. She did feel drawn to Mr Jennings, but what right had she to let her heart stray? He was not a man who could have her heart, no matter how good-looking or charming he might be.

Marianne stood.

"Thank you, Father. You've given me much to think on."

Walker studied her. She had a determined look about her. It was easy to recognize. Both his daughter and wife sported that look when they had a tough job they wanted to accomplish. But happy as Walker was that his daughter was taking this seriously, his heart knew great compassion.

"I'm glad, Marianne, but I also want you to know that I wouldn't have chosen this for you. I'm sorry for the hurt it's brought you."

Marianne's face softened, and she leaned close to kiss his cheek. "Thank you, Father. I've just been so emotional about this that I'm trying to be quite firm with myself."

"And I commend you, but keep in mind that God understands emotions. Don't leave them all behind."

Father and daughter shared a smile and a hug before Marianne left her father on his own. Walker prayed for his daughter as she left, knowing that if she followed her pattern from childhood, she was headed to see her mother.

≈ ≈ ≈

Lydia found Marianne in the garden much later that day. The younger woman was bent over cutting a blossom, and when she straightened, she found her dearest friend watching her.

"How are you?" Lydia asked.

Marianne set her basket aside and walked toward Lydia. Arm in arm the women began a slow promenade through the yard and expansive gardens.

"It was so unexpected, Liddy. I'm still in shock." Marianne glanced over at Lydia. "I'm quite surprised that he told you."

"I was also stunned when he confided what he'd done, and my reaction made him even more agitated."

"Was he angry with me, do you think?"

"More at your reason. Palmer commented after Jennings left that my brother is probably growing weary of the censor. Your rejection on the grounds of his faith was just one more reminder."

"That was not the only reason I gave him," Marianne said. "Did he tell you that?"

"No. What did you say?"

Marianne thought for a moment about the way she'd worded things before answering, "I reminded him that Penny isn't that many more years in need of a mother, and in less than ten years' time he'll find himself with a wife he no longer needs."

"You said that to him?"

"Yes."

"And what did he say?"

"Nothing. The whole conversation was very brief. He presented his proposal as though addressing a business gathering. I told him why I couldn't accept and then asked if my answer would alter my being able to see the children. He said no it would not, thanked me, and went on his way."

Lydia found herself trembling all over again. She didn't wish to be overly dramatic, but on behalf of Marianne and her brother, this was very upsetting to her. That her brother could make an offer for Marianne's hand in this way simply never occurred to her. He obviously felt in something of a desperate situation and was trying to do his best, but that didn't completely pardon his treatment of Marianne.

"Are you angry with me, Lydia?" Marianne asked quietly, cutting into Lydia's tortured thoughts.

"Not in the least! Why would you ask such a thing?"

"I don't know. I just thought you might be a little upset with the way I answered Jennings. I tried to be kind, but I don't know if that's possible in such a situation."

"Marianne, there was nothing else you could do. Having you for a sister-in-law would be like a dream come true, but only if I've another brother hidden away somewhere who would fit God's criteria for your husband."

Marianne found this comical. She laughed a little, and Lydia laughed with her. It was what they both needed.

"I know he meant it as a compliment," Marianne eventually said. "And I meant it when I told him I was honored, but even though his feelings are not involved, I'm sure he couldn't help but be slightly put off by me."

"And what of you? Were you not hurt, even though your feelings aren't involved?"

The look that crossed Marianne's face on this question was so telling that Lydia stopped. The two women looked at each other a moment before tears filled Lydia's eyes.

"I need to tell you," Marianne began, "that I'm working on this. My father was good to point out that I had no business even letting my heart stray the small bit that it has. I can see the disappointment in your eyes, and I'm sorry, Lydia."

Lydia put her arms around her and held her close.

"It's not that, Mari," she whispered. "It's thinking how much more painful it must have been to hear my brother's offer and have at least a small portion of your heart wanting to say yes."

Marianne found it to be the sweetest thing on earth to have Lydia understand. They kept talking as they made a full circle in the garden, and when they arrived back at Marianne's basket, Lydia hugged her again.

"I've got to get back. Jennings was called away to London, so we're back to seven children at Tipton."

Marianne thanked her for coming and walked her to her carriage, but in the back of her mind was another word of thanks, this time to God that she wouldn't have to face Jennings just yet. Sunday was two days away, and she hadn't been looking forward to it at all.

≈ ≈ ≈

London

"How do you explain the bruises on the child in question?" Judge Harris asked, spearing Mrs Smith with his eyes.

"I saw no bruises," she said innocently.

"No, I don't suppose you did." The judge's voice was cold, and some of the confidence left Mrs Smith's face.

Tense and silent, Jennings watched the proceedings, hoping the judge would not forget to call Megan for her testimony. The older man seemed distracted, and Jennings could not gauge how this ordeal would turn out.

"Where is the child?" the judge asked, and Jennings inwardly groaned.

"She is staying with my sister," Jennings answered, hoping the judge remembered him.

"But you have a witness, do you not, Mr Jennings?"

Jennings could have sagged with relief.

"I do, sir. Miss Megan Cornell."

"Approach," the judge said when Megan came to her feet.

Staying very businesslike, the judge questioned Megan, or at least began to question her. Not five minutes passed before there was a commotion at the back of the room. Nearly all heads turned, and when the noise escalated, the judge demanded an explanation.

A finely dressed and extremely confidant man stepped forward. He made just one statement, but it was enough to stop the judge's interview with Megan and to make Jennings' blood boil with rage.

≈ ≈ ≈

Thornton Hall

"The children are where?" Jennings asked Mr Collins in disbelief, as though he'd not understood him the first time.

The staff had not seen this aloof side of Jennings for many weeks, but Mr Collins still answered with his usual calm.

"The children are on an outing with Miss Walker. Shall I send for them, sir?"

"Do you know where they went?" Jennings asked, working to calm the emotions inside of him.

"They are on foot and ventured off from the gardens."

Prior to being turned down by Marianne, Jennings would have thought nothing of this, but this, along with the events in London, put Jennings in a mood most foul.

"I'll go look for them myself," Jennings finally retorted, sounding none too happy about the prospect and moving to the stairs with plans to change from his traveling suit. He stopped just a few steps up. "Why aren't they at my sister's?" he demanded, having just realized what was wrong.

"The children at Tipton have fallen ill, sir—summer colds. Your sister did not want Thomas, James, and Penny exposed."

This was calming news. At the mention of Marianne Walker, Jennings' imagination had run in several directions. It was good to know that he'd been far off the mark in each and every case. An hour later, however, when he had changed and was walking along the path and found them at a distance, some of his earlier misgivings returned.

Was this woman filling in for Lydia in hopes that he would ask for her hand once again? Had she changed her mind for some reason? Jennings nearly shook his head at his whirling thoughts. He had no reason to think any of those things, but Palmer was right: His pride was sticking out a mile over this.

With this thought, Jennings slowed his pace. From a distance he observed the foursome as they stood under a tree. They were discussing something in Penny's hand. As he watched, Penny started and dropped whatever she'd been holding. Marianne and the boys laughed as James bent to pick it up.

"Did it tickle?" Jennings heard Marianne ask as he neared.

"No, but I thought he might bite."

"Maybe it's a she," James suggested.

"Well then, you'd only get bit if she heard you," Marianne said quietly, and the children laughed.

"Hello!" James said, the first to spot Jennings as he neared.

"Hello," he replied, his voice sounding reserved even to his own ears.

The children began to talk to him, but Marianne's face flushed and then paled. She remained in the background and didn't speak until all was quiet. Because she didn't look at Jennings, she wasn't sure if he was looking at her, but the children suddenly were. Her glance included them all.

"Well, I'd best be off."

"Must you?" James began, but Marianne was already moving toward the path.

"Thank you for coming out with me, children," she said before adding quietly, "Welcome back, Mr Jennings."

The four of them were silent as they watched Marianne walk swiftly away, but it didn't last long before Penny spoke her mind.

"Did you send Marianne away?" she asked.

Jennings turned and looked down at the sad face staring up at him.

No, I didn't, Penny, he answered silently, *but neither did I welcome her.*

"Maybe she had other plans," Jennings suggested.

"No," Thomas inserted. "She was free all day."

Jennings was at a complete loss. The children seemed out of resources with Marianne gone, and Jennings was swamped with doubt over the way he'd treated Miss Walker. The tall man cast about, his eyes looking around for something to do, when he spotted a bug.

"You were looking at something when I came up. What was it?"

"A caterpillar," James told him, his eyes still looking down the path from time to time. Marianne was out of sight, but he must have hoped she would return.

"What color was it?"

The question worked for a time. They walked the path a bit longer and even found a few more bugs, but it didn't take long for Jennings to see that the children were not having the fun they'd had with Marianne. No one complained when Jennings suggested that they head back to Thornton Hall or when he closeted himself in his study. Just fifteen minutes later he sent a servant to Tipton, missive in hand.

~ ~ ~

"How are the children?" Jennings remembered to ask Palmer much later that day, even when he was eager to say what was weighing most heavily on his mind.

"Still down. Everyone has a raw throat and little energy."

"Is Lydia ill?"

"No, but she's growing tired as well. I'm keeping a close eye on her," Palmer added, just when he could see that Jennings was going to tell him to do so. "Tell me," Palmer went on, having witnessed Jennings' edginess. "How did the trial go?"

"Dreadful. Some smooth-talking solicitor showed up out of nowhere, saying he was there to represent Mrs Smith and the Dashwood family, for whom she'd worked for years. He said there had to be some horrible mistake because the woman had been a wonderful nanny for years. Smith herself managed enough tears to catch the judge's eye, and the next thing I knew, she was being let off."

Palmer shook his head. "I wonder who she knew to pull off that little trick."

"I don't know, but I wasn't very happy with the outcome."

Palmer nodded but didn't comment further. He knew the trial was not the reason Jennings wished to see him, but he wasn't going to initiate that conversation.

"I didn't send for you so we could discuss the trial," Jennings said. "I have to ask you something."

"All right."

"You believe the children to be Christians, do you not, Palmer?"

"I've talked specifically to each child, Jennings, and, yes, I do."

"And Miss Walker? You feel she is also, don't you?"

"Most certainly."

Jennings leaned forward in his chair. "Do you think the children would be more comfortable around me if I was a Christian? Do you think they feel some sort of barrier or wall because of this faith business?"

Palmer was thoroughly stunned by the question and didn't bother to hide it. He took a moment to think about his reply and realized he needed answers to some questions first.

"Have you by any chance been reading the Bible, Jennings?"

Jennings came to his feet.

"I've tried, Palmer. All the time I was in London I tried, but what kind of God would let Mrs Smith go free? I don't think I can accept this God of the Bible. He doesn't make sense."

"Let me ask you something, Jennings. If you were God, and you could see that Penny was walking along a path that would take her directly past a poisonous snake, might you put a hole in her path to stop her?"

"I might."

"But then she might break her little ankle. The snake would hear the commotion and slither away without Penny ever knowing he was there, but you would have saved her from a worse fate."

Jennings stared at Palmer.

"Would you want Penny angry with you forever over something you couldn't explain but you knew to be for her best?"

Jennings sat back down, his hand to his forehead. His sigh was a mixture of despair and frustration.

"I tell you, Palmer, this is the most humbling thing I've ever known."

"Well, then, we're getting somewhere."

Jennings looked at him.

"You see, Jennings, God can't save men who think they don't need Him. Humility is where it begins. Your sin will separate you from God, but His forgiveness, if you will accept it, will draw you so close that you'll never be lost again."

"And do you think it would change my relationship with the children if I became a Christian?"

Palmer smiled. "I do, Jennings, but you know very well that you can't do it for them. This is between you and God. No one else."

Jennings knew that was very true. Tempted as he was to be angry with Pastor Hurst, Jennings knew that he was truly upset with God and his own feelings of inadequacy.

"Try something, Jennings," Palmer suggested. "When you go to bed tonight, read in the book of Luke. Start at chapter 22 and read to the end of the book. Those passages cover the death, burial, and resurrection of Jesus Christ. They cover the way He was punished when He hadn't committed a single wrong. They cover the way He forgave the ones who killed Him.

"The act of His death is the defining event for the Christian. You can't really understand what God wants of you until you understand the sacrifice His Son made on your behalf. Read it and talk to me about anything that doesn't make sense."

"All right," Jennings agreed. "I'll read it tonight."

"Good. I need to get home to Lydia. Come and see me tomorrow if you want to talk."

"Thank you," Jennings told Palmer as he stood and walked him to the carriage. Darkness now full in the sky, he stood for a long time on the drive before going in and finding the Bible he'd put away as soon as he arrived back from London.

Chapter Fourteen

"Miss Walker, may I have a word with you?"

Marianne could hardly believe her ears, but she agreed with as much decorum as she could muster and accompanied Mr Jennings toward an open spot in the churchyard. She turned to him as soon as they were alone and looked up.

"I fear that I was rude to you on Friday when I returned from London. You were gracious enough to spend time with the children, and I didn't thank you."

"Please do not concern yourself, Mr Jennings. I was only sorry that I interrupted your homecoming."

"Not at all. Please do not stay away from Thornton Hall. The children were very sorry to see you leave."

"Thank you. I shall visit again soon."

"I'll tell the children to plan on you."

The couple parted company at that point, but Marianne had all she could do not to gawk at the man. He was warm and gracious, nothing like the cold individual who had come down the path on Friday. Marianne wished she could ask someone about the matter but didn't know who it could be. Lydia might know, but she was still at home with the children.

Only at that moment did Marianne remember that she had something for Penny. She searched for the Jennings family but could not find them. When her parents located her to tell her of their plans, she was still standing undecided, Penny's small handkerchief in her hand.

≈ ≈ ≈

Having done what he knew to be right, Jennings had gathered his own brood and headed for home. His reflection on his treatment of Marianne could not be ignored. She had been on his property with his children, doing him a favor, and he'd treated her as an interloper. He only hoped that she would take him at his word and visit the children. He was not overly comfortable in her presence, but in this matter he would have to put his own feelings aside.

"Are we going to Tipton?" Penny asked, much the way she did every day.

"No, Penny. I think we'd best give them more time."

"I miss Emma and Lizzy."

"I know you do."

"Thomas," James asked from his seat directly across the carriage, "what did Pastor Hurst mean when he talked about a mother being made by her own child? He said it was a miracle, but I don't know what he was talking about."

Jennings didn't either. He missed that statement altogether, so he listened for Thomas' answer as well.

"Not just any mother and child, James, but Mary and Jesus. Jesus was there at the creation of man, so He made the woman who gave birth to Him."

"What do you mean Jesus was there at the creation of man, Thomas?"

This question came from Jennings, silencing everyone in the carriage.

"Well," Thomas tried after a moment "in Genesis it talks about man being made in *our* image, and the "our" in that passage means the Trinity."

"What is the Trinity?"

Thomas opened his mouth but drew a complete blank. He'd heard the word his entire life, but no matter how swiftly his brain scrambled for the answer, he couldn't find the meaning at the moment.

"I'll think of it, sir, but right now I can't remember."

Jennings nodded and sat back in thoughtful silence. He certainly wished that the family at Tipton was well. He'd had no questions about the Luke chapters even though he'd been surprised by what he read, but if this account from Thomas was true, it was an amazing thought, and he wanted answers.

The children stared at each other and then at Mr Jennings before sitting back as well. As a rule, James did not bring up topics from the Bible in front of Mr Jennings, but he'd been so taken with this statement that he'd forgotten himself. Now he wished he could take it back.

They pulled up in front of Thornton Hall and climbed from the carriage. Not until that moment did they realize that another carriage was behind them. It was far down the driveway but clearly coming their way.

"That's the Walkers' carriage." Thomas was the first to recognize it.

"Is it Marianne?" Penny wished to know, jumping a little in excitement.

"I think it must be. Do you see Mr and Mrs Walker?"

"I can't tell yet."

While they discussed this, the carriage drew up and Marianne's face appeared in the window. The family went toward her.

"Hello," she greeted them. "I missed you after church, Penny, and I wanted you to have your handkerchief."

"Thank you. Can you come out?"

"I think not, dear. I'm joining my parents at the Hursts'."

"Marianne," Thomas asked swiftly, seeing his chance. "I can't remember what the Trinity is."

"Oh, I can tell you, Thomas. The Trinity is God the Father, God the Son, and God the Holy Ghost."

"That's right! Thank you," Thomas said with a smile and began to turn to Jennings.

"And what does that mean exactly?" Jennings asked, having been close enough to see and hear all.

Marianne had not expected a question from Mr Jennings and wished her father were here to speak to him on biblical matters, but she still answered.

"The Trinity is first mentioned in Genesis when God says that man is made in "our" image, "our" being the Father, Son, and Holy Spirit. It's God in three distinct persons. The best explanation might be in the first chapter of Mark when Jesus is being baptized. God the Son, Jesus, is standing in the water. The Spirit descends in the form of a dove and lands on Jesus' shoulder—that's God the Holy Ghost. Then God the Father speaks from heaven."

Jennings' face was so intent on this information that for a moment he said nothing. The children were aware of his demeanor and remained quiet. Marianne didn't know what to do. She needed to get to the Hursts', but she did not want to interrupt if Mr Jennings was trying to think.

"And you say that God is in all places at all times?" he finally asked.

"Yes."

"Which God? The Father, Son, or Spirit?"

"They're all the same God, Mr Jennings, but with different roles. The Father rules in heaven and is over all. Jesus became God-Man so He could live on earth and die for sins. The Spirit ministers in the hearts of believers."

"So God the Father doesn't minister to Christians?"

"Yes, He does, but it's the Spirit's unique role to minister to believers through Scripture."

"How can He do that?"

"Because He's three in one. He's Father, Son, and Spirit at all times, everywhere."

Jennings took another span of time to contemplate this, and Marianne knew she must leave.

"Children," she said quietly, her eyes mostly on Thomas, "I'll see you later this week."

Thomas nodded right away and began to take James and Penny away.

Jennings, his eyes on a distant spot, didn't notice their departure.

"Mr Jennings?" Marianne tried when they were alone.

The thoughtful man looked at her.

"May I tell you something?"

"Certainly." Jennings' eyes were now intent on Marianne.

"When my father was searching, a man told him that while God loves questions and that everything He wants us to know is in His Word, there might come a time when you need to stop working to figure it all out, realize you need a Savior, and fall down on your knees. My father has always said that those words helped him tremendously."

For the space of several heartbeats, Jennings held her eyes and let the words sink in. At last he said "Thank you" in genuine appreciation.

"I must go," Marianne said.

"Of course," Jennings nodded, backing up so the carriage could move on its way.

He walked slowly to the house, still not realizing that the children had gone ahead and that Thomas was praying for his guardian as he never had before.

≈ ≈ ≈

Jennings had never experienced a sleepless night. Yet he heard the chimes at midnight, one, two, three, and four. He had readied for bed at the usual time, but that had done little good. His heart in a quandary, he paced the floor of his room, checked on the children, stared out the window, lay back on the bed, and repeated the process for hours.

Sometime after four o'clock, he went for the Bible on his writing desk. He opened it but didn't look at the words. With a hand to the pages, he prayed.

"Holy Father, I don't know what's wrong with me. I yearn for something. I think it must be You, but I don't know where to start."

Jennings thought of the happy life he saw in the parishioners of Pastor Hurst's church. The women were shy and sweet around him, not bold and brazen as they were at the parties in London. And Pastor Hurst himself! He had not turned out to be anything like Jennings had remembered.

And all of these thoughts ran through his mind before he made a close inspection of the Palmer family. There was no denying the genuineness of their faith. The children were well behaved and respectful. They adored their parents and enjoyed each other. Rarely did he see a squabble between them, and when he did, it was worked out with kind words, not accusations and shouting.

And Palmer and Lydia—Jennings didn't know another couple who enjoyed each other more. They worked together even in tense situations, and unlike many other marriages Jennings had witnessed, they were devoted to each other and not joined in name only.

"I'll go tomorrow," Jennings prayed quietly. "I'll see Palmer tomorrow, Father God."

Even as he said this, Jennings wondered to whom he should be praying: the Father, Son, or Holy Spirit. Suddenly he was more tired than he'd ever been in his life. He went back to his bed and lay down, his heart a mixture of burden and peace. He had so many questions, but he was certain that Palmer would have the answers.

~ ~ ~

Blackburn Manor

"Are you all right, dear?" Mrs Walker asked of Marianne at the breakfast table, her hand reaching for the teapot.

"I didn't sleep well," the younger woman admitted, still not understanding why, as she absently accepted a hot cup of tea.

"Was it something you ate?"

"I don't believe so." Marianne reached for the toast rack. "Mr Jennings was on my mind, and I prayed for him a good deal."

"That's not surprising, dear." Mrs Walker moved the butter dish closer to her child. "The conversation you had with him on the Trinity was most unusual. It was bound to stay on your mind."

"You're probably right," Marianne said as she used the butter and preserves. "I sense that he's ready to listen."

Mrs Walker smiled. "I remember the day that happened for your father."

"Mother," Marianne interrupted her. "I can't remember how long before Father you came to Christ."

"Almost a year. I said little of the matter in those days. Your father was having a terrible struggle, and my peace seemed only to rattle him more."

"I recall some of that. I mostly recall the peace in the house once the matter was settled."

After exchanging a smile, the ladies ate breakfast in silence. Marianne was tired, and Mrs Walker's mind had strayed again to a husband for her last daughter. She had been at peace over the situation for some weeks, but now she felt restless and anxious again.

Reaching for the newspaper, she scanned the words, but her mind was more prayerful than it was attentive to reading. Not all the anxious thoughts in the world would bring a man for her Marianne before God's timing was right, and it was time to remember that.

~ ~ ~

Tipton

"Is it truly so simple, Palmer?"

"Salvation is from God, Jennings—it's remarkably simple for Him. What it isn't, is easy. I don't mean for God, but for us. You can't plan to live your life as you please once you've made that step. Salvation means you belong to Him. You no longer live for yourself. That doesn't happen overnight, and all believers fail repeatedly, but the goal is to live for Christ each day."

Jennings sat in silence. Seven weeks ago he wouldn't have believed he could be having this conversation, but his heart was so ready, his mind so settled, that he couldn't wait another day. He hadn't even given eternity much thought, but he knew he needed help in his life. He needed peace and wisdom for the children, and suddenly it was perfectly clear that God could give him those things.

"What do I say?" Jennings asked.

Palmer opened his Bible. "Ephesians 2:8-9 says, 'By grace are ye saved through faith; and that not of yourselves: it is the gift of God, not of works, lest any man should boast.' Our salvation is from God, Jennings, but we do have something to do. Romans 10:9-10 says, 'If thou shalt confess with thy mouth the Lord Jesus, and shalt believe in thine heart that God hath raised him from the dead, thou shalt be saved. For with the heart man believeth unto righteousness; and with the mouth confession is made unto salvation.' Do those verses make sense to you?"

"Yes, but I'm still not sure what I need to say."

"Let me show you a verse from Acts. It's in chapter sixteen, verse thirty-one. A man has just asked Paul and Silas what he must do to be saved, and this is what they tell him: 'Believe on the Lord Jesus Christ, and thou shalt be saved.'"

"So I need to tell God that I believe in His Son?"

"Exactly. We come to God for salvation when we realize we need a Savior and can't save ourselves. It's your heart before God, telling Him what you need. There's not a perfect prayer. If you're admitting that you're a sinner in need and you want Him to take care of that need, God will do it."

Jennings' hands covered his face. Palmer couldn't tell if he was praying or not, so he remained quiet.

"I didn't sleep much last night," Jennings said quietly, his hands coming down. "I can't help but wonder if God wasn't involved in that."

Palmer waited. When he didn't reply, Jennings looked over at him.

"Can I take care of this today, Palmer? Can I pray now, or must I be in church for this?"

"You can take care of it right now."

Jennings tipped his head back, his eyes open and looking up.

"Father God, I need You. I can't do this on my own. My sins are many, the worst of which is my belief that I didn't sin at all. I can see now that I sin every day. I believe the words I read in Luke. When Your Son died, He commended His spirit to You. I wish to do the same. Please save me. Please help me to raise Thomas, James, and Penny. Amen."

Jennings looked across the room and then over at his brother-in-law. Palmer did nothing to hide the moisture in his eyes.

"Where's Liddy?" Jennings asked quietly.

"I'll get her."

Not two minutes later Lydia was returning with Palmer, her face full of hopeful anticipation.

"Jennings?"

He met her in the middle of the room.

"It's settled, Liddy. It's all taken care of."

Lydia could only hug him. Jennings hugged her back. How many years had she prayed, and now in just a few months of his being with them, he had seen his need.

"When will you tell the children?" she asked.

"I'm not sure."

"They might figure it out on their own," Palmer suggested, and Jennings smiled.

"They might."

Suddenly the group laughed. It was a laugh born of relief, peace, and a measure of fatigue. Nevertheless it felt wonderful, and especially so when the little girls came looking for them just minutes later.

≈ ≈ ≈

"Which pony is this?" Penny asked of Emma as Jennings got the cart underway.

"I think this is Bessy."

"She's pretty."

Jennings, barely listening to the little girls' chatter, sat amazed at the way life continued. He was not the same person. Just that morning the most astounding change had happened, but life still had to be lived. A small part of his mind wanted to stop people and tell them what had occurred, but because he didn't do that, it made him more aware of the people in his life.

Never before had Jennings realized what a marvelous staff worked for him. They were efficient, and his life and home ran smoothly and comfortably because of the well-oiled wheels they created. He wasn't going to start gushing over them and make a fool of himself, but he did wonder if any of them had a personal relationship with God. Did any of them realize that nothing they did on this earth was as important as knowing God and His Son?

"Why did we stop, Uncle Jennings?" Emma suddenly asked him.

"Well, now, I guess I wasn't paying attention. Walk on," he ordered the pony who looked quite content to be standing and doing nothing.

"Let's stop and pick flowers!" Lizzy suggested after they made a turn and were headed past the barn. "Can we do that?"

"*May* we," Emma corrected her.

"May we, Uncle Jennings?"

"I think that would be fine. What will you collect them in?"

"Our bonnets!" Penny chimed in, but Jennings didn't think that the best idea.

"There's a little space in the rear. Maybe we can put them there."

As though they'd been promised the moon, the girls tumbled from the cart and into the field of wildflowers with great abandon. In little time at all, they had flowers aplenty and only one scare with a honeybee.

Amid all this, Jennings found himself doing it again: He picked a flower, a small yellow bloom with a dark center, and for the first time thought about its creation. His mind wandered to the book of Genesis, and he wondered if the creation of flowers was covered in those chapters.

"Mr Jennings?"

Jennings looked down to see Penny addressing him.

"Yes, Penny."

"I have to be excused."

"We'll go with you, Penny," Emma offered before Jennings could reply, and that man watched as the little girls began to move to the trees.

"Go where, Emma?" Jennings finally managed.

That little girl stopped and turned.

"To the secret spot. The one we go to with Marianne."

This said, the girls continued on their way. Jennings did not take them seriously until he saw that they were indeed headed directly into the trees. He hurried to catch up, his long legs covering the distance in a hurry, but by the time he arrived, he found nothing. He was on the verge of calling out when he heard soft female voices.

Following the sounds, he realized the girls were inside a group of bushes. Talking all the while and with the occasional giggle, they took matters into their own hands. Not until that moment did he realize that they'd said Miss Walker brought them here.

Jennings didn't know the last time he'd wanted to laugh so hard. The lovely, dignified, always-a-perfect-lady Marianne Walker brought these little girls to the forest for their personal needs when the house seemed a bit far away.

He decided suddenly that he didn't wish to be caught waiting too closely for the girls, so with chuckles still shaking his shoulders, Jennings made his way back out of the trees to wait at the edge of the copse. He didn't have long to linger. The girls appeared a short time later, but in those few moments he realized that he wanted Miss Walker to know of his decision. He wasn't certain how he should go about it, but it was suddenly important to him that she know.

"Uncle Jennings? I think we should take our flowers back now."

Jennings looked to where the girls had walked beyond him, back to the field. They had stopped when he didn't follow.

"You're going to have to keep your wits about you, Jennings," he muttered to himself as he moved to join them. "All right, girls. We'll take the flowers back."

Skipping and laughing all the while, the little girls went to scoop up their treasured bouquets and head to the cart. Bessy was just about asleep by then, but Jennings roused her with the reins and they ventured back to the house.

Jennings turned his head to look down at his three charges, and they chose that moment to look up at him. Their smiles were like a tonic for his wandering thoughts. Asking questions about their favorite flowers and gaining fascinating answers, he talked with the three of them all the way back to Tipton's front door.

Chapter Fifteen

Thornton Hall

"I wish to tell you something, Thomas," Jennings began that evening when the two of them were alone.

"Yes, sir?"

It had seemed easy in his mind, but now, looking into Thomas Jennings' open and trusting eyes, the guardian was at a loss for words.

Thomas continued to wait, his expression not changing, but the longer the silence continued, the tenser he became. He shifted a bit in his seat, and that was enough to snap Jennings from his wordless state.

"I've been taking care of myself for a long time, Thomas, and when a man does that he doesn't believe he has many needs." Jennings stopped and studied the young man's face. "Then you and Penny and James came into my life. I'm sorry for your loss, but I'm not sorry for my gain. You know better than anyone how ill-equipped I was to see to your needs. And not until I got to know my sister and Palmer again did I realize the real source of having one's needs met."

Thomas began to smile. "If I may say so, sir, you seem rather at peace today."

Jennings smiled back at him. "I had no idea, Thomas. I didn't know that anyone could know for certain. My heart was burdened down. I didn't see how much until the burden was lifted."

"Thank you for telling me, sir. I'm extremely glad for you."

"And I for you too, Thomas," Jennings admitted soberly. "I wanted to know God so that I could be the guardian you needed."

Thomas found that he couldn't speak. His young heart had worked hard to trust in God's care when he missed his father so much, but at times he felt so faithless. His throat began to close in an alarming fashion. He suddenly rose and went to the window. He stood still, hands clenched in his pockets in an effort to contain himself, and after several moments he turned, ready to face Jennings.

"I don't think we thank you enough for everything you've done, Mr Jennings. Please accept my thanks now."

"I appreciate that, Thomas, but don't feel that you must constantly shower me with thanks. None of you are in the habit of taking things for granted. I witness that fact every day."

Thomas nodded, but his face didn't look overjoyed. Jennings had observed young Frank with that expression one day, and Palmer had immediately asked his oldest son what was on his mind.

"If there is something you need, Thomas, I hope you'll tell me."

Thomas came back and sat down, a move so mature that Jennings could only stare at him.

"I don't know if I can term it a need, sir, but I have been thinking of Morehouse," Thomas told him.

"I think it's time to make a date to visit," Jennings responded, needing no other prompting. "Your birthday is in eleven days. Lydia is planning a party. Why don't we go a week or two after that?"

"That sounds excellent."

"Which shall it be? A week or two weeks?"

They consulted a calendar and saw that two weeks put them into August, a warm time of the year.

"Two weeks, I think. The breezes at Morehouse are nice at that time of year."

"Not to mention your brother's request to go sea bathing."

"Will we do that?"

"Certainly."

Jennings witnessed a smile on Thomas' face that he had not seen before. Years melted from his already young face, and he laughed.

"Sea bathing! Penny's going to talk of nothing else."

"And what about you?" Jennings asked, suddenly wanting to offer this child the world in a silver spoon. "Will you enjoy it?"

"Yes," Thomas said, his mouth still stretched into a smile. "I'll enjoy it."

Before Thomas could finish his answer, a knock sounded on the door. James came into view, book in hand.

"Oh, here you are. I lost track of you, Thomas."

"I thought you'd gone to bed, James," his brother said.

"I was reading in the chair and fell asleep. Then I woke and checked your room. You weren't in bed, so I thought I'd find you."

"We've just been making plans to visit Morehouse and go sea bathing."

"Sea bathing?" James questioned, his face lighting up as Thomas' had. "When is this?"

"A few weeks after our birthday."

"Does Penny know? She'll talk of nothing else."

Jennings laughed, and the boys laughed with him.

"We'll tell her in the morning."

"Why can't we tell her now?" James asked.

"She's sleeping," Jennings said simply.

"No, she's not. She was awake and followed me down."

Jennings went to the door of the study and there in the dark hallway staring up at him with a serious face was a dark-haired moppet in a pink flannel gown.

"Come along," he invited, and Penny raced inside and into the large chair Jennings had been occupying. Jennings was not put off in the least. He went to the chair, scooped her up, sat down, and deposited her in his lap.

"We have good news for you," he said, ignoring her large eyes. "We're going sea bathing."

"Sea bathing?" Penny perked up, completely forgetting in whose lap she sat. "I can come?"

"Yes, you can. After your birthday we're all going."

"And Marianne? Marianne can come?"

"Yes," Jennings said with a bit less enthusiasm but remembering that at some point in the past he had said as much.

"I wish you could marry Marianne."

Silence descended on the room, a total and devastating silence that lasted the better part of a minute, until Thomas, his voice telling of his horror, took his sister to task.

"Penelope Jennings, you apologize this minute!"

"I'm sorry," she said, scrambling from Jennings' lap in fear.

Seeing her reaction, Thomas was instantly sorry for his tone and would have spoken up, but Jennings beat him to it.

"Come here, Penny," the older man bade. "Come back so I can tell you something."

Penny went back to him with no intention of returning to his lap, but as soon as she was close, Jennings took her back on his knee.

"You must never fear telling me how you feel, Penny. I won't be angry with you. You can always tell me. And by your statement, I assume you wish you had a mother."

"Marianne," Penny admitted quietly, a slight quiver in her voice. "I wish we had Marianne."

"She's very kind, Penny. I can see how you would feel that way."

"You could like her," Penny went on almost pleadingly, shocking her brothers so that their mouths fell open. "Emma said her parents liked each other and then fell in love. You could like Marianne."

Jennings looked into her earnest little face and eyes before smoothing the riot of hair from her brow.

"It does work that way at times, Penny, "liking" turning to "loving," but not always. You understand, don't you?"

"Yes."

She sounded so sad about it that Jennings didn't know what to say. It was a natural yearning on her part, but that didn't mean he could fix it.

"I think we've stayed up late enough," Jennings finally suggested. "I'm for bed, and you should be too."

Goodnights were said as the room emptied. Jennings followed the children slowly, planning to check on everyone once they were settled. Lantern in hand, his eyes caught a large map of the earth—one of his favorites—that had been hung in the hallway. He stopped to study it, wondering at the last time he'd even noticed.

There was a time in his life when his own pursuits and interests were his world. Jennings went on to the children's rooms, not giving the map another thought.

"I'm going sea bathing," Penny told Megan as she brushed her hair the next morning.

"You are?"

Penny nodded. "After my birthday."

"You don't have a birthday coming up, do you?" the housekeeper gently teased.

"I'll be seven."

"Seven is a very big girl, but I don't know if that's big enough to go sea bathing."

"It is! I've gone for years."

"Have you? Do you swim, Miss Penny?"

Another nod answered this query. "Papa used to say I swim fine."

"Did he go in with you?"

Penny nodded. "James and Thomas too."

"Won't that be fun," Megan commented as she put the finishing touches on Penny's hair and tied the little bow at the back of her dress.

"Maybe you can come, Megan," Penny stated.

Megan smiled at this, not wanting to dampen the child's spirits, but not the least bit interested in doing something that would either drown her or cause her to be chilled to death.

"You're all set, Miss Penny."

"Thank you."

"You're welcome. Breakfast is on the table. You'd best scoot."

The little girl was out the door a moment later. Not ten steps into the hallway she encountered Mr Collins.

"I'm going sea bathing."

"Are you, Penny?"

"Yes. So are James, Marianne, Mr Jennings, and Thomas."

"Well, now, won't that be fine."

Penny smiled at him and went on her way, but only until she spotted Bates, who was just coming from one of the rooms downstairs. Cook was the next to hear her news, and at last Penny arrived at the breakfast table.

"Where have you been, Penny?" James asked.

"Seeing Cook."

Thomas caught on immediately.

"Was she glad to hear you're going sea bathing?"

Penny nodded and reached for the toast.

"Don't tip your juice, Penny," Jennings entered the room in time to say. He sat down at his place, reached for his napkin, and continued to watch his youngest charge. "Do you suppose there is anyone at the table who is excited about going sea bathing?" he teased, seeing a moment too late that he shouldn't have. Penny jerked in surprise to tell him she was, and over went her juice.

The little girl looked upset about this incident but didn't apologize. Megan was called in to clean up, and things were put to rights. After prayer was said and the meal began again, Penny wanted to know only one thing.

"Will we still go sea bathing?"

Jennings nearly choked on his coffee for laughing.

≈ ≈ ≈

Blackburn Manor

"I wanted to come yesterday, Mari, but there was no time."

"Mr Jennings came to Christ, Lydia? Yesterday morning?"

"Yes!"

Marianne's sigh was long and deep.

"You're not going to believe this, but I couldn't sleep on Sunday night and ended up praying for your brother off and on all night."

"He told us he got almost no sleep that night, and that's why he came to see Palmer Monday morning."

Accompanied by their own laughter, the women hugged.

"Tell me about it."

Lydia recounted the story, and for a time they talked about the changes that had come in the last few months—

no contact with Jennings for so many years, and now almost more activity than Lydia could handle.

"And there's more," Lydia eventually went on. "I think I'm expecting."

"Lydia Palmer!" Marianne scolded. "You had no business coming over here in the carriage."

"That was Palmer's reaction, but then we talked and realized that I have to be somewhat normal, risks or not."

Marianne calmed a bit.

"I'm pleased for you, Liddy—you know I am. I just don't want to see you ill again."

"I know you don't. I told Nigel to take it very slowly, and he did. I'll do the same on the way home."

"How far along do you think?"

"About six weeks."

"And you feel well right now?"

"Yes. I sense things will go better this time, but maybe that's wishful thinking."

"Be wise, Liddy. Don't be afraid to slow down and use caution. I'll help with the children or whatever I can do."

"Thank you."

For a moment Lydia stared at Marianne. A thought had just occurred to her, and she was surprised that it had taken this long.

"What is it?" Marianne asked under the scrutiny.

"Mari, my brother is a believer now. You don't have to guard your heart any longer."

Marianne smiled a little before saying, "Yes, Liddy, I do. He isn't in love with me. Before God the union would be righteous, but I've no desire to be in love alone."

"Of course you don't." Lydia reached for her hand. "That was thoughtless of me."

"Not at all. You just want to see me happily married and are beginning to think like my mother: It's never going to happen!"

Lydia laughed at Marianne's perfect imitation of her mother's face and voice.

"How did the children take the news about Jennings?"

"My children or his?"

"Both."

"Well, ours were very pleased, and all of them prayed for Jennings last night before bed, but Jennings was going to handle things with his own, so I haven't heard."

"I can't help but think that Thomas will be especially pleased."

"I think you must be right. His heart is sensitive to spiritual matters, and I think he's felt it most keenly that Jennings has not shared his father's faith."

"If only Godwin had known how valuable his training would be. God certainly went before Thomas Jennings."

"Yes, He did. It makes me remember my own mortality and urges me to make sure the children are claiming Christ for their own and not just imitating Palmer and me."

"That's a wise thing to pray for."

"And hopefully we'll have a fifth little person to include in that prayer."

Marianne smiled. "We'll pray for that as well."

Lydia had to be leaving, but the women took time to pray together. Mrs Walker checked on them just as they began and joined in their prayer time.

Marianne sat alone after her friend left and while her mother was working on the daily post. Her mind traveled to Jennings and the children. She so wished he'd never asked her to marry him and then realized that God's hand was moving even then. Nevertheless, it made her dreadfully uncomfortable in his presence, and she so wanted to spend time with the children.

"Well, he did ask you to visit the children," Marianne reasoned to herself, wondering how much of a coward she might turn out to be. She decided not to be a coward at all!

I'll go at the end of the week, Marianne told herself, also concluding that it might be best not to think of it again so she wouldn't change her mind.

≈ ≈ ≈

Thornton Hall

"I'm going sea bathing," Penny told Marianne the moment she saw her. "After my birthday."

"You are?"

The twosome were visiting in the parlor. At the moment they were alone.

"Yes. And do you know what?"

"What?"

"You can come."

"I can?"

Penny nodded. "Mr Jennings said."

Marianne doubted that would actually happen, but she still smiled and hugged the little girl close.

"I'm going to be seven."

"Yes, you are, and in just a matter of days."

"Thomas and James are older. Thomas will be thirteen and James will be eleven."

"That is old," Marianne said. She tried not to smile, but it was nearly impossible. Penny Jennings was one of the most adorable, winsome children Marianne had ever known. Every thought and feeling showed on her face, and when she was comfortable with a person, her warm and engaging personality emerged quickly.

"Where do you go sea bathing?" Marianne asked.

"At Weston-super-Mare. We always go there."

"What do you wear?"

"I have a bathing costume. It's blue with stripes."

"That sounds..."

"Hello," James said from the door before Marianne could finish.

"Hello, James. I hear you're going sea bathing and having a birthday."

James smiled.

"Penny is excited."

"Aren't you?"

"I am too," he admitted.

"Here you are," a fourth person said as he stepped across the threshold. Marianne stood when Jennings entered the room. "Please excuse my tardiness. I had some pressing business."

"Penny was keeping me company," Marianne explained as they all took seats.

"Thank you, Penny," Jennings said before addressing their guest. "Has my sister spoken to you about the birthday party?"

"Yes, she has. We're planning on being there."

"Good. It should be a fine time. Also, the children and I are planning an outing to their home in Bristol, and then on to Weston-super-Mare for some sea bathing. The date is set for the first weekend in August. Will you join us?"

Jennings actually watched Marianne begin to shake her head to decline, a hand going to her throat. But that was before she looked down at Penny, who was on the footstool at her feet. Her eyes then shifted to James' smiling, expectant face. Forcing her hand to her lap and her eyes to her host, she answered.

"I will join you, Mr Jennings. Thank you so much."

The most amazing feeling of tender compassion that Jennings had ever known filled his heart. She had wanted to decline. It was written all over her, but for Penny and James she'd accepted.

And what of my proposal? Had she wanted to accept that day? Had acceptance been the deepest feeling in her heart, but had she forced herself to decline in the name of her faith?

"We'll have such fun," James piped in, and Jennings hoped he hadn't been silent too long. He wanted to be alone with his thoughts, but that wasn't possible at the moment.

"Is it a long drive to Weston-super-Mare?"

"Not from Morehouse," James answered. "Just a few hours."

"And will we stay at Morehouse or just visit?"

"I should think we would stay," James stated logically. "Will we, Mr Jennings?"

"Probably, James, but I think I'll send word ahead and ask if they can manage a visit."

"Why would they not?"

"I don't know how much of the staff stayed on, James. Megan and Mr Collins will be with us, but the staff at Morehouse might need some warning at the very least."

James was very accepting of this, and to everyone's surprise, he began to tell them about the house in detail. Thomas joined them before his brother finished, choosing to sit quietly, but then he looked at their guest.

"I was hoping you'd come soon."

"Why is that?" Marianne wished to know.

"I was thinking a trip through the maze might be fun."

Marianne laughed before asking, "Is it very hard?"

"Yes."

"No."

"At times."

The answers varied with the child. Thomas ended it by saying, "If you get terribly lost, we'll come and find you."

Marianne shook her head in mock dismay.

"I was thinking parlor games or a walk through the park today, and here you want to lose and confuse me. Is someone going to be with me?"

"I will," Penny volunteered.

"It's actually easier if you're on your own," Thomas said. "Too much advice about where to go next only confuses the matter. We'll wait for you at the end."

"How will you know if I'm lost?"

"It should only take you about ten minutes. If you're not out in that time, we'll come for you."

"What if you can't find me?" Marianne asked, and for a moment Jennings caught a very real hesitancy in her eyes.

"We'll find you," Thomas assured her with extreme confidence, and as a group the children came to their feet.

Marianne saw no help for it. Amazed that she'd been talked into this, she accompanied this band of shanghaiers to the yard. Not until they were out standing next to the maze did she notice that Mr Jennings had not joined them.

Chapter Sixteen

"Here's the entrance," James directed. "We've been through it so many times you'll probably find our footpath. If you get very lost, call out. We'll come for you."

"You can do it," Penny added.

"You can even pray if you feel a need," Thomas teased her, thoroughly enjoying her answering laugh.

The three watched as she entered. Marianne looked back long enough to shake her head at them and then forced herself to walk within the walls of shrubs, a solid foot over the top of her head. She heard the scramble of the children's feet as they dashed away from the entrance and knew she was truly on her own.

She soon learned that James was right. Footprints could be detected from time to time and for a while she followed them. Soon a feeling of claustrophobia began to surround her, but she pushed the panic away. In less than three minutes everything looked the same. Marianne wandered for a time and then stood quite still, her arms folded tightly over her chest as she worked to remain calm and review all her options.

She finally had the idea that some of the walls might not be as high as others and began to look up. When she did, she looked directly into the handsome face of William Jennings where he stood at Penny's window. With a finger to his lips and a smile in his eyes, he began to direct her.

"Go back," he mouthed as he pointed behind her, and Marianne walked until she came to a break in the path.

With nods or shakes of his head and the occasional hand direction, he took her to the end of the maze. Marianne heard the children just beyond her and looked up one last time to throw Jennings a beaming smile and mouth a word of thanks. He disappeared from the window a moment later, and Marianne emerged from the maze.

"You made it!" The children welcomed her as if she'd been gone for ages.

"Was it hard?" James asked.

"Very!"

"How did you manage it? Did you pray?"

"Well, I looked up," she said, just holding her laughter. "And that seemed to help."

"How did she do?" Jennings, suddenly on the scene, asked innocently.

"She made it through."

"Well done. I wonder if Cook would have any refreshments on hand to be enjoyed on the veranda. It's been a hard morning of work."

"We'll go see!" Penny volunteered, and the three children ran in the direction of the house. Jennings and Marianne began a slow walk toward the rear veranda.

"Thank you," Marianne said quietly. "I was feeling a bit frightened."

"I could see that."

Marianne blushed, wondering how long he'd been watching her stumble about in a near state of panic.

"You could have told the children," he said.

"I didn't wish to disappoint them."

"Just as you didn't wish to disappoint them by declining the trip."

Marianne looked at him gratefully, glad he understood. "I'm so sorry it's worked out this way," she said, her voice telling of her regret. "I know it's not your choice to have me along. I just didn't know how to say no, especially to Penny."

Jennings was opening his mouth to tell her she was under a wrong impression when the children ran to join them. He regretted the interruption deeply but saw no help for it.

"Cook says she'll have it ready before we can sit down."

"Well, lead on," Jennings directed as they continued toward the house, but Penny didn't leave them, so he wasn't able to clear the matter with Marianne.

The activities continued on the veranda with cool fruit drinks and cakes, and the children shared more about their home and past times at the sea.

It occurred to Jennings that the children, although growing more comfortable with him, were already very at ease with Miss Walker. He'd known this all along, but it was most interesting to observe firsthand. Watching them, he realized that at least part of it was her ability to ask good questions. Jennings could have listened to her all day.

"If you were looking for a spot at Morehouse in which to curl up and read a book, where would that be?" was Marianne's next question.

"There was a good chair in the small parlor. Do you remember that one, James?"

"Yes, we used to race for it."

"And what about here, James? Where would you read at Thornton Hall?"

"I have a grand chair in my room. I think I could sit in it all day."

"And you, Penny? Where do you like to look at books?"

"Here or at home?" she asked, and mentally Marianne flinched. How many months would it take for this little girl to see this as home? And how did her words make Mr Jennings feel? Marianne glanced at him, but his expression gave nothing away.

"Both places," Marianne encouraged her.

"At Morehouse I like to be by the fire. Here I like to be..." her voice trailed off as she thought. "I don't know."

"Well, you'll have to find a special place to call your own."

"Will you help me?"

"Certainly. We'll look around your room and see if you have just the spot."

"And what about you, Miss Walker?" Jennings put in, surprising her. "Where would you go for a good read?"

"Oh, well, I think if the day were fine, I would venture outdoors, but I also like the window seat in my room."

It was a simple question, but the nod Jennings gave and the way his eyes watched her caused Marianne to blush. She could have pinched herself. She was doing it again: behaving like a school girl.

"Is anyone ready for a walk?" Marianne asked in an effort to get her mind off her red face.

"You look a little warm, Marianne," James said innocently. "Are you sure you wish to?"

"I'm fine, James. It's sweet of you to ask."

"Well, then," Thomas inserted, "shall we be off?"

Marianne thought she stood with the children and was right with them but suddenly found herself alone with Mr Jennings. She glanced up to find his eyes still on her.

"I'm not sorry you are accompanying us on our trip, Miss Walker," he began without preamble. "I only hope you can enjoy yourself."

Marianne could only stare at him for a moment. She had expected nothing like this and knew not what to think.

"Thank you," she barely managed as she heard the children call for her.

"We had best join the children."

"Yes," Marianne agreed but still hesitated. "Mr Jennings?"

"Yes, Miss Walker."

"It's only just occurred to me that you might have had plans today. Should I tell the children we'll walk at another time?"

"Not at all. I'll just come along and learn."

Marianne started off the veranda but stopped.

"Learn?"

"Your technique. Why the children like and respond to you."

To this Marianne was utterly speechless. She finally left the veranda, glad that Lydia had told her of her brother's decision. Had she not known of it, she wouldn't have understood the complete change in the man.

As it was, it was so astounding that her heart and mind could hardly reckon with it.

≈ ≈ ≈

"That was hard!" Frank said when he met Thomas outside the maze at Thornton Hall the very next day.

"I would tell you that Marianne made it with ease, but we found out later that Jennings was in Penny's window directing her."

Frank's head went back as he studied the rear windows of the house.

"That's Penny's room that looks right down?"

"Yes. We never even saw your uncle, and the next thing we knew, Marianne was coming out. James and I thought her most clever. We went for a walk in the park, and she confessed."

"Do you think they planned it?"

"I don't know." Thomas' voice was thoughtful. It did seem to him that Jennings and Marianne were rather aware of each other lately, but he wasn't sure if that was what he was seeing or not.

"Let's go riding," Frank suggested.

"All right. I think Jennings is in his study with your father."

The boys went that way, unaware of the discussion going on inside.

~ ~ ~

"Life just goes on, Palmer, but I'm not the same."

"That's an excellent explanation, Jennings. Most days are lived in a regular way, but what makes it different for us is the big God that lives inside of us."

"I've been reading the Bible."

"Good. You'll probably need to do that every day."

"What do you think of my starting in Genesis?"

"I think it's perfect," Palmer told the new believer. "It's the beginning. I can't think of a more logical way to read a book."

"You know, that's been part of my problem. I haven't seen God for the logical being that He is."

"He is logical. At times it's beyond our human comprehension, but God doesn't act without reason."

"I'm looking forward to seeing Pastor Hurst tomorrow," Jennings said, his face showing excitement. "I want to tell him what a help he's been."

"He'll enjoy that."

"Come in," Jennings called to whoever had knocked on the door. "Hello, gentlemen!" he said on seeing the boys. "What can we do for you?"

"We'd like to go riding. Will that work out?"

Jennings looked to Palmer.

"I think so," Palmer gave permission. "Keep it to about an hour."

"All right. Thank you."

The young men left in a hurry, excitement filling their eyes.

"What did the children think of your news?" Palmer asked next.

"Thomas and I spoke first, and we talked for quite some time. I know he was pleased. James and Penny only smiled at me. Penny also told me she had Jesus in her heart."

Palmer smiled.

"That was sometime after she asked me if I would marry Marianne."

Palmer's mouth opened.

"She said that to you?"

"Yes. Her brothers were very upset with her, but she wants Marianne for a mother, and I told her she could always tell me how she feels."

Palmer said nothing. Questions came to mind, but Jennings' face was so thoughtful and serious that he felt as though he'd be intruding to voice them.

Heavenly Father, he prayed instead. *Help Jennings and Marianne. If Your plan puts them together, make it so clear to them. Help the rest of us to stay out of the way and let You work. And thank You, Father. Thank You for saving Jennings.*

Palmer thought he could weep at the goodness of God, but he didn't want to do that right now. Instead he suggested they check on the boys. Jennings stood up swiftly enough that he knew he'd made the right choice.

∾ ∾ ∾

"What did you get them?" Walker asked of his wife and daughter after the three of them had loaded into the carriage for the ride to Tipton. On this day the Jennings children had become thirteen, eleven, and seven respectively.

"A book of maps for Thomas, a compass for James, and a small tea set for Penny's doll," Marianne answered.

"The boys are interested in maps, are they?"

"Yes. It seems to be a Jennings-Palmer passion. I guess Godwin Jennings also loved maps. I can always find young Frank and Thomas bent over one when I stop at the house."

"Palmer has liked them since he was a lad himself," Walker put in. "I remember how well he liked that large one my father gave me."

"The one with the black background?"

"That's it. He could study it for hours."

The remainder of the ride was uneventful, and when they arrived, two other carriages could be seen.

"Looks like quite a party," Mrs Walker commented.

"I think only the Hursts." Walker studied the other conveyances. "The other carriage is Jennings'."

"Imagine," Mrs Walker continued, still amazed. "All three of them born on the same day."

The Walkers joined the party that was just getting underway. Penny was delighted to see Marianne and hugged her as soon as she entered the large salon. Happy chaos was in high order for the next few hours. The children, Palmers, Hursts, and Jenningses alike, along with the adults in the group, played games on the lawn and enjoyed two different cakes.

When it was time for the gift opening, the children received a variety of gifts and were pleased with each one. Jennings ended up next to Marianne's chair and bent close to speak to her.

"Where did you find that small tea set?"

"I ordered it in Collingbourne, but I'm sure Benwick got it from London. Had you looked for one for her?"

Jennings smiled. "No, you'll have to come over after the party and see what I plan to give them."

"They don't have your gifts yet?"

Jennings shook his head no, showing his pleasure without the obvious smile. Marianne was dying to ask him what he'd bought but didn't feel free to do so. She thought she might take him up on his offer, however, and go see for herself.

The gift opening over, Marianne happened to look up and gain a good glimpse of Lydia's face. She looked pale and weary.

"How are you holding up?" Marianne asked when everyone had begun to move and she could get to her without overdue notice.

"I'm tired."

"I think this should have been scheduled at Thornton Hall."

"Now that I'm weary I would agree with you, but at the time it sounded like such a good idea."

Thankfully the party did not last overlong. Pastor Hurst, Mrs Hurst, and their four children were the first to leave, and not long after them, Marianne's parents went on their way. Palmer assured Marianne he would see that she got home when she told him she wanted to stay on a bit.

"Here, Liddy, sit down," Marianne ordered when the salon was quiet. The children had run off in various pursuits. Only the two women remained until Jennings returned. From just a few steps inside the door, he watched Marianne fuss over his sister. Something was wrong—he was sure of it—and he intended to find out what it was. He walked to the settee where Lydia was now comfortable and looked down at her.

"Lydia?"

"It was a nice party, wasn't it, Jennings?"

Jennings' look was telling. He sternly held his sister's eyes before turning to Marianne.

"Since my sister isn't going to tell me why she looks exhausted, Miss Walker, I hope you will do me the favor."

Marianne had all she could do not to tell him. William Jennings could be practicing law! She opened her mouth but looked to Lydia in time. That woman was laughing.

"He can be frightening, can't he, Mari?"

Marianne dropped into a chair, her face a bit pink. She still hadn't said a word.

Palmer entered the room, Judith behind him with glasses and a pitcher of cool water. Jennings held his tongue until the servant left, but only until the door was closed behind her.

"Palmer, I want to know what Lydia's hiding from me. Now be a good man and tell me."

Palmer didn't even hesitate. It was a delicate subject for mixed company, but these were the dearest people in the world to him.

"Lydia was expecting a year ago and lost the baby in a rather difficult way. She's now expecting again, and though she feels better this time, she's going to be taking it easy."

Jennings speared Lydia with his eyes. "So that's why you just had a birthday party for three children? That's your idea of taking it easy?"

"I didn't do that much, Jennings," she began.

"You led the games, Lydia, and played the hostess. Had I realized—"

"I wanted to," she cut him off. "It was my way of showing the children, and you, how much I care."

Jennings could say nothing to that. He realized he was much too upset, took a seat, and willed himself to calm down.

"It was the first birthday without their father," Lydia went on. "I wanted it to be special. Who knows how he would have handled it. Maybe they never had parties, but I wanted them to enjoy the day."

"Thank you, Liddy," Jennings said sincerely. "I know the day was special for them, but neither the children nor I would want you ill, not for any reason."

"I do feel better this time, Jennings; honestly I do. Things seemed to be askew from the very start last year, but I shall be taking it very slowly."

"Don't forget, Jennings," Palmer added, "school starts again soon. Lydia will have even more time to rest then."

Jennings nodded. He realized his reaction stemmed from a certain amount of fear. He had been absent from his sister's world for many years—his own choice, certainly—but the thought of not having her when he was only just seeing how precious she was had frightened him very much.

Amid this turmoil of thoughts, he realized Marianne hadn't said a word. Actively listening, she was sitting among them looking from one to the other. Jennings began to watch her and found he couldn't take his eyes away. There was something altogether soothing about this woman. She was lovely to look at, but more than that, she didn't demand attention from anyone.

"I think a cup of tea sounds good, don't you, Lydia?" Marianne suddenly asked her friend.

"Oh, yes, Mari. Ask Judith, would you?"

"Certainly."

"I think maybe some small sandwiches too, Mari. I don't believe Liddy ate much during the party."

"And what are the children doing?" Lydia asked a few moments later.

"I'll check," Jennings volunteered, not wanting her to move.

And there it was happening again, Jennings realized as he strode from the room. All of them were carrying on in a normal way, but with God living in their hearts. It was such a phenomenal truth to Jennings that he pondered it often.

Jennings' mind was on his new discoveries and not on where he was going when he left the salon. Thinking he'd left Palmer, Lydia, and Marianne behind, he was especially surprised when he walked along the hall and ran directly into Marianne.

"Are you all right?" he asked after nearly plowing her over.

"Yes, thank you. I'm sorry, I was not attending."

"Neither was I."

For a moment they stood in awkward silence.

"Are you leaving?" Marianne asked at last.

"No, I was going to check on the children, but I've just remembered that I mentioned the children's gifts to you. I'm going to have them brought here so my nieces and nephews can enjoy them also. If you stay you'll see them."

"Oh, thank you. I'll plan on that."

For a moment silence reigned again. Jennings' eyes were intent on Marianne's face, and Marianne was looking up at him from time to time, her eyes uncertain.

"I'd best get back to the salon," Marianne said.

"And I to the children."

Jennings stepped to one side so Marianne could pass, but he didn't move on his way. He stood watching until she was out of sight.

≈ ≈ ≈

"You have birthday gifts for us here?" Thomas questioned Jennings an hour later, following him down the hall, the other six children in his wake.

"Yes. Come along to the parlor and sit a moment. I'll come for you soon."

Frank, Walt, Emma, and Lizzy all trailed after the Jennings children, not wishing to miss a thing. As soon as they were in the room, Jennings went to his sister.

"Are you sure you're up to this?" he asked softly. "It's not too late to send everything back to Thornton Hall. The children will understand."

"I've been sitting here for more than an hour, Jennings. I wouldn't miss it if you begged me."

Jennings nodded and turned to the children.

"Walt, do you have your pocket watch?"

"Right here," the little boy answered as he pulled it from his small vest pocket.

"Very good. The seven of you sit tight. We're headed out of doors. You follow us in three minutes. Can you do that?"

The children squirmed with excitement as they agreed to this, and questions followed the adults as they exited, questions that were not answered.

"I'm excited, and it's not even my gift," Marianne commented as they neared the front door.

"We'll want to position ourselves so we can see their faces," Jennings said as he brought up the rear. What he didn't realize is that he missed his sister's and Marianne's faces. When they stepped out and saw the two horses, pony cart, and pony, their mouths dropped wide open.

"Oh, my," was all the ladies could say. Palmer had been in on the surprise for some weeks.

"Do you think they'll be pleased?" Jennings asked, his face showing how much he was.

"I think they'll be ecstatic," his sister proclaimed. "There's just one problem."

"What's that?"

"How will you ever top it?"

The adults were chuckling over this when the children joined them, their reaction all that Jennings could have hoped for.

Within minutes the girls were begging for a ride, and Frank and Walt were talking of getting their own mounts so the four of them could be off.

"Thank you," James said for the fifth time, his eyes telling of his wonder and pleasure.

"You're welcome," Jennings told him, but he could have thanked the child right back. He was learning that giving presents to these children was like giving a gift to himself. But it was more than that: He felt a little more like a father every day.

Chapter Seventeen

There had been a change in plans. The first idea had been to go directly to Morehouse and then on to an outing that included sea bathing. But the weather had turned very warm, so when Marianne left with the Jennings family two weeks later, their first destination was the sea.

"I should have spoken to you about this before we left," Jennings said to Marianne from across the carriage some thirty minutes into their ride, "but I thought the boys and I would share a room, and if you don't mind, Penny can be in with you. Megan is along if you'd rather not."

Marianne could feel Penny's eyes on her as she answered.

"Share a room with Penny?" she sounded doubtful. "Does she snore very loudly?" Marianne looked down at the little girl beside her as soon as this was said and smiled. Penny laid her head against Marianne's arm and stared up at her with all the adoration she felt.

"I think we'll do fine together."

"Penny would fit on our bed," Thomas added, doing a little teasing of his own.

"I'll be smashed," Penny said, her face comical as her head came up.

"It might be cozy."

Penny frowned at him. "I want to be in with Marianne."

"And so you shall," Jennings said. "Thomas is only teasing."

Penny still frowned at her brother.

"You've no reason to be so sensitive, Penny," Jennings went on mildly. "It's all right."

Penny took the rebuke well, her face relaxing. Marianne, not wanting to be a part of family discipline, had turned to the window. It had been years since she'd been to Bristol and beyond, and she found she was looking forward to it. The scenery varied from that at home, which made it interesting.

If she felt a bit odd about being with Mr Jennings and his children, she did her best to hide it. The children were so excited, and she was finding Mr Jennings most solicitous. What the days at the sea would bring, as well as those at Morehouse, was impossible to predict, but Marianne was determined to give the others a good time.

For a moment Marianne thought about the past week. One evening she had ended up at Tipton when Jennings and the children had been there. After supper the four adults had sat talking over coffee. It was at that time that Jennings shared some of what his thoughts had been prior to his visit to Palmer the morning he was saved.

"I felt almost a fearful peace. It makes no sense when I say it, but that's the best way to describe my mind that night. I knew that something had to change between God and me, and that made me afraid, but I was confident and peaceful that Palmer would have answers.

"At the same time I wondered if I'd waited too long. I don't think God waits forever, and maybe He was tired of my stiff neck. The children were so confident. I'd heard them pray a few times, and such trust seemed beyond me, but then I prayed and told God how much I needed Him, and I know He heard me."

"Look at the horses!" James suddenly exclaimed.

Everyone crowded to the left side of the carriage to see a small herd of horses running hard through the fields.

"I think my horse will miss me," James said a bit wistfully when they all sat back.

"It's not long that we'll be gone, James," Marianne said compassionately.

"You can make up for the absence by going for a long ride when we return," Jennings suggested. "You might even find the weather more suited when we get home."

With that everyone fell quiet. It was warm in the carriage, but the cool sea breezes awaited them. For a time, each one was left alone with his or her thoughts.

≈ ≈ ≈

"There was a softening in you, Jennings." Waiting downstairs at the inn for the gentlemen to join them, Marianne found herself remembering back again. *"Even before you came over to see Palmer that morning, you had started to change."*

"I think you must be right, Lydia. I had been inhospitable to Miss Walker," Jennings said with a glance in Marianne's direction. *"Six months prior to that time I would have thought nothing of it, but this time I knew I had to speak with her."*

"And did you?" Palmer asked.

"Yes. She was very gracious and even took me at my word and visited the children."

"That was all before I knew they were going to send me through the maze," Marianne put in, her voice light.

"Did they really?" Lydia asked on a laugh.

"Yes. I'd still be in there if a little help hadn't materialized."

"Who helped you?"

Jennings and Marianne exchanged a look on that question, but neither one answered.

"How is your room?" Jennings asked Marianne, snapping her from her reverie.

"Our room is fine, isn't it, Penny?" Marianne addressed the little girl beside her.

"Yes. We have a bed."

"Good!" Jennings said with a smile down at her. He took note of the fact that her face looked freshly washed and her hair newly combed, and realized the little girl was certainly rooming with the right person.

"How did you fare with the boys?" Marianne asked.

"We're quite comfortable ourselves. They're coming behind me with plans to walk to the water. Does that suit you?"

"That suits me very well," Marianne told him.

Are you always so sweet? Jennings asked her in his mind, his eyes on her face. *Have you always been so ready to see to others' needs, or did you learn over time?*

The question was especially close to Jennings' heart just now because he found himself weary at times. It had never once occurred to him that parenting was a full-time venture. With preparing for the children's birthday and getting ready for this trip, he felt as though he'd had no free time in weeks.

"We have a map," Thomas said triumphantly, waving it over his head as both boys joined the group.

"Are we sea bathing now?" Penny wished to know.

"Not until tomorrow, Penny," Jennings decided with a moment's thought. It wasn't that long to supper. "Shall we be off for a walk on the beach?"

"I'll lead the way," James offered, but Thomas reminded him that he had the map.

A "discussion" followed this interchange, and Jennings had to intervene.

"Let's not start our holiday with an argument," he ended the quiet speech he gave the boys. Both knew they were being selfish and agreed to study the map together.

"It was unfortunate you had to witness that," Jennings said for Marianne's ears alone as they walked from the inn. "They're usually better behaved."

"That's true, but they're still human."

That statement proved to be very true just five minutes later when the boys got somewhat turned around and Jennings ended up studying the map.

"Human," he whispered to Marianne with a smile as he lifted Penny onto his arm, his body turned at an angle so he could offer a hand to Marianne for the short walk down the stairs to the sand.

At last they were on the beach. Marianne tied Penny's bonnet a bit tighter and urged James to button his coat, and then they were off. Many families, couples, and singles were out on this fine day, and Jennings and Marianne walked slowly as the children explored and led the way.

"You have been to the beach before?" Jennings inquired.

"Not for years. I'd forgotten the scents that come on the wind."

"Some more memorable than we'd like," Jennings uttered quietly as he took Marianne's arm to navigate her around a dead fish, causing her to laugh.

"Oh, look at the kite!" Marianne suddenly cried—even the children heard her—and all five of them stopped to watch the object already high in the air.

From there the group observed the last of the sea bathers and the last trips for the bathing machines. Marianne had never seen such contraptions, and Thomas explained how the covered, wheeled carts that were pulled by horses or donkeys worked.

"You can rent a bathing costume or take your own inside. It's very private, and while the cart goes to the water, you change. Once changed, you open the door and go directly into the sea. When you climb back in for the ride up to the beach, you change back again."

"That's marvelous!" Marianne was enchanted. "Will Penny and I both fit in one bathing machine?"

"Certainly."

"What if I don't swim well?"

"They don't go out very deep, so you'll just remain close to the bathing machine."

"Do you swim at all?" Jennings asked, concern showing in his face and tone.

"I do a little, but as I said, it's been many years."

The concern did not leave Jennings' face, and Marianne did not want to spoil the outing.

"I'll just see that Penny gets into the water," she said, landing on an idea and voicing it with excitement. "How would that be?"

"No!" the children began to protest, wanting her along.

"I'll tell you what," Jennings cut in. "Miss Walker and I will discuss it and come up with the best plan."

It was not what the children wanted to hear—they wanted Marianne to enjoy the water as they did—but they let the matter drop.

"I'm hungry," James suddenly announced, and Penny took no time to tell of her empty stomach as well.

Thinking that they had all of tomorrow to enjoy the beach, Jennings pragmatically ushered the group back the way they'd come. Once at the inn they took time to freshen up, planning to meet in the dining room for supper.

Jennings was almost to his room with the boys when a housekeeper stopped him.

"Mr Jennings, does Mrs Jennings need some extra towels?"

"It's Miss Walker," he corrected her kindly, "and why don't you check with her in her room down the hall?"

"Oh!" the maid responded with a start. Clearly embarrassed, she moved quickly on her way.

Jennings turned back to use the key to his door and found two sets of eyes watching him.

"It's a logical mistake, don't you think?"

"Yes," James agreed. "And now it's easier to understand why Penny wanted you to marry Marianne. I never noticed it before, but you already look like you're married."

Jennings was heartily surprised by this, and his face showed it.

"James meant no disrespect, sir," Thomas put in.

"Thank you, Thomas. I was not offended, just unaware. I would wish to be very careful of Miss Walker's reputation, and I hope we haven't given the wrong picture."

Looking old beyond their years, the boys nodded, and Jennings finally opened the door. They made their preparations to go back downstairs with few words exchanged, but all minds were moving. Each one was thinking on the conversation from the hallway.

~ ~ ~

"I don't have to swim. I would be happy to watch."

"We arrived at the end of the day today," Jennings reasoned with her. "It will be very warm tomorrow, and you'll want to cool off.

"Here is what we'll do," Jennings continued, using the voice that was hard to argue with. "I'll come over to you as soon as the door to your bathing machine opens."

"I can stay in the shallow part so you can play with the children."

"You could still drown, and I won't risk it."

Marianne frowned at him, and since he was clearly intent on having his way, Jennings looked right back, his face calm.

At the same moment, they remembered they had an audience. The public room was nearly empty, but three other people shared their table. They turned to look at the children, who were all watching them with unabashed curiosity.

"Thomas," Jennings began, "if you're finished, why don't you, James, and Penny take a walk out front?"

"All right."

"Are they married now?" Penny asked Thomas as he took her from her chair.

He hushed her and rushed away but did see her point. Jennings and Marianne had acted and looked like an old married couple while having their debate.

Jennings watched the threesome on their way, and when he looked back at Marianne, he could see she was hiding laughter.

"Penny's remark?"

"Yes. I find her amusing—so guileless in her curiosity."

Jennings took a slow drink of his coffee. Marianne was not looking at him, but he watched her over the rim of his cup.

"You look lovely tonight," he said as he set the cup back down.

"Thank you," Marianne said with a shy duck of her head.

"The children and I, not to mention your family, would never get over it if something happened to you. I've no cruel intentions of embarrassing you or tarnishing your reputation further, but I must make certain you don't drown."

Marianne looked into his eyes.

"Has my reputation been harmed?"

"At least one of the maids thought we were married. I'm sure our walk last evening helped her form that conclusion."

"I could be the children's nanny," Marianne suggested.

"Not dressed as you are and walking by my side."

"True."

"And even now, I've sent the children away from the table. At least having them with us does not suggest that you're here alone with me."

"I'll go out with them," Marianne said immediately and began to rise.

"All right. Are we settled on the matter of sea bathing?"

"I think so, but I don't believe I would have come if I thought I was going to be such trouble."

Marianne exited before Jennings could reply. He understood how she could feel that way, but sea bathing was just one small aspect of the entire trip. He was surprised that she didn't realize how much she was needed.

~ ~ ~

Marianne kept her focus on the little girl with her. She had changed into her bathing costume, and while it covered her from head to foot, a woman was very self-conscious when not wearing a corset in a man's presence, and she knew as soon as the door opened that Mr Jennings would be there.

"All right, ladies," the driver said from outside their shuttered window just after the bathing machine came to a stop.

Penny lit up like a candle upon hearing the man's words and reached for the door. Marianne, not quite certain what to expect, watched as she swung the door open and jumped.

"Penny!" Marianne came swiftly after her.

"She's fine." The deep voice of Mr Jennings came to her ears just as his hand took hers. "Are you going to jump?" he asked.

"Are the children all right?" Marianne questioned, looking anxiously beyond him.

"Swimming like fish. Shall we join them?"

Marianne forced herself to step out into the water.

"Oh!" she couldn't stop the gasp that escaped her when the cool water soaked through to her skin.

"Are you all right?" Jennings asked, still holding her hand.

"It's a bit cool."

"That's putting it mildly," he said, a twinkle in his eyes. "Here we go!"

Marianne was wading in water only up to her knees at this point, and she walked along to the children who were already wet from head to foot. They were delighted that she joined them, and in no time at all, she was very wet herself.

What followed were two glorious hours of swimming and playing in the water. Marianne didn't know when she'd had such fun. She spent most of her time sitting on the sea floor, water nearly to her neck, and laughing at the antics of the children. Mr Jennings proved to be a fine swimmer, and at one point he and Thomas struck out in a race. Jennings had the advantage and won easily, but he let Thomas hang on his back for part of the return trip.

When the children showed signs of becoming water-logged, everyone changed and sought refreshments from among the stands on the beach. All a little drowsy, they took their time at a seaside table for five.

"Will we go to Morehouse tomorrow?" Thomas asked.

"We can, or do you wish for one more day at the sea?"

To Marianne's surprise Penny and James did not immediately vote to stay. They were quiet as they relished their drinks and biscuits.

"I think I'd like to go tomorrow," Thomas said. "Will we have time to stay a few days?"

"We can stay, Thomas. And if you feel an extended visit is necessary, you just speak to me."

"Thank you, sir."

They ate and talked for more than an hour. It was a slow time without interruptions or schedules to keep. Eventually they changed again and went back into the water and then back to the hotel for supper, but it was a day in which forever after James would say that time stood still; minutes had stretched into hours and hours felt like days.

By the time they reached their rooms to retire for the night, Jennings was so drowsy he could barely ready himself for bed. He was sitting on the side of the bed and staring at nothing when someone knocked on the door.

"Mr Jennings?" The innkeeper himself stood outside.

"Yes."

"A lady asked me to give you this," he said, pushing a paper toward him. "She's down by the fire, 'oping to see you."

Jennings pulled a coin from his pocket, thanked the man, and then closed the door.

The boys watched him read the note, his face thoughtful.

"Thomas," Jennings directed, turning to him, the note going to his pocket, "lock the door. Open it for only me. I won't be long."

"Are you leaving?" James asking, feeling so tired he thought he could cry.

"Just down to the common room, James. Go ahead to sleep. I'll be back shortly."

Jennings had said all of this while slipping back into his jacket. A moment later he was out the door and to the stairs. He took them down and entered the room, a bit darker than he remembered, and the moment he did, a woman stood from her seat by the fire.

"Mr Jennings?"

"Yes."

"I'm sorry to disturb you, but I would beg a moment of your time."

"Please sit down, Mrs..." Jennings began.

The woman didn't answer but did resume her seat. Finely dressed and not young, she was terribly distracted, her hands twisting her handkerchief into knots.

"Are you unwell?" Jennings asked from the seat opposite her, his heart wrung with a certain measure of compassion.

"No, sir, I thank you, but I must tell you something. It's about Mrs Smith."

Jennings' frame tensed, but he sat still, his mind racing with what this woman could want.

"I thought a huge injustice was being committed," she began apologetically. "I thought I was doing the right thing when I hired Mr Hayter to represent her. Mrs Smith was our nanny for years. I thought she was wonderful. My daughter was always so quiet and well behaved." Some emotion overcame the woman just then, and she stopped to compose herself. After a deep breath, she continued very quietly.

"I don't see my daughter very often; she's moved far from London," the woman said in obvious pain and regret. "But I did see my daughter after the trial, and from her I learned the truth." The woman raised tortured eyes to his. "Mrs Smith was horrible to my Elisabeth. She was cruel and impatient and made sure the bruises didn't show."

It was too much for the woman. Even knowing her daughter was no longer in harm's way, the thought of what she'd been through was too much for her.

Jennings remained quiet while the woman cried, his heart so thankful that it hadn't taken years to learn of Penny's pain. Nevertheless, he didn't think anything could be done to reverse the decision of the judge. The trial was over. He could speak to a lawyer about entering new evidence, but would this Elisabeth, who now lived far from London, wish to testify? And if she was willing, would they find Mrs Smith again?

"I don't suppose anything can be done by the courts now," the lady continued, "but I had to come to you. I had to make it right with you."

"Will you tell me your name?"

"Mrs Dashwood of Bath. I was to your home at Collingbourne. I talked to your man. He was kind enough to tell me where you'd gone."

"Thank you, Mrs Dashwood. I shall look into this when I return. If the courts do want to hear further testimony, they might need to hear from your daughter."

"She would be more than willing to have her say about Mrs Smith. I shall write to you at Collingbourne so you'll have my address. If you need Elisabeth, contact me."

And with just a soft word of goodbye, Mrs Dashwood rose and exited. Jennings stood by the fire long enough to hear a carriage pull away and assumed she was safely on her way. He mounted the stairs slowly, thoughtfully.

Thomas opened the door, his eyes searching out some kind of reassurance. Thankfully Jennings caught his anxious gaze.

"I'll tell you in the morning, Thomas," he answered the unasked question. "Get your rest now."

"There's nothing wrong with Penny or Marianne, is there?"

"It was nothing like that, Thomas—just a woman desperate to set the record straight."

Thomas nodded.

"Goodnight, sir."

"Goodnight."

The lantern was still burning next to Jennings' bed. He could see that James was sound asleep and assumed Thomas soon would be. In light of that he felt free to burn the lantern a bit longer, and he reached for his Bible.

Tonight his mind was on God's sovereignty. He remembered how frustrated he'd been when Mrs Smith had gotten off, but it hadn't been long after that when he'd understood how God had been in control the entire time.

Jennings had it in his mind to look for a verse that spoke of God's sovereignty when he found himself in the first chapter of Second Timothy. He began to read, going over things slowly when they did not make sense, and stopping in his tracks on verse five: "When I call to remembrance the unfeigned faith that is in thee, which dwelt first in thy grandmother, Lois, and thy mother Eunice; and I am persuaded that in thee also."

Jennings had not been reading the Bible long, but even at that, he couldn't recall reading about a man's mother and grandmother in this way. It sounded to him as though Paul credited Timothy's faith to his mother. And then his mother's faith to her mother.

Jennings read it several times over, determining to ask Palmer or Pastor Hurst if this was usual. He thought about it as he readied for bed—he was now well and truly tired— and even after he lay down. The lantern still on, Jennings raised himself up and looked over at the other bed. The boys were sound asleep.

Jennings eventually turned the lantern down and laid his head on the pillow. His mind as full as it was tired, he fell asleep with the children in his prayers.

Chapter Eighteen

"Her name was Mrs Dashwood," Jennings explained to Marianne and the children at the breakfast table about his evening visitor. "Mrs Smith worked for her years ago, and just as with you, Penny, she was not kind. Mrs Dashwood didn't know this at the time. She sent a man to represent Mrs Smith at the trial, and because of his defense the court let her go free. Later when she spoke with her daughter, she learned the truth."

"Is Mrs Smith coming?" Penny asked.

"To find us? No, Penny. We know about her. She won't want to be anywhere near us."

"So the lawyer lied?" Thomas asked.

"No. Mrs Dashwood thought Mrs Smith was being unjustly tried."

"How could she not know about her own daughter all those years?" James asked, his small brow lowered.

"I don't know, James. I'm only glad we found out so soon."

Penny suddenly found all eyes on her. She looked at Jennings.

"I didn't like her."

Jennings reached over and touched her small hand.

"It's all over now. There's no need to worry."

Jennings urged the children back to their breakfasts, but before he could return to his, he caught Marianne's eyes on him. Before she dropped her gaze he thought he saw approval there. He wondered on it until they were in the carriage and on their way.

≈ ≈ ≈

Morehouse was beautiful, set on a hill amid trees of great variety. The small band of travelers were quiet as they approached. The handful of staff began to gather when they were still a long way off, and James was the first to spot them.

"Look, it's Murch."

"And Mrs Murch!" Penny added.

The children tumbled from the carriage almost before it could stop and ran to these faithful servants.

"How are you, Master Thomas?"

"We're fine, Murch. Please meet our guardian, William Jennings, and a friend of ours, Miss Walker."

"Welcome to Morehouse."

Penny was hugging Mrs Murch in a way that reminded Jennings of her relationship with Cook, and he now understood why the children had shown such kindness to his staff. And all of this was before stepping through the doors of Morehouse.

One of the grander homes Jennings had ever seen, the foyer alone was spectacular. The woods were all a bit dark for Jennings' taste, but the staircase that rose from the foyer area to the second floor was unparalleled. He was on the verge of telling the children how impressed he was when he realized they had moved as a group away from him.

Jennings and Marianne watched as the children silently but resolutely approached the double-wide open doors of a study, presumably their father's. His large desk sat directly in the middle of the room facing the door, and the children were drawn to it as though under a spell.

Jennings kept his place, but Marianne went as far as the doorway to watch.

They all seemed to be attracted to their father's desk chair. Remaining silent and watchful, Marianne slipped in and sat on one of the sofas.

James ran his hand along the smooth leather back of the chair and then buried his face against it to cry. His tears prompted Penny's. She stood with her arms wrapped around the nearest armrest, her sobs coming unchecked. Thomas was in no better condition. He didn't touch the chair or his siblings but looked down at the desk, tears flowing freely down his face.

Marianne cried as well but didn't move to the children. She knew that Jennings had come to the doorway, but she couldn't turn to him. She could only cry and watch the heartbreak of these children she loved.

Thomas was the first to contain himself. He used his handkerchief and then glanced around the room. Only then did he notice Marianne.

"Why are you crying, Marianne?"

"Because I'm so sorry for your pain."

It was too much for the oldest child. He again succumbed to tears. Hearing Marianne's voice, Penny went to her, and it wasn't long before the others joined her on the sofa.

Large windows allowed a stunning view of a valley to the north, and a smattering of sunlight cast a glow on shelves of books and keepsakes.

"It's a wonderful room," Marianne said after some minutes. The tears had slowed, and all was quiet. Jennings had taken a chair nearby as the sofa was full.

"He read to us here," Thomas said. "Almost every night."

"What did he read to you?" Jennings asked.

"Many poems and plays, and always a verse from the Bible."

"He let Penny have a corner of his desk," James filled in.

"Right there." Penny pointed to the nearest one.

"What did you do there?"

"I had paper like Papa. I wrote numbers."

It wasn't hard to imagine for Jennings or Marianne. Jennings did the paperwork for his own estate, and Marianne had watched her father for years.

A servant stepped into the doorway just then—it was Murch—and all five of them looked up.

"Excuse me, sir. Mrs Murch has refreshments if anyone is thirsty," he offered.

Jennings turned to Thomas.

"What do you think, Thomas?"

"I'll show you the way," he said with his usual show of maturity. When he came to his feet, the rest of the group followed.

They ate, visited some, and had a tour of Morehouse. Then Jennings and Marianne were shown their rooms. Supper was served several hours later, a fairly light meal, before Jennings suggested they make an early night of it. It was over breakfast the next morning that the real conversation began.

"I think the three of you should go through the house and choose things you want to have with you at Thornton Hall," Jennings said at the first meal on their second day. "You arrived in London with little more than the clothing on your backs, and you might wish to have certain things— even your beds if you like these better."

It was obvious that Thomas and his siblings had not thought of this, but the idea appeared to please all of them.

"There are some items I would wish to have," Thomas said. "I don't think I could stand to see the house bare, but an item or two would be rather nice."

"Is my dollhouse too big?" Penny asked.

"I'm sure not, Penny. We can arrange for that if you like."

The table fairly buzzed with talk after that. While the children discussed items of interest, Jennings turned to Marianne.

"Do you think you could go along with Penny this morning and make a list of what she wants? I'll have the boys start their own lists—I might even go with James—and we'll look them over after lunch."

"I'd be happy to. Do you want me to steer her in any particular direction?"

"I think not. I want to know what she wants. If we need to trim the lists before the end of the day, that's fine."

"Very well. We'll do our best."

They did not linger over breakfast. All three children were eager to get started.

"Well, Miss Penny," Marianne said when they were alone in the dining room, "where would you like to start?"

"Upstairs."

"Lead the way."

Marianne had said this in a lighthearted manner, unaware of how serious Penelope Jennings felt about this first item. The two entered a bedroom, a masculine room with almost no frills. The room's furnishings could only be termed practical. Over the dresser, directly across from the bed, hung a portrait. Penny stopped before it.

"I want this."

Marianne could only stare.

"Who is it, Penny?"

"It's my mother."

For the first time Marianne understood why Penny often stared at her. The resemblance was not perfect, but very distinct. For a moment Marianne couldn't say anything, and during this silence, they heard James and Jennings come down the hall.

"This way," James said as he walked in. "Oh, hello, Penny. I thought you might put Mother's portrait on your list. I was coming to add it to mine."

Now it was Jennings' turn to stare. He looked at the woman who had given birth to Thomas, James, and Penny and then to Marianne. There was no missing the similarity.

"Did you know?" Jennings asked her.

"Not until a few seconds ago."

"Have we never told you?" James asked Marianne.

"I'm sure I would have remembered, James. Penny stared at me rather intently when we first met, and while I wondered why, I never figured on this."

"Well, I'm glad you both want it," Jennings said. "We'll hang it in Thornton Hall wherever you choose."

This statement was greeted with smiles before the partners went on, James with Jennings and Penny with Marianne. Both pairs took notes and debated about various items. Penny cried when she saw her father's shoes, but her eyes were dry when the children were once again in their father's study. Nevertheless, they all crowded close and looked at the desk chair.

"The room would be awful without it," James proclaimed. "I want to remember it here."

"As do I," Thomas added, putting his oar in.

Penny looked uncertain but said nothing.

Marianne felt a rescue was needed.

"Is there another item, Penny, here on the desk or in the room, that would give you a special memory?"

Almost immediately Penny's eyes landed on her father's pens and inkstand. Just moments later they were added to the list. The boys also chose items from their father's study— a map for James, and a picture, one that had always hung over the fireplace, for Thomas. By the time they had settled on these items, it was nearly time for lunch.

Lists in hand, they gathered around the table for that meal—excitement evident on every face—with questions as to how the items would get to Thornton Hall.

"I'll make the arrangements tomorrow, and then we'll leave the next day," Jennings told them. "If you think of something else, just inform me, but don't feel panicked that you might be leaving something special behind. We can visit again, and if that won't work, we can always write Murch and describe the item you want. Once arrangements are made, it might take a few weeks until things arrive, but it will feel like Christmas when they do.

"And don't forget," Jennings tagged onto the end, "we'll be accompanying the Palmers to London for school clothes not long after we arrive back. Maybe by the time we return from London, your Morehouse possessions will have arrived."

The children were very excited about all of this, and a bit of coaxing was needed to get James and Penny to eat.

"I have to make sure all the doll furniture is inside" was one of Penny's reasons for not wanting very much of her food, but Jennings stepped in.

"You have to be able to think clearly so nothing is forgotten, Penny, and you can't do that if you don't eat properly. I'll ask Murch to get you a box so all the furniture can be packed securely, but I won't do that until I see that you've eaten."

"Yes, sir."

"Good girl. James, you're looking a bit distracted as well. Work on your meal."

That child nodded, pulling his eyes from the list next to his plate and reaching for his fork.

Jennings reached for his fork as well, but before he could eat he caught it again. When he looked up, Marianne's eyes were just leaving him. Before she dropped her gaze, however, he saw her eyes filled with approval.

≈ ≈ ≈

"Will you read me a story?" Penny asked of Marianne that night at bedtime.

"I would love to read you a story, Penny. What shall we read and where shall we read it?"

Penny went for a fat volume on her bedroom shelf and then surprised Marianne by taking her hand and leading her downstairs. She went to her father's study.

"Penny, are you certain that you wish to read in here?"

The little girl nodded, and Marianne went to the sofa they had snuggled on just the day before. She opened the book and began to read, her soft voice very soothing to the little girl tucked under her arm.

In less than five minutes James joined them. He sat on Marianne's other side and listened, his eyes gazing across the room with an occasional glance at the page. Penny looked at the drawings whenever the page included one, but in less than twenty minutes her small head was limp against Marianne.

"Shall I finish this chapter, James? Would you like to hear it?"

"Yes, please."

Not until Marianne smiled at him did she realize they were being watched. She looked up to find Jennings in the doorway. He stood still and watched her. As their eyes locked, Marianne couldn't help but wonder how long he'd been standing there. For several long moments she couldn't look away. Thankfully James' shifting was enough to put her back on task. She read the page she was on before glancing up again to find the doorway empty. With her mind only half on the story, she finished the chapter as James wished her to do.

≈ ≈ ≈

They would head for Collingbourne directly after break-fast in the morning. The day had been full of activities as official lists were filled out and someone was hired to move the items, but now the stories had been read, the children were sleeping, and the house was quiet. Nevertheless, Marianne could not rest. It had done so much for her to see where the children had been born. They had chosen won-derful items to follow them to Thornton Hall, and in the course of the hours spent at Morehouse, they had shared many things with both Marianne and Jennings.

Marianne, still not ready for bed, found she needed one last glimpse of the study that was so dear to them. She descended the stairs, her feet quiet, and sought out the beloved room. With a full moon shining in through the large windows, she needed no lantern. The moonlight bounced off of nearly every surface, and when she had looked her fill, she went to the windows and looked out on the moon-washed valley. She didn't know how long she had been standing there when she heard a sound behind her. Jennings stood just inside the room.

"Restless?" he asked as he moved to join her.

"A little," Marianne admitted, her gaze going back out-side. "I wanted to be in this room one more time because it's so important to the children."

"I had the same thoughts. I feel that I know so much more about them than I did before."

For a time they stood in silence, enjoying the view, not needing words.

"Miss Walker, will you marry me?"

Marianne turned, her face showing her surprise, but no words came forth.

"Our situation was not the same the first time I asked you," Jennings continued, his eyes watchful of the profile that had been turned to him. "I understand fully why you had to decline, and although my faith is new, it's most genuine.

I know the children love you, and your kindness with them is beyond compare. I would wish for you to partner with me in raising Thomas, James, and Penny."

"Oh, Mr Jennings," Marianne began, still not able to look at him as every move of her hands showed how flustered she felt. "I'm not sure you realize how swiftly time moves. Penny's just turned seven!" She said this as though the child in question was closing in on thirty. "In such a short time she'll be ten and then fifteen. If she retains even a fraction of her loveliness, you'll be sending suitors away day and night, but one will come along and she'll be gone, and then you'll be in possession of a wife you no longer need." Marianne had yet to look at him and still did not when she shook her head in a definitive fashion. "I must say no, Mr Jennings. I must spare you from a trap you can't even see."

This very anguished speech out in the open, Marianne turned and hurried from the room.

Unlike the first refusal, Jennings felt no anger. He stood watching Marianne rush away from him, knowing only deep regret that he had asked for her hand in such a poor fashion. Twice now she had referred to herself as a wife he would not need. Jennings knew now that Marianne Walker would never be a person he didn't need, but as to how to go about convincing her of this fact, he had not a clue.

"Penny?" Thomas asked his sister when she slipped into his room early on their last day. "What are you doing up?"

"I need to talk to you."

Before Thomas could ask the subject, James came in behind her. He watched in some amazement as the two climbed uninvited onto his bed and looked at him.

"We want Jennings to marry Marianne."

"And what, James Jennings," Thomas began slowly, still working to get the sleep from his brain, "can we possibly do about that?"

"Maybe we can tell Jennings about Marianne," Penny suggested. "Maybe he doesn't know how nice she is and that she loves Jesus."

"It's not that simple, Penny. Jennings may be our guardian, but he's not our father. At least, not in the same way."

For a moment the children were quiet. For the last year of Godwin Jennings' life, his children had been asking him if he would ever marry again. There had been no prospects at church, but Penny was growing older and noticing men and women together, and the first questions had come from her.

"It's not the same," James agreed, "but he has been kind. If he doesn't want us to question him, he can tell us and we'll leave the matter alone."

Penny perked up over this idea, and Thomas had to smile. He wondered how long they'd been hatching this plan but then realized that if he was honest with himself, he'd had more than a few thoughts about Jennings and Marianne as well.

"So what did you have in mind?"

As though uncorked, Penny and James began to speak at once, both excited and full of ideas. Thomas listened in wonder and began to catch some of their excitement as well. Before the three parted to dress and go down to breakfast, they were sure they had a subtle plan.

Even the children noticed that Marianne was quiet on the ride home. Jennings worked hard to keep his eyes from her, but the new emotions he was feeling coupled with his attraction toward her were making it a very long ride toward Collingbourne. He found himself thankful that Blackburn

Manor was situated to the west side of the village, giving him a valid reason to take Marianne home first and be alone with his thoughts soon.

He hadn't counted on the children. They had no more bid Marianne goodbye, the carriage still in her driveway, than the comments and questions began.

"Marianne believes in Jesus," Penny said simply.

Jennings stared at her but didn't comment.

"I've seen her read her Bible and pray."

"Have you, Penny?" James asked as if he found this unusual and very interesting.

"Yes. She told me that she tries to memorize a verse every week. Sometimes she can do it, and sometimes she can't."

"It was certainly nice that she could come along on our trip," Thomas now inserted.

"I was thinking the same thing," James added. "She was such a good sport about sea bathing when she wasn't a good swimmer, but then I think Marianne is a good sport about most things."

It was not lost on Jennings that the children were watching him. The comments went on for a time. Almost without exception something would be said, and then three pairs of eyes would come his way.

"Did you enjoy having Marianne along, Jennings?" James finally asked.

"Yes," he said truthfully, now having fully caught on and wanting to shout with laughter.

"Do you think she's nice?" Penny wished to know.

"I do, yes," Jennings was able to say in complete honesty, his voice softening even as he thought of Marianne Walker's sweetness.

"I can't help but wonder why she's never married," James said, his eyes conspicuously directed out the window this time.

Jennings' hand came to his upper lip. He wasn't going to touch this one, no matter how subtle James thought he might be, but the urge to laugh was almost unbearable. He wondered what these three would do if he were to confess to them that he'd already asked the lady in question to be his wife—not just once, but twice.

"I hope she'll come to visit us soon," Thomas said, this time with only Marianne on his mind. "She was quiet on the ride home. I hope she hasn't grown weary of us."

"I'm sure not," Jennings said, hearing genuine concern in Thomas' voice. "We have had long hours in the carriage, and she might have been tired."

"Will she come and visit us soon? Did you ask her to?" Penny wished to know.

"I didn't, Penny, but we can certainly extend an invitation anytime you like."

For a time the children let it drop. Nothing they had said had prompted Jennings to admit that he was interested in Marianne, and they didn't want to take their idea too far. It popped into James' head that maybe Marianne was the one they should have been hinting to, but then he remembered that the man does the asking and put this idea aside.

Although, his young heart reasoned even as Thornton Hall came into view, *the lady in question has to be ready with an answer. It probably wouldn't hurt to drop a few hints to Marianne as well.*

This determined, James contemplated a time when he could discuss it with his siblings. They had to work as a team on this, or Jennings might not get the message. Even as the carriage stopped before Thornton Hall and they moved their stiff limbs to climb out, James was hatching a plan, believing himself to be utterly undetectable as he mentally plotted.

Had James but known it, Jennings was on to the three of them. His heart a mixture of tenderness and amusement, he could hardly wait to see what they would next attempt.

Chapter Nineteen

Blackburn Manor

"How was your trip?" Mrs Walker asked when she embraced her daughter in the foyer at Blackburn Manor.

"Very nice and interesting all at the same time," Marianne said, setting her things aside and even kicking her shoes from her feet.

"Come and tell me."

The women sequestered themselves in the sitting room, and Marianne began to recount the trip.

"It was going quite well," she ended her story, "until he asked again to marry me."

"When did this happen?"

"Last night at Morehouse. We were alone in the study; the children were in bed."

"What did you say?" Mrs Walker asked quietly, even as she could read the answer in her daughter's pained eyes.

"I said no. I rattled on, probably making no sense, and then rushed away. I must admit that the journey home was a bit strained."

"Did he give a reason why he asked again?"

"Yes. He said he understood my first refusal, but that his faith is very genuine, and he truly wishes me to partner with him in raising the children."

"Oh, Mari, I'm sorry you had to go through that."

"You don't think I should have said yes?"

"At one time I would have, but not when I think about his not loving you. I want you to be cherished, and unless you're going to be, you can just stay right here where I know it will happen."

They were words that Marianne would cling to in the time to come. Even as she recounted the story to her mother, she had doubts about refusing Mr Jennings. However, she would not settle for anything less than love. Marianne knew this deep in her heart, but unless she worked to keep it at the forefront of her mind, she might be tempted to doubt her own sanity.

Mr Walker ran them to earth just a few moments later, and he too wished to know of his daughter's trip. His words nearly echoed his wife's when he learned of the second proposal, and when Marianne finally left their company to read for a while in her room, she was certain she'd done the right thing.

Thornton Hall

"I want to show you something," Penny said to Marianne when she visited a few days later.

"All right."

"It's in my room."

Almost out of nowhere James materialized. Marianne greeted him but continued to follow Penny upstairs. James trailed in their wake.

"It's a shelf," Penny said, pointing to a small wooden shelf mounted on the same wall as her headboard and level with her pillow. Placed on the shelf, with very little room for anything else, was Mr Pat.

"Oh, Penny, that's grand! A shelf for your special rabbit."

"Mr Jennings gave it to her, just for Mr Pat," James informed her.

"How kind of him."

"He does other kind things as well," James went on. "He's letting us bring just about anything we want from Morehouse."

"I remember," Marianne said with a smile, stopping James a bit.

He recalled suddenly that Marianne was often part of their life. What could he tell her about Jennings that she would not already know?

"And we're going to London for school clothes," Penny said, also forgetting that Marianne knew of this.

"When will you leave?" Marianne asked.

"Next week, Monday."

"That will be nice."

"Mr Jennings is often nice," James said, knowing that it sounded a bit forced, but so wanting Marianne to be ready when Jennings asked for her hand.

"Is everything all right, James?" Marianne asked him.

"Yes," he said, although his face said otherwise.

Penny chose that moment to ask, "Do you like Mr Jennings? Do you think he's nice?"

In an instant a cold feeling ran down Marianne's spine. If Jennings had put the children up to this, she found it most distasteful. It didn't seem to be his style, but where did all of this come from?

"I think a walk in the park sounds nice," Marianne said in an effort to divert her own chaotic thoughts. "Is anyone interested?"

James knew he had to give up. He'd seen an odd look on Marianne's face and now had the impression that something was bothering her. The thought made the little boy feel uneasy.

"We'll come with you," James said right away. "But we have to do something first. Would it be all right if we meet you downstairs?"

"Certainly, James."

Not at all sure she liked this turn of events, Marianne
made her way from the room. She descended the stairs, her
mind distracted. She didn't see Jennings at the bottom of the
stairs until she was almost on top of him.

"Good day, Miss Walker."

"Oh!" Marianne was startled. "I didn't see you."

Ignoring her flushed face, Jennings asked, "Did you find
the children?"

"Yes," Marianne said, not feeling very warm toward her
host just now. She used little eye contact as she continued.
"Penny, James, and I are going for a walk."

"I hope you have a nice time." Jennings bowed and
moved on his way. It was clear to him that she was not comfortable around him, and for the sake of the children, he
determined to stay out of the way, at least for the time being.

Marianne watched him walk away, her heart in a
quandary. She was heartily relieved to see James and Penny,
who had just determined together to drop all hints, coming
down the stairs. They left on their walk just moments later.

≈ ≈ ≈

"How did that foot seem?" Jennings called to Thomas as
he rode back toward the stables on his horse, Nicholas.

"Good as new. He didn't miss a step."

Jennings held the bridle as Thomas swung out of the
saddle, the young man's face flushed from the activity.

"Do you think James wants to ride for a time?" the boy
asked.

"He's on a walk with Miss Walker and your sister, but
you can probably find them in the garden and ask him."

"I might do that."

"Ride down the path. They're sure to hear you coming."

Thomas jumped back into the saddle in a flash and set
off at a brisk canter. Jennings had a word with the stable

master before following slowly. He came at an angle to the rear of the house, and for that reason he spotted Marianne at the edge of the garden. Not willing to rush the view, he came to a complete stop and for a time just watched her. At first his mind was nearly blank, but then he found himself begging God for direction, and beyond that, patience.

≈ ≈ ≈

Marianne was going to wait for refreshments on the veranda, but since the children had gone inside and a particular bloom, a Great Willowherb if she remembered correctly, had caught her eye, she moved from her seat. She was bent slightly and was studying the bright pink petals when she heard movement beside her.

"How did you fare on your walk with the children?" Jennings asked as he came up beside her.

"Fine, thank you," Marianne answered, only just glancing at him, still feeling most unsettled over her earlier thoughts.

"Did Thomas find James?"

"Yes."

"Did they go riding?"

"Not yet."

Save the wind in the trees, silence fell on this stilted conversation. Marianne wished Jennings would move on his way or that she could think of something worthwhile to say.

"Something is wrong, Miss Walker, and I wish I knew what it was."

For some reason, the words irritated her. Marianne faced Jennings, her eyes stern.

"The children seem to think that I need it pointed out to me what a kind man you are. I don't like the direction of my thoughts, but it has occurred to me that you've spoken to them."

Marianne had no more said this when she noticed both James and Penny watching them from a window near the veranda. They stood side by side, and Thomas appeared behind them a moment later.

"Spoken to them about what?" Jennings asked once he'd followed the direction of her gaze and turned to see the children as well.

"About your proposal."

"I certainly have not," Jennings said, sounding none too pleased. "It's none of their affair."

Marianne was so relieved that for a moment she said nothing.

With another glance at the children, Jennings calmly spoke.

"I do believe, however, that we are the focus of a conspiracy."

Marianne looked at him. "What do you mean?"

"You are not the only one the children are working to persuade."

Marianne had all she could do to keep her mouth closed. "They spoke to you about me?"

"Almost before you could exit the carriage when we returned on Wednesday."

Marianne looked as stunned as she felt.

"Am I to assume that you put them up to it?" he questioned.

"Mr Jennings!" she began before seeing the twinkle in his eyes. Marianne laughed, a hand to her warm cheek, and found herself calming.

"Someone needs to explain to them," Marianne said with a small shake of her head. "It's only fair."

"And what exactly needs to be explained?"

Marianne looked slightly flustered but still said, "Well, that they've misunderstood the situation."

Jennings didn't reply. At the moment he didn't know what to say, but then he wasn't given a chance. Mr Collins had come outside to inform him that he had a visitor.

"If you'll excuse me," Jennings said with a bow and left her.

Marianne realized almost immediately that the situation had not been rectified, but at the moment she felt there was little she could do.

A glance to the veranda told her that the children had come out. They were sitting as though ready to eat, but they were looking at her.

Reminding herself that it wasn't really her place to set the record straight, Marianne joined them, determining to simply enjoy their company and leave the parenting to Mr Jennings.

≈ ≈ ≈

"I need to speak with the three of you," Jennings began that evening after he'd gathered the children in the small salon. Looking at their faces, he could almost guess their thoughts: They believed trouble was headed their way in a big hurry.

"It has occurred to me that I have been remiss. Palmer reads the Bible in the evenings to his children, and you said that your own father was in the habit of doing that. I think it's time we begin our own evening tradition in the Bible."

The relief on their faces was almost comical. Jennings reached for the Bible next to him to keep from laughing.

"Is there a particular book where you would like to begin? If not, I'll read to you from Genesis, since that is where I'm basing my own personal study."

"I think Genesis would be fine," Thomas said, his voice sober.

Jennings read, and the children listened. He spoke to them of his excitement about what he was reading, but even then the children were somewhat reserved. Jennings only hoped the reading of the Word wasn't the reason, and when they asked if they could be dismissed, he let them go.

"That was frightening," Thomas said to his siblings the moment all three of them were alone in his room. "I thought we were in for it. We've got to drop these hints about Marianne. If they're going to find each other, then it will happen. We've got to keep out of it."

James nodded, but Penny sat looking at her brother.

"Can I still pray?" she asked in a small voice that shamed her brothers completely.

"Yes, Penny," Thomas said with a gentle touch to her head. "You can do what we should have been doing all along. Just remember to ask in God's will, and believe that whatever His will is, it's for the best."

Penny nodded, her small face looking more at peace. Thomas offered to walk her to her room, not bothering to creep or sneak. For the first time in days, he didn't feel shifty and ashamed of himself.

He saw Penny into bed and even gave her a kiss before he went back down the hallway. When he did, it was to find James in the doorway of Jennings' room.

"Thank you for reading to us," James was saying.

"You're welcome, James. I hope we can do it each night."

"We would like that, sir."

"Thank you and goodnight," Thomas added before following his brother toward their rooms.

More than an hour later, having checked on the children one last time, Jennings shut his door to ready for bed, his thoughts on the day. As was becoming a habit, his mind moved to Marianne Walker. She had wanted the children to know that they'd misunderstood the situation, but Jennings couldn't bring himself to tell them that. He wasn't sure they had.

≈ ≈ ≈

Tipton

"Was it me, Palmer," Lydia asked her spouse just after they arrived home from church on Sunday, "or did Jennings seem rather preoccupied with Marianne?"

"What did you witness?"

"That he seemed incapable of keeping his eyes off of her while we were visiting after the service."

"I caught that as well."

Palmer said nothing more, and Lydia stopped him from going into the house.

"Well?"

"Well, what?"

"What do you think?"

"I think I'm hungry, and I want something to eat."

"No, Palmer—what do you think of Jennings' actions?"

"I think that we don't have any facts, and that speculating leads nowhere."

"But it's so fun," Lydia said in utter seriousness.

Palmer laughed at her.

"What?"

"You're funny."

"I don't want to be funny; I want to know what's going on in my brother's mind."

"I'm afraid it's none of our business."

Lydia sighed. He was right, but she didn't want him to be.

"And besides, you've got other things to concentrate on."

"That's true," Lydia had to agree. They were leaving for London in the morning, or at least planning to, but if Lydia wasn't absolutely sure she should make the trip, Judith was going instead.

Husband and wife walked indoors to check on the children and have something to eat, William Jennings forgotten for the moment.

≈ ≈ ≈

"Miss Walker is here," the housemaid told Lydia not thirty minutes after her family left for London.

"Oh, please send her in."

The women embraced in the middle of the room before Lydia noticed the bag in Marianne's hand.

"Are you going on a trip, Mari?"

"Yes."

"Where?"

"Right here."

"You've come to stay with me?"

"Until you feel you need some time alone, yes."

"But how did you know I didn't go to London?"

"Palmer stopped and asked me to surprise you."

Lydia hugged her again before inviting her to get cozy in a chair.

"Do you feel terrible about not going?" Marianne asked, her feet tucked up comfortably and her shoes kicked off.

"A little. I know it's for the best that I not make that trip, but it's so fun to be there to select the fabrics and patterns. Judith has gone with us every year to help me, and the children adore her, but I naturally wanted to go along."

"Well, we'll have fun," Marianne comforted her. "And the children will have dozens of stories for you and keep you busy for a week after they arrive back."

"I suppose you're right, but I might have my moments of tears."

"Completely understandable. I shall just cry with you."

Lydia laughed.

"Did you notice anything in your brother yesterday?" Marianne asked suddenly.

"Yes! I even spoke with Palmer about it."

"What has come over him, Liddy?"

"I don't know. He stared at you for the longest time."

"Palmer asked him a question he didn't even hear."

"You don't suppose," Lydia began, but Marianne shook her head.

"Let us not suppose, Liddy. You might find that I lead the crying sessions this week."

Lydia let the matter drop, as did Marianne, but if the women had been vocal about it, Jennings was still on both of their minds.

≈ ≈ ≈

London

"I'd forgotten the comfort of this room," Palmer said, his feet on the ottoman, his head back against the fine red leather of the chair. They had arrived at Aydon midafternoon.

"It is rather nice, isn't it?" Jennings said from his place opposite the fireplace. It was a warm night and no fire was needed, but the trip had been a long one, and a few hours alone in the study, the children in bed, seemed to be the soothing prescription needed.

"One of Lydia's regrets about not coming was how much she wanted to see this house again."

"You'll have to bring her next year."

"Yes. Maybe we'll come on our own and have a little time away."

"You should. I may be here some when the children are in school, but I'm enjoying Collingbourne more than I ever dreamed, so this place will probably stand empty most of the year."

"Is it just Collingbourne that you enjoy, or are there other things?"

Jennings smiled. "That was subtle."

"I wasn't trying to be subtle. After you spent so much time staring at Marianne on Sunday, Lydia wanted to know what you were thinking. I told her that speculation was pointless." Palmer paused. "I also told her it was none of our business, and here I just asked you."

Jennings had a good laugh over this, but when the chuckles eased, he was ready to talk.

"You, Lydia, and the children certainly add to my warmth for Collingbourne, and the church family goes without saying, but I will admit to you that the presence of a certain woman has made things a good deal more interesting."

"When did all this begin?"

"I don't know. It was just suddenly there, making me think that I'd been more aware of her than I realized. I even asked her to marry me again."

Palmer was clearly startled.

"I handled it better this time, but she still turned me down."

"How did you handle it better if she said no?"

"I mean in my heart—my reaction to the rejection. After she said no I realized that I went about things the wrong way. I wasn't the least bit angry, just determined to do things differently next time."

"Next time?"

"Yes. I'm not convinced that Marianne doesn't have feelings for me, but she thinks—and who could blame her—that I'm only looking for a nanny. When she realizes she's wrong, I think she'll accept me."

"You sound confident."

Jennings fell quiet on this remark.

"What did I say to cause the pensive look?"

"I'm not confident, Palmer—at least not in my having a future with Marianne. I would hope for it, but I just don't know."

"Well, if you'll take a bit of advice from an old married man, I suggest you find a way to express your feelings. Marianne is loved at home. Why would she leave the love of her home to go to a place where she's not sure where she stands? If you can show her your heart, then at least she'll know what she can expect from you."

It was excellent advice for Jennings. He was not afraid to show his feelings, but without some sign from the lady herself, he wasn't sure what tack to take.

"I'll do it," he said quietly, and Palmer even asked him about the remark, but Jennings didn't hear him. That man's face told how far away his thoughts were just then, and Palmer wasn't even sure Jennings remembered he was in the room.

Chapter Twenty

The horse ride to Blackburn Manor helped clear Jennings' mind. He was simply going to extend an invitation to Marianne. He could have sent it by servant, but this gave him a reason to see her during the week.

The boys—Frank, Thomas, Walt, and James—were all headed back to school the following Monday. The families were planning a small party on Saturday, just five days off. They all wanted Marianne to come, and Jennings had offered to invite her.

He was shown into the large salon, and that was where Marianne found him.

"Hello," she said quietly, still wishing she could be herself in his presence. She'd been getting better until he had asked for her hand again.

"Hello. I hope I'm not disturbing you."

"Not at all. Please sit down."

"I've come to invite you to a small gathering," Jennings said from across the small room, his hat on his knee. "The boys all head off to school on Monday, and this Saturday we're going to have a meal together."

"Of course I'll come, thank you. Thornton Hall or Tipton?"

"Thornton Hall."

"And the time?"

"About five."

Conversation ran a little thin at that point, and Marianne brushed an invisible speck of dust from her lap and tried not to fidget.

"I didn't see your parents when I came in. Are they well?"

"Yes, we are all well, thank you."

And after that brilliant exchange, silence reigned again. Jennings was perfectly happy to sit and look at the woman across from him, but Marianne was all but climbing out of her skin with nerves and embarrassment.

"Would you find me presumptuous if I asked you..." Jennings began, and Marianne found herself holding her breath, "to tell me your own salvation story."

Marianne's sigh was nearly audible. She thought if he asked one more time for her hand, she might go mad.

"I would be happy to tell you," she answered, feeling a bit drained with relief and so starting out quietly. "There was a time in our lives when everything seemed fine, at least on the surface. We went to church every week and were very good. Then a man came along who opened God's Word and told us we were not good. That announcement turned things upside down for a time. Some people left the church family in a rage, but others wanted to know more. My mother was one of them.

"She came to Christ, as did two of my older siblings. My father was furious. He was so angry with Pastor Hurst that he nearly forbade mother to attend, but he didn't. So she kept on, and it was her peace and cheerful spirit that got my attention. Even though my father was unbearable during those months, she persevered. When I asked her about it, she told me what had happened in her own life. I had heard similar words from Pastor Hurst, but not until my mother said them did they truly make sense. She was living out this new belief. When she showed me the verse about being a new creature, I knew I wanted that for myself as well."

"How old were you?"

"Sixteen, but it feels like yesterday. Many of our neighbors and friends came to Christ in a steady stream. At one time there were only a few godly men; now there are more godly men than women. Families are being raised to love and follow Christ. Nearly all of Collingbourne has been changed by the revival.

"We certainly have our areas of weakness, and we've had our share of hurts, but God is moving ahead of the Collingbourne church, and it's been the most exciting thing I've ever seen."

"Thank you for telling me. I was talking to Pastor Hurst recently about the role Lois and Eunice had in Timothy's life. He said that Scripture proves over and over again that a father's involvement in a child's walk with Christ is beyond value, but that God uses mothers as well. Your mother and you are certainly a picture of that, as were Timothy and his mother."

"I never thought of it quite that way."

"When did your father come to Christ? What were the circumstances around that?"

"God made no sense to my father. It took many months for him to see that he was viewing God through circumstances, not viewing his circumstances through God. In the end, my father had no choice but to admit that he was lost and afraid. It was a lovely day when he came from his study and told us that he'd gotten things straightened around with God. We weren't even certain he understood what was expected of him—he hadn't gone to church with us very often—but his life gave evidence to the fact that he was a changed man and still is."

"And you say your siblings know Christ?"

"Two of them do. My oldest siblings, James and Elinore, do not. They were gone from Blackburn Manor when Pastor

Hurst came, but they ask questions when they visit, and they listen. We keep praying."

"I'll pray also."

"Thank you."

For some reason, Marianne found this conversation quite intimate. Having Jennings know about her unsaved family and praying for them was very private and special. She was not sorry she told him, but suddenly the room felt rather warm and close.

"I shall not keep you any longer," Jennings offered, having witnessed the blush in her cheeks. "We'll see you on Saturday?"

"Yes. Certainly."

Marianne saw him out and ended up blushing again once they were out on the drive. From the saddle, Jennings stared at her, his gaze holding her own and making her feel breathless. When he left, she took a moment to puzzle over this odd mixture inside of her: Part of her heart was glad to see him go; the other part wished he would stay.

≈ ≈ ≈

"Is he still here?" Walker asked of his wife when she slipped into the study.

"No, I think he just left."

"You didn't go in and speak to him?"

"I just arrived back. Did you go in?"

"No."

For a moment the two looked at each other.

"A man does not come calling on a woman for no reason, Liz," Walker said sincerely. "He hasn't taken her no for an answer."

"Should you speak to him?"

Walker thought on this.

"If he loved her, she would accept him, correct?"

"Yes, I'm sure of it."

"Then I'm staying out of it, at least until one of them comes to me. If he can't find a way to prove that he loves her, then he doesn't deserve her."

"And if he doesn't love her?"

"If he doesn't love her, why does he bother coming around?"

Again husband and wife looked at each other, but this time both were out of words.

Tipton

"Well, hello," Palmer greeted his wife on Saturday morning.

Lydia smiled and stretched, her hand bumping the headboard of the bed. She had slept long and hard, or rather it felt like she had, and for the first time in weeks, she was rested.

"What time is it?"

"Almost noon."

Lydia sat up.

"No, Palmer! I have a hundred things to do."

"No, you don't. The party is at Thornton Hall. You have nothing to do."

"We're taking food and some small things for the boys."

"Judith is seeing to all of that. I told her you were to sleep. I've already been over and had Bible study with Jennings. Everything over there will be ready on time. *You* have nothing to do, Lydia Palmer."

Said in that tone, Lydia knew she had no choice. She felt fine—she truly did, nothing like before—but Palmer was not taking any chances.

"Can I even get out of bed?" she asked, a bit miffed at him.

"If you want to," Palmer replied with a smile. He knew she was upset with him but that she would think it through and get past it.

"I'm hoping for a boy," Palmer suddenly remarked, causing all of Lydia's irritation to drain away.

"Why?"

"This might be our last. A little boy would have adventure and fun on his own."

Lydia put her hand out, and Palmer joined her on the bed.

"I'm sorry I was cross at you."

Palmer leaned to kiss her. "Forgiven. Want me to rub your back?"

"Why don't I rub yours?"

"We could take turns," Palmer suggested, a distinct glint in his eye.

Lydia's smile was very warm as her husband leaned to kiss her again.

≈ ≈ ≈

Thornton Hall

"I'll help you." Penny was at her most convincing as she, Emma, and Lizzy stood at the mouth of the maze on Saturday afternoon. "I know the way."

The young visitors did not look convinced. They glanced at the tall shrubs before them and then back at Penny.

"We can do it," Penny tried again, but the Palmer girls shook their heads. Penny looked most unhappy with them and tried again to assure them, but it wasn't working. Lydia came along just in time.

"Are you going into the maze?" Lydia asked.

"No," her daughters said in unison.

"Why ever not?"

"We'll get lost."

"You know the way, don't you, Penny?"

That little girl nodded, looking grateful that someone understood.

"Well then, let's go!"

"You'll go with us, Mama?" Emma asked. This put the excursion in a whole new light.

"Certainly. I'm sure that Penny can get us out. If not we'll shout and carry on until we're rescued."

Amid much laughter, the four set off. Penny was a determined little leader, not pausing very often in indecision and even showing the girls a few points of interest along the way.

"This is the duck head," Penny offered, stopping at a hole in the hedge.

"Oh, I see it!" Lizzy exclaimed.

Lydia had to bend some to be at the correct level to view it, but she could see how the hole would remind one of a duck's head.

"And there's a flower up here," Penny added as they walked along. "James wanted to pull it, but I said it helps me remember which way to go."

Hiding laughter, Lydia took Penny's word for this as the flower sat in an area that could only be leading in one direction.

"And this—" Penny the guide continued, "this is where I got lost the first time."

"What did you do?" Emma asked, eyes large.

"I cried," Penny said simply, and Lydia's hand came to her mouth until she could control herself.

"I think Emma meant to ask how you got out."

"Oh, I just went the right way."

Lydia followed in the wake of this seven-year-old logic, very pleased she hadn't missed this little outing.

"Are we headed the right way now?" Emma asked.

"We are! Come on!"

Penny picked up the pace, and Lydia's daughters ran after her. She didn't worry about losing them—their laughter and chatter were easy to trace—but remembering that the older two girls were headed off to school soon after the boys departed was not something she cared to think about at the moment.

∾ ∾ ∾

Liddy and the girls have just started through the maze. You can catch them!

Palmer's words rang in Marianne's ears as she exited the house, went along the side of the building, and headed to the gardens and into the maze. Confident that they were just ahead of her, and buoyed by the fact that she'd been inside before, Marianne boldly followed.

Things went well for the first few minutes, but in very short order the walls of greenery closed in around her, and Marianne became uncertain of the way. She tried one direction and then another, not sure if she was making progress or not.

She stopped and looked back, wondering if she'd missed something. Even though she had just been that way, she went back around the corner and ran straight into Jennings' waistcoat. He reached to steady her, and she looked up.

"Are you lost?" he asked kindly.

"Yes," she answered, looking more than a little distressed. "And you're not in the window!"

Jennings smiled down on her and brushed a stray curl from her cheek.

"This way," he offered, directing her right back the way she'd come. Once he got her turned around, he took her hand and led her to the exit, letting go only as they stepped out to join the group already assembled in the garden.

"Thank you," Marianne said quietly as she looked up at him.

"You're welcome," Jennings answered, working not to reach for her hand again. She had initiated eye contact for the first time, and his heart was doing funny things in his chest.

"You made it!" Lydia congratulated them as they moved into the garden.

"It's time for cake!" someone else was heard to say, and the party moved indoors. They feasted on fresh fruit, small sandwiches, scones, biscuits, cheese and sausage rolls, and cake. They drank tea and milk, before leaving the table and getting comfortable in the large salon. Once there, Palmer asked the boys to share a bit.

"Tell us something you're looking forward to, something you're thankful for, something you're not too keen on, and something you'll miss. Frank, why don't you start us out."

"All right."

That young man stood, smiling at his father's twinkling gaze before addressing the group.

"I'm looking forward to seeing my school chums again. I'm thankful that Thomas will be along this school term. What else was there?"

"Something you'll miss, and something you're not overly keen about."

"Oh, right. I'll miss some of my freedom being at home and all, and I'm not too keen on being away from mum when she's waiting to have a baby."

Lydia smiled at her oldest, her heart burgeoning with love as he sat back down and smiled at her.

"Thank you, Frank. Thomas, can you go next?"

"I think so." He rose as well. "I'm thankful for Mr Jennings, who wants us to call him Jennings, but I can't quite make myself do it, and also for my friendship with Frank. I'm looking forward to some of my favorite classes and getting a first glimpse of the school. I'm not all that keen to be away from Thornton Hall and Penny for the next weeks, and I'll miss everyone here."

Marianne thought if they kept it up she would be in tears. This was not the first year they would be going away, but having to say goodbye to the Jennings children as well as the Palmers was proving to be harder than she thought.

Walt was next with the list, giving several items he was not that excited about and having to be reminded to name something for which he was thankful. People were still chuckling at him when James began. He stood and faced the group, saying that he would miss his horse but that he was thankful for the holiday they'd taken to sea bathe and visit Morehouse.

"I'm not in a hurry to go back to school at all," he shared for the item he wasn't keen on, "so in light of that, I guess I'm looking forward to term ending and a chance to come home."

The adults laughed again, and when they quieted, Jennings spoke.

"Thank you, gentlemen. I've never suggested anything like this before, but I wonder if now wouldn't be a good time to pray together. It might be the last chance we get."

"That's a splendid idea," Palmer remarked, and everyone bowed their heads. Palmer began and Jennings ended. They asked God's blessing on the boys, that they would learn well and apply knowledge to their hearts. They also prayed that they would be diligent in their daily reading of God's Word, and that those verses would be life changing forevermore.

With prayer time over, everyone was up for a few games in the yard. The children trooped out first; the adults followed more slowly.

"You look thoughtful," Jennings remarked to Marianne as he walked behind her. The Palmers had gone ahead.

"I was thinking about how much I'll miss them."

"It's going to be very quiet around here," Jennings agreed.

"You'll have to find someone to keep you company," Marianne said without thinking.

"Are you offering?" Jennings' already deep voice dropped even lower, and an unfamiliar feeling centered itself around Marianne's heart. She turned to him, her eyes wide, and began to stammer.

"I think the children...games are outside...they're probably looking for you..."

Without warning, Jennings bent and kissed her lips.

"We'll join them, shall we?" he said, looking much calmer than he felt.

"Yes, that's a good idea," Marianne agreed, her voice soft and bemused.

With a hand to her back, Jennings made sure she went in the right direction. He wasn't sure the kiss was the best thing to have done, but it was obvious he'd gained her attention. It might backfire on him somewhere along the line, but at least it was a start.

Jennings looked across the carriage at the little girl with the dark hair and wondered what she was thinking. She hadn't cried when she said goodbye to her brothers, but she looked rather lost and alone as the carriage pulled away from the school to take them home.

Jennings had volunteered to take the boys. Pastor and Mrs Hurst would collect them for their first break, the Palmers would take them back, and then Jennings would collect them again at the term's end, all of which were some time away. Penny would be headed off very soon herself, but the seven-year-old and her guardian had approximately two weeks together.

"Are you all right, Penny?" Jennings asked.

"Yes."

"Are you sad?"

"A little."

"Do you want to look at one of the books you brought along?"

"No."

Jennings searched his mind for a way to comfort her. He decided on logic and a bit of distraction.

"I think it's normal to feel bad when you miss someone, Penny, but don't forget, you'll be seeing Marianne soon for your archery lesson. Won't that be fun?"

"What day?"

"I don't know, but I should think we could go this week."

"And she'll teach me?"

"She said she would."

Penny smiled a little. Jennings smiled as well. He was glad that Penny could learn the sport, but having an excuse to see Marianne suited him very well.

They'd had a fine time at the party, his last real opportunity to be with her. Jennings did nothing to disguise his interest that day, and he was pleased when Marianne looked his way often. He didn't think he was imagining anything that wasn't there, and unless he was utterly delusional, Marianne Walker was interested in return.

While his thoughts dwelt on the woman who had claimed his heart, Jennings found himself praying for her and then the boys. When Thomas came to mind, Jennings also thought back on one of the last conversations he'd had with that young man.

"Mr. Jennings, could I have a word with you?" Thomas asked before they could leave for school.

"Of course, Thomas. What is it?"

"I feel I must confess something to you. I wish I'd done so weeks ago."

Jennings listened, giving Thomas all the time he needed.

"James, Penny, and I got it into our heads that you needed to wed Marianne. It's none of our business whom you marry, and we said some things when it wasn't our place. For that I apologize."

"Thank you, Thomas. I assure you I was not upset by anything you said, but I do thank you."

Jennings could tell that it was the last thing Thomas needed to do. This job done, he was ready to go to school. Not for the first time, Jennings felt amazed by this young man. He was remarkably special and mature, and Jennings could only thank God that Thomas had come into his life.

"I have to be excused." Penny's words from across the carriage brought Jennings back to the present.

Jennings hit the roof with his fist, and the coach immediately began to slow. Thankfully, there were woods nearby. Jennings alighted from the carriage with his small charge, glad that she seemed comfortable with his accompanying her, and then waited patiently while she scooted around a bush to take care of the business at hand.

She didn't dawdle, and in little time they were back inside, the carriage plunging into motion again.

"Will you read to me?"

"I should like that, Penny. Why don't you come over here?"

Penny joined him, and much the way he'd seen Marianne do, he tucked the little girl under his arm and held the book so they could both see.

Jennings would not have guessed her tired, but in less than ten pages, her little head was drooping. Jennings shifted her on the seat until she could stretch out while he moved across to give her room. For the longest time he studied her sleeping face. Like the boys, she was a miracle to him.

Had I been the one to die, Jennings found himself telling the Lord, *I would not have left a single space to be filled, but Godwin Jennings is missed so greatly, and his hard work lives on in the lives of his children. I know that Your hand has moved here, Father, and Godwin himself would probably be the first to tell me so, but I needed to see how selfishly I'd been living my life. Help me to put You and the children first. Help me to show Marianne how I feel and to be gracious if she rejects me yet again.*

Jennings suddenly realized that he was tired as well. Thinking that Penny had the right idea, he stretched his legs at an angle, getting as comfortable as he could manage. He went back to praying, but it didn't last long. He joined Penny in a nap a few miles up the road.

Chapter Twenty-One

Thornton Hall

The letter from Jennings' London solicitor started without formalities. Jennings read it in his study the very day after he and Penny arrived back.

> *The information you sent was both fascinating and frustrating. To think that Mrs Smith walked away from charges she was guilty of is maddening news. I'll be contacting the judge this week in hopes of reinstating the case. If you've omitted anything, send it immediately as every scrap of evidence might count, but I must warn you that even if the judge does find grounds to reopen the case, the chances of finding Mrs Smith are poor. She wasn't a small woman, but her type can often make themselves invisible.*
>
> *I'll keep in touch.*
>
> > *Sincerely,*
> > *Jas. Flemming*

Jennings set the letter aside, his eyes thoughtful as he looked out the window. The letter Mrs Dashwood had promised him was already in his files. On paper, that lady had repeated much of what she'd said at the inn that night, and of course she'd included her address. She had also thanked Jennings for his graciousness and understanding.

Jennings could feel himself tensing. He hadn't been as understanding as he seemed. The whole affair was abhorrent to him, and he was none too happy about Mrs Dashwood's admission. Anger spiraled within him just as someone knocked on the door. He stopped just short of barking at whoever it might be, knowing that there was no excuse for such behavior.

"Come in," he managed in a calm tone. When Penny walked in he was very relieved that he'd not taken the head from her shoulders.

"Hello, Penny. Did you need something?"

"May I write to James and Thomas?"

"You certainly may." Jennings decided to snap out of his ill humor—remembering also to confess it—that very instant. "Why don't you sit here by my desk and use my paper and pens?"

Penny skipped with excitement over this idea. Jennings set her up to the side of his wide desk, and when she began, he sat and watched her small bent head and serious brow.

I've got to leave Mrs Smith with you, Lord. Penny is safe, and You got my attention on the matter. Thank You that it didn't last for years. I don't want Mrs Smith loose to hurt another child, Lord, so please help the judge to be wise when he reexamines the case, but help me to leave it in Your hands without anger or thoughts of revenge.

"I can't spell 'tomorrow,'" Penny looked up and said.

"I'll help you," Jennings replied and spelled the word for her.

"Thank you."

"You're welcome. What's going on tomorrow?" Jennings asked before Penny could continue.

"My archery lesson," Penny said as if he should know this, "with Marianne."

Jennings opened his mouth to tell Penny that he had not as yet arranged the matter but changed his mind. A drop-in visit to the Walker household might prove to be very fun. He wasn't trying to keep the lady off balance, but right now he wasn't sure of another way to go about this. It would help to know what Marianne thought of him; indeed, it would settle the matter completely, but that fact was still a mystery, quite possibly even to Marianne.

Jennings' eyes went back to Penny. He knew with that little girl in tow it was unlikely that he'd be turned away. Was it fair to use her that way? Jennings didn't examine that question too closely. Marianne had agreed to an archery lesson, and Penny's guardian was simply taking her at her word.

∾ ∾ ∾

Blackburn Manor

"I've a letter from your sister," Mrs Walker told her daughter.

"Which one?"

"Caroline this time. Elinore wrote about your visit to her, and she wants to know when you're coming to Rode Manor."

Marianne smiled. A few months back she would have jumped at the chance to visit her sister and family, but right now something in her heart wanted to remain in the area.

"Tell her I'll come when the weather cools."

"The weather has cooled," her mother argued.

"Later," Marianne stated. "Tell her I'll come sometime later."

Mrs Walker didn't press her daughter—she even went back to the afternoon post—but her daughter's response lingered in her mind for quite some time.

∾ ∾ ∾

Tipton

"How did you pinch it?" Jennings asked a tearful Penny as she allowed him to examine her finger. Supper was over, and the adults were sitting in the rear yard. Until Penny was injured, the girls had been enjoying a new ball Lizzy had received for her fifth birthday.

"The door slammed."

Jennings took the little girl into his lap, his eyes still on the offended digit. Emma and Lizzy hovered nearby, Lizzy with tears of commiseration in her eyes.

"It's a little red, so it might throb for a time," Jennings told her. "Why don't you sit here until it feels better?"

Penny laid her head against him, her face woeful with self-pity.

Watching her, the Palmers smiled. She was so cute, even when she was sad, and snuggling in Jennings' lap made her look all the littlier and more appealing.

"How is it?" Emma asked, her face concerned.

"It's better."

"You can hold the ball," Lizzy told her, ready to hand it over.

Penny thanked her and took it in her lap.

Jennings turned back to his sister.

"I've been meaning to ask you how you feel lately, Liddy. You look so well that I take for granted that you feel the same."

"I do feel well, thank you."

"Other than needing more sleep, you're much as you always are," Palmer added.

"I think so," Lydia agreed.

Soon Penny had recovered, and the three girls, ball in hand, went back to their play.

"She's so relaxed with you, Jennings," Lydia said when the little ones were gone. "It's lovely to see."

Jennings smiled in agreement. "This morning she wrote letters at my desk. I helped with her spelling."

"Would you say the two of you have gotten closer with the boys gone?" Palmer asked out of curiosity.

"Yes. She searches me out much more often, and of course in the evenings it's just the two of us reading the Bible. Her knowledge of Scripture is impressive, and she's not afraid to ask questions." Jennings suddenly laughed. "I just remembered back to the first time I tried to interact with Penny. It was while we were still at Aydon at the dining table. When I finished speaking to her, Thomas said to me, 'It wasn't that scary, was it, sir?'"

The Palmers laughed with him.

"How do you think they're doing?" Jennings wished to know, his mind having obviously gone to the boys.

"I think well," Palmer reassured him. "It's old stuff for Frank and Walt, and they will be helped when they see school through the eyes of newcomers like Thomas and James. Your boys will be helped when they follow the lead of our boys who have been there. It's a good combination."

"That makes sense, but it's still difficult not knowing."

"A huge trust issue," Palmer agreed.

This was no more said than the girls were back, wishing for adults to join them in the game. Palmer and Jennings agreed, leaving Lydia with only her thoughts for company, something that suited her very well. Jennings' words had brought all four boys keenly to mind. It was lovely to have time alone to pray.

≈ ≈ ≈

Thornton Hall

"Can we ride horses to Blackburn Manor?" Penny amazed Jennings with these words as they walked to the carriage on Thursday morning.

"You don't have a riding horse, Penny."

"I could ride with you."

Jennings' brows rose. He'd never considered it.

"You could, couldn't you?"

Penny nodded, her eyes excited.

"I think I need my horse," Jennings said to the footman.

"Right away, sir."

The carriage that had been readied for them was returned to the stables.

"Do you want to wait inside or walk ahead to the stables?"

"Let's walk."

Jennings realized very suddenly that if he'd known the pleasure of having children long ago, it would have altered the way he lived his life. He put his hand out, and Penny took it.

"It's nice today," he commented, smiling when Penny looked up at the partially cloudy sky, evidently just noticing.

"Do you think it's nice at school too?"

"Your school or where the boys are?"

"The boys."

"It's hard to say. Your school is close enough that the weather is probably the same, but the boys could be having any type of weather."

This conversation took them almost to the stables, with one brief stop to look at flowers.

"Do you know what I hope, Penny?"

The little girl looked up at him.

"I hope you never lose your love of flowers or forget who made them."

"God made them."

"Yes, He did. I wish someone had told me that when I was your age."

"Did your father love Jesus?" Penny asked, nearly stopping Jennings in his tracks.

"I don't know, Penny," he answered slowly, having thought of this only a few times since his conversion. "We never spoke of it, so I'm not certain he did."

"Someone should have told him," she said simply.

"Yes, Penny, I do believe you're right."

To the stables and in the saddle a minute later, they set off, Penny utterly delighted to be up so high and moving so fast.

"Go faster," she called at one point.

"This is fast enough," Jennings said on a laugh, thinking it wouldn't be the end of the world if Marianne was not available; he and Penny could just keep riding.

≈ ≈ ≈

Blackburn Manor

"You have visitors," Mrs Walker told her daughter, her eyes trying to hide her delight. "Mr Jennings and Penny."

Marianne's brows rose, but she left the flowers she was arranging, checked her hands for stains, and went to the salon.

"Well, Penny," Marianne said when she opened the door and that little girl ran to embrace her. "What a nice surprise!"

"We hope you'll think so when you hear why we've come," Jennings put in but didn't elaborate.

Marianne looked down at the little girl still hugging her legs.

"I came so you could teach me to shoot the arrows."

"Oh!" Marianne said and got no further.

"If we're disturbing you, Miss Walker, we can certainly make it another day.

"Not at all," she denied, but her tone and voice were not convincing. "I'm just not certain I'm the one to teach her."

"You don't want to?" Penny asked.

"It's not that, dear. I would be happy to, but Mr Jennings is more accomplished, and I only thought—" Marianne stopped when the other two occupants of the room stood staring at her, their faces open and expectant. She truly did not see herself as the person for this task, but clearly she was the only one who thought that way.

"Well, then, let's head along to the yard and begin."

Penny took Marianne's hand, and not until they were outside the salon did Marianne realize that Jennings was coming along as well.

"If you have things to do, Mr Jennings, feel free to leave Penny with me."

"On the contrary; I was hoping to watch. I might learn something."

Marianne waited for him to smile and tease her, but the eyes that watched her were warm and serious.

"Well, then," she repeated, nearly at a loss. "We'll go right out."

Once outside, Jennings took pity on the nervous teacher. Extra equipment was being set up on a table a good way from the target. Settling in a yard chair there, Jennings gave Penny and Marianne some space to work, but he was still able to observe.

It didn't pass his notice that Marianne put her back to him as she began to explain. She took several minutes to define the dangers and caution Penny against pointing the arrows toward people, the house, and even the dogs.

Penny tried the bow one time, and Marianne could see it was going to be too long.

"Wait here, dear," Jennings heard her say just before she started his way.

She came to the table and began to study the equipment laid there. She had begun to gather the smaller bow and arrows in her hand when she looked up into Jennings' eyes.

"I love you," he whispered softly.

Dropping everything she was holding and in a complete panic, Marianne could not even look at Jennings. Her actions were so flustered that his heart turned over. She knelt down toward the grass to gather the items at her feet.

"Here, let me help you," Jennings offered as he bent to the task.

"It's all right," Marianne said in a breathless voice, even as she took the things he was handing her. Her hands shook as she straightened and laid the arrows neatly on the table.

"Do you want me to come over to the target and help you?" Jennings asked quietly, his eyes never leaving her face.

Marianne knew where the question had come from. This was not the time to be upset. Someone could be hurt. But if he knew that, why would he have said such a thing to her? Maybe he hadn't planned it—maybe it just came from deep in his heart.

Stop it! Marianne said to herself, taking a breath and slowly lifting the bow and arrows in her hands. She was still not ready to look at him.

"We'll be fine," she said softly. "Thank you for offering."

For just a moment Marianne managed to raise her eyes to his. What Jennings read there caused him to muster up every ounce of self-will he possessed. Not even aware that he was on his feet, he stood for some time and watched the two "ladies" he loved. When at last he remembered to sit down, it was because he was no longer certain his legs would continue to support him.

Tipton

"Well, Marianne, where did you come from?" Palmer asked from his place at the head of the dining room table.

"Oh, I just flew in on a cloud." Marianne's voice was very merry. "Hello, Lizzy; hello, Emma."

"Hello, Marianne."

"Do you suppose I could have a word with you, Lydia?" Marianne managed, but only just.

"Certainly."

Marianne knew that her friend was not done eating, but this would not wait. Wanting to drag her to move faster, Marianne went to the closest room, the library, and over to the sofa. Lydia, a bit bemused, followed.

"Your brother loves me," Marianne said softly the moment Lydia's seat touched the upholstery.

Lydia laughed.

"And when did you figure this out?"

"This afternoon when he told me."

Lydia stopped laughing.

"He said this to you?"

Marianne nodded, her face wreathed in soft smiles.

Lydia put her arms around her friend.

"Oh, Mari, I could cry."

"It's wonderful, isn't it?"

"Yes. Did the two of you talk?"

"No. Penny was with us, and I know Jennings wants to spend time with her right now."

"But your time will come," Lydia put in.

"I hope so."

"So he doesn't know how you feel?"

"Not directly."

"Everyone all right?" Palmer asked from the door.

The women didn't answer but turned and smiled at him.

"Well, now, everything looks well."

"Come in, Palmer," his wife bade, laughter in her voice. "Marianne has lovely news."

≈ ≈ ≈

Thornton Hall

"Are you ready, Penny?"

"Yes."

"Are you certain about Mr Pat?" Jennings asked her again.

The little girl looked over at the shelf that held her treasured possession.

"Yes," she said with very little pause. "I have Mama's quilt."

"All right. We'd best get to Tipton so you can be off."

"Is Lydia coming?"

"I think just Palmer is taking you girls."

"Can we ride to Tipton?"

Jennings almost shook his head in amazement. Since the first time he allowed her in the saddle with him, riding was all she wanted to do.

"I think we should not arrive windblown and dusty, but we will ride again when you return."

Penny looked satisfied with this plan but wanted to go out and say farewell to Jennings' horse. He escorted her, keeping her well back, and at last they were in the carriage, his heart asking himself if he was ready for this.

They were at Tipton before he had an answer. The family was out front, Marianne with them, and Jennings climbed from the carriage, his heart dealing with more emotions than he expected.

Lizzy was in tears by her mother's side, and the group said little. Before Jennings was ready, Palmer said it was time to leave. Penny had just come back from hugging Marianne and Lydia, and now looked to Jennings. She was dry-eyed, but her face was sober.

"Come here," Jennings called to her as he hunkered down to her level.

"Megan packed all you need, but if we forgot something, have the matron write me."

"Okay."

Jennings looked into her face, his hand coming up to cup her small cheek.

"I love you, Penny."

"I love you, Mr Jennings."

Jennings could not get her into his arms fast enough. He scooped her close and hugged her for a long time, her little arms hugging him back. Still in his embrace, Jennings walked to the carriage and put her inside.

The goodbyes were brief, and in that there was mercy. The women waved to the carriage for a long time, but Jennings only stood and stared after it. When it was finally out of sight, he looked over at Marianne to see her watching him with sweet compassion.

"The girls' school is much closer," Lydia comforted him. "You can visit so easily."

"And don't forget," Marianne added, "she's with Emma."

This brought fresh tears from Lizzy, and Lydia led the way inside. Jennings wasn't ready to visit and make light conversation and was thankful Marianne and his sister understood. They prayed for him as his carriage pulled away, neither one wanting to tell him that it never got easier.

Chapter Twenty-Two

Marianne did her best not to look expectant or disappointed, but when Sunday morning came and went, and Jennings greeted her with the Palmers but made no move to single her out, her heart filled with confusion and questions—questions that she could not answer. One person could answer them, but right now he seemed very far away.

"Did you see Mr Jennings this morning?" Walker asked of Marianne on the carriage ride home.

"Not to speak to."

Her father made no comment one way or the other, and Marianne read nothing biased in his expression. Nevertheless, Marianne waited at home all afternoon. She received no visitors.

She climbed into bed that night with many thoughts but only one that she would act on: *Maybe it's time to visit my sister after all.*

≈ ≈ ≈

Jennings had never in his life been so idle. It made no sense. He'd lived for years on his own, never lacking a moment, but now, with the children gone, he was nearly at his wit's end.

He thought long rides on horseback would do the trick, but they only made him miss Penny. Seeing the portrait of the children's mother brought back memories of their time at Morehouse. And the quiet bedrooms upstairs were the worst. They seemed to mock him with their emptiness.

Jennings caught up on his business correspondence, including a letter to Mrs Dashwood, letting her know that his lawyer was on the job, but to date, Mrs Smith had not been located. He had more time to read and study his Bible, and he was learning a lot, but it didn't completely dispel the loneliness that lingered in his heart.

About the third day he took to writing personal letters. He'd already received one from each of the boys, and had read them five times.

Mr Jennings, Thomas began,

> *School is exciting. I enjoy most of my classes and professors. Yesterday we had a lively discussion on Napoleon. The entire class was involved. The professor even mentioned an outing we might take, but he didn't say exactly where we would go.*
>
> *Did Penny get off well? I wonder if she cried or if going with Emma was enough. I know I enjoy having James and the Palmer boys nearby. We see each other every day, and Frank and I have done some studying together.*
>
> *I've got a paper to write that must be handed in tomorrow, so I had best close. Give my best to everyone there. Say hello to Marianne for me, and please ride my horse if you have time.*
>
> *Sincerely and with affection,*
> *Thomas Jennings*

James' letter was different, but no less dear to the lonely guardian.

Dear Mr Jennings,

How are you? How is my horse? I hope someone will have time to ride him so he doesn't think he's been deserted. Walt and I have several classes together. He's funny. Is Penny all right? Did she go to school with Emma? Tell Marianne I've seen wild-flowers she would enjoy. I'm looking forward to the term break, being at Thornton Hall, and seeing you. Thank you for all of our school needs.

With regards,
James Patrick Jennings

Having read the letters, Jennings started his own. He wrote to the boys about everything he could think of. He gave a detailed account of Penny's getting off to school and even told how much they had enjoyed their daily rides.

He was able to tell the boys that he was riding their horses as well as his own, and that both animals were in fine shape. He ended his letters to them with the item that was most on his heart.

I know where we've left off in our Bible reading, and we'll be sure and share in that time whenever you are home. I miss you boys very much and pray that you are well. Thornton Hall is a dif-ferent place without you.

With deep affection,
William Jennings

Jennings followed the letters to the boys with a note to Penny. For a time his heart was calm, but he found himself pacing the next day before the post arrived.

He spent too many days this way. Jennings should have been thinking more clearly about the matter, but it took more than a week for him to realize that this was the time he'd waited for. He'd told Marianne he loved her, but with Penny still home, he felt he couldn't spare the hours to call on her.

As he finally rode away from Thornton Hall, Blackburn Manor his destination, he wanted to laugh at his own foolishness. He hadn't seen a lot of Marianne since that day he'd declared himself in her yard, but what he had seen told him she was not adverse to his company.

Blackburn Manor came into view, and Jennings' heart skipped a beat. For the first time in days the children had receded from the forefront of his mind. He couldn't wait to see Marianne Walker.

"She's away right now, Mr Jennings," Mrs Walker said kindly, completely mastering the smile that wanted to break through. "But please, come in and sit down."

"Thank you," Jennings said graciously, his heart so disappointed that he could hardly think. He had ridden up with such excitement and nearly leapt from his horse's saddle, only to have Marianne's mother calmly dash his hopes to bits.

"How are you, Mr Jennings?" the lady of the house asked once she'd seen her guest comfortably seated.

"I'm well, thank you. And you, Mrs Walker?"

"We are very well, thank you. Did the children get off to school as planned?"

"Yes. It's been a bit quiet without them."

"I remember those days," Mrs Walker said, and Jennings did his best to attend. It wasn't lack of interest on his part so much as extreme distraction, a point that came home suddenly when he realized his hostess was no longer talking but sitting quietly and watching him.

Jennings gave up. He knew from the look in her eyes that she had him figured out.

Feeling more than a little embarrassed but also somewhat desperate, Jennings asked, "Would it be presumptuous of me, Mrs Walker, to ask when Miss Walker plans to return?"

"Not at all, Mr Jennings, but I can't tell you. Marianne wasn't firm on her plans when she left."

Jennings took this in stride.

"In light of your graciousness, Mrs Walker, may I also ask what day she left?"

"Yesterday."

Not many words could have been more disheartening.

With a kind smile, Mrs Walker stood, allowing Jennings to excuse himself. When he thanked her, it was most sincere, but as he took his leave he wondered where all his good sense had gone. Had he realized only a day sooner how poorly he was taking the children's departure, he might have seen Marianne by now, been able to speak with her, and reiterate what was in his heart.

Halfway home, Jennings filled with new resolve. Marianne was away from Blackburn Manor, but that situation would alter. He would simply check each and every day until she returned. He had a most desperate need to see that lady, and he would not give up until he had!

$$\sim \quad \sim \quad \sim$$

Tipton

"Have you seen Jennings lately?" Lydia asked of Palmer.

"Not since Sunday. He was looking for Marianne."

"She was at Caroline's on Sunday. I think she still is."

"Why do you ask?"

"Lizzy said she wanted him to take her out in the pony cart. I thought if he was missing the children overly much, it might help to play with her."

"Oh, he's missing them all right."

"How do you know?"

"I know."

Lydia waited for Palmer to explain, but he didn't go on, although it wasn't all that hard to figure. Palmer always missed the children as much as she did. Nevertheless, he might be talking about something else. Lydia's stomach was feeling a bit upset at the moment, and she thought that eating might help. As she rang for Judith, she determined to check with her husband at a later time in order to confirm her suspicions.

≈ ≈ ≈

Blackburn Manor

Mrs Walker had words of hope for the first time in four days.

"She's not here, Mr Jennings," that lady had said. "She took a walk in the park."

Jennings couldn't stop his smile.

"Do you mind terribly, Mrs Walker, if I don't stay?"

"Well, I do have a lovely new book on flowers I wanted to show you," she said with great regret.

Jennings paused. The two stared at each other until Jennings laughed. Mrs Walker could not hold the act; her mischievous eyes gave her away.

"Go, Mr Jennings," Marianne's mother said with a laugh of her own. "And don't come back until you've found her!"

That man had needed no further urging. Jennings knew that if it took the rest of the day, he would stay in the forest until he located Marianne Walker. He'd been riding for less than ten minutes, but it felt like hours. The temptation to call out was mighty, but he held his peace and prayed.

Five minutes later he spotted her dark head. Surprise lifting his brows, he saw that she was in the identical spot where she'd previously hurt her ankle. Sitting on the ridge, eyes toward the valley, she remained rather still, just as before. Jennings dismounted and strode toward her. He stood looking down on her, his eyes warm.

"Hello," he said at last.

"Hello," Marianne said, feeling her cheeks heat, although her eyes remained on his.

"This is a familiar place," Jennings commented, amazed at how satisfying it felt just to gaze at her.

"It is," she agreed, "and isn't it ironic, I seem to have hurt my ankle again."

Taking her at her word, Jennings went down on one knee even as he realized she sounded quite pleased about the fact.

"Shall I check it?"

With a swift movement, one that belied an injury, Marianne moved her dress even farther over her ankles and feet.

"There's no need," she said, her voice almost playful as her eyes watched him. "I believe it's already quite swollen."

Jennings worked at not smiling, but one peeked through. Their eyes held for several more lovely seconds before Jennings slowly leaned forward and brushed her lips with his own.

"Do you know what you've been doing to my heart?"

"I think I must."

Jennings kissed her again.

"Will you marry me?"

Marianne sighed quite audibly.

"I feared you would never ask."

A moment later she was on her feet and in his arms.

"I'm sorry it took so long for me to come to you."

"I think I understand. It was about the children, wasn't it?"

"Yes. It was foolish, but I felt completely forsaken. It took me several days to see what I was missing with you. I still miss them, but my time is finally free for you."

"You're sure?" Marianne teased him. "I could go away again."

His arms tightened around her.

"I don't think so. I'm going to see your father straight away and have the matter settled."

"What matter would that be?"

Jennings looked deep into her eyes.

"I'm going to tell *him* that I love his daughter and want to make her my wife. And I'm going to tell *you* that there will never be a time when I don't need you."

"Even though you now know how deceitful I can be?"

"On the contrary," Jennings said as he lifted her in his arms. "Your ankle is swollen. I'd best carry you."

Marianne's laughter sounded in the forest before the man she loved escorted her home. And just as he'd promised, he asked for an audience with her father and settled the matter straightaway.

Epilogue

Marianne Jennings leaned toward the window of the carriage as the horses drew it closer and closer to Thornton Hall, her eyes scanning the acreage for signs of the children.

"I see Penny," Jennings said from beside her, having spotted the little girl first. "She's just seen the carriage."

Husband and wife laughed as the little girl ran in circles of excitement. They laughed again when she threw herself at them the moment they emerged from the carriage.

"Welcome home," Thomas greeted as he emerged from the house.

"You're back!" came from James.

"How are you?" Marianne asked, trying to hug and kiss them all at once.

"We're fine."

"When did you arrive?" Jennings asked as he led his family inside.

"Yesterday."

The children had been taken from school for a special weekend so they could witness the vows of William Jennings and Marianne Walker, but that had been nearly a month past. The newlyweds had taken a long trip with plans to arrive home for the children's week off. The Palmers and Hursts had done duty to get them to Thornton Hall so the "new" mother and father could drive directly there.

"And we're here a whole week!" Penny said.

"Yes, you are," Marianne agreed, now in the drawing room and taking that little girl in her lap. "And we are going to have a wonderful time."

"Did you sea bathe?" James had to know.

Jennings and Marianne both laughed.

"Yes! It was very cold, but we couldn't resist."

"When will we go again?"

"I think next summer," Jennings told him. "When the weather warms."

For a moment they all looked at each other.

"We hoped you would marry," Thomas admitted. "We wanted it for a long time."

"I prayed," Penny put in.

Marianne hugged her again and smiled at Thomas before looking to her husband. His eyes were on her, and for a moment they exchanged a look that didn't need words.

"I need to show you something," Penny said next.

"All right. Where is it?"

"It's in my room. I made it at school."

This was the way Jennings and Marianne spent their first day at home. The children thought of tidbits from school that they wanted to share or showed off art or papers they had worked on. Meals were relaxed and informal, and conversation was easy. Marianne had left on her honeymoon right after she was married, so she'd never lived even one day at Thornton Hall, but she could already tell she was going to like it.

And as lovely as the day was, it didn't hurt her feelings in the least when it was time for the children to retire and she could be alone with her husband.

Jennings' mind was running in the very same vein. He wasted no time taking her hand and leading her to their room.

"Am I dreaming," Marianne said in his arms, "or am I really here with you?"

"You're here," Jennings said softly, as though trying to believe it himself.

"And the children—they're mine now, aren't they?"

Jennings smiled. "Each and every one, for better or for worse."

Marianne held him a little closer. She wasn't foolish enough to think that there would never be a worse, but right now, close in her husband's arms, his head lowering to kiss her, it was the last thing on her mind.

About the Author

LORI WICK is one of the most versatile Christian fiction writers in the market today. Her works include pioneer fiction, a series set in Victorian England, and contemporary novels. Lori's books (more than 2.5 million copies in print) continue to delight readers and top the Christian bestselling fiction list. Lori and her husband, Bob, live in Wisconsin with "the three coolest kids in the world."

Books by Lori Wick

A Place Called Home Series
A Place Called Home
A Song for Silas
The Long Road Home
A Gathering of Memories

The Californians
Whatever Tomorrow Brings
As Time Goes By
Sean Donovan
Donovan's Daughter

English Garden Series
The Proposal
The Rescue
The Visitor

Kensington Chronicles
The Hawk and the Jewel
Wings of the Morning
Who Brings Forth the Wind
The Knight and the Dove

Rocky Mountain Memories
Where the Wild Rose Blooms
Whispers of Moonlight
To Know Her by Name
Promise Me Tomorrow

The Yellow Rose Trilogy
Every Little Thing About You
A Texas Sky
City Girl

Contemporary Fiction
Bamboo & Lace
Beyond the Picket Fence (Short Stories)
Pretense
The Princess
Sophie's Heart